DAREDEVIL'S
APPRENTICE

BY

LETHA ALBRIGHT

Letha Albright

MEMENTO MORI MYSTERIES

Memento Mori Mysteries
Published by
Avocet Press Inc
19 Paul Court
Pearl River, NY 10965
http://www.avocetpress.com
mysteries@avocetpress.com

AVOCET PRESS

Library of Congress Cataloging-in-Publication Data
Albright, Letha, 1952-
  Daredevil's apprentice / by Letha Albright.
     p. cm.
  ISBN 0-9705049-4-2
 1. Women journalists—Fiction. 2. Cherokee Indians—Fiction.
3.Oklahoma—Fiction. I. Title.
  PS3601.L34 D37 2002
  813'.6—dc21

Printed in the USA
First Edition

Suppose this happens. The world looks
tame, but it might go wild, any time.

—William Stafford

1

The wind always blows in Oklahoma. It's such a fact of life that we don't even need extra words for it like they have in other places—chinook, Santa Ana, sirocco. Here, we just say it's windy.

The day my friend Lucie Dreadfulwater killed Dale Nowlin, the November wind rattled the rafters of the barn in which they faced each other. Only the two of them could say what happened that day, and they're both dead. No one is left to tell their story except me.

I wasn't there, but now, after all this time, I think I know how it happened. If I close my eyes, I can see it playing like a B-movie at the drive-in. And no matter how often I watch, I can't change the ending.

The wind blew from the north, and its cold fingers crept through the cracks of the old building and pooled in the dark corners with the brooding disregard of a ghost.

The barn was Lucie's, and the middle-aged woman and the older man warily circled each other in the center of the floor. Lucie held a hoof knife low in her right hand; Nowlin gripped a two-by-four with both hands like a baseball bat. Other than the life-and-death drama under the loft, the barn was empty. Even the barn swallows had vanished.

Lucie Dreadfulwater's eyes were black pools. It was as though her ancestors had come up from the depths and watched through her. The war women of the Cherokee nation. Her eyes flickered back and forth from Nowlin to the door beyond him.

She had been cleaning the left front hoof of her quarter horse when Nowlin walked through the door. Lucie steadied the pastern between her knees and leaned into the horse's shoulder. Bent to her task, she hadn't recognized the man's silhouette until he spoke.

She straightened and slapped the horse on the rump, signaling him through the open door into the corral. He shied away from Nowlin then rushed past him.

Lucie held onto the knife. Perhaps she didn't even think about it. Perhaps it was just a tool that she had been using. Or perhaps even then she knew where she and Nowlin were headed.

Lucie's black hair fell down her back in a thick braid. Her body was short and compact, and she moved with the grace of a panther. Was it that athletic menace that made Nowlin pick up the board? It had been propped against a bale of hay, as though it waited for his hand to choose it.

Nowlin's face was creased like old shoe leather, and his mouth twisted down like the mask a storyteller dons when telling tales of war and disaster. He walked with a limp, but his arms were powerful. Or maybe it was the bulk of his jacket that made him seem muscular. It was unzipped, and his belly stretched his knit shirt and hung over his belt.

What secrets did he tell Lucie? What words sealed off their choices one by one and turned the skirmish into a life-and-death struggle?

As they circled each other, the acrid scent of desperation filled the air. Every sound was magnified in the fierce concentration of the moment: the soft pad of shoes on straw, the creak of rafters, the moan of wind through the eaves.

Nowlin feinted once with the board as though he was trying to slap the knife from Lucie's hand. She jumped back, and they resumed their dance.

Nowlin had the advantage of size; Lucie, agility. He rushed at her, swinging the board. Lucie tripped over a piece of broken harness on the barn floor, and the hoof knife plunged into Nowlin's groin, the full weight of Lucie's body behind it. Bright red blood spurted from his severed femoral artery.

Lucie rolled away from Nowlin, the knife still clenched in her hand. The man dropped to his knees onto the straw-carpeted floor, clutched the wound and screamed, "Bitch!"

The blood pulsed between his fingers like oil pumping from the ruined fissures of Oklahoma's red earth.

Their eyes locked for one long moment. Lucie's were dark and calculating; Nowlin's were panic-stricken. Nowlin was a registered nurse, and as his heart pushed blood out of the deep gash, he noted that he was dizzy and light-headed. Clinical symptoms of a fast-falling blood pressure.

The knowledge that he was dying charged Nowlin's panic. "For God's sake, help me!" His voice was hoarse and broken. He lay on the floor, his legs drawn up in a fetal position.

He saw Lucie drop the knife and fold her arms. "You think we're even now," Nowlin said. "You don't know the half of it. You and your damned Cherokee ancestors. Damn you all to hell."

While Lucie hugged herself, the pool of blood spread and Nowlin grew pale and quiet.

2

I sat in the publisher's office at the *Green Country Journal* drawing squares in my reporter's notebook while David Menckle, my boss, droned on the phone. What a messed up, pointless life. I had left the daily grind of a small-town newspaper only to end up as a staff writer for a second-rate regional magazine that always promised more than it delivered—in both pay and content.

The weather didn't help my mood. The cheery woman on KTUL out of Tulsa had promised Indian summer, yet when I had left the house that morning, clouds blanketed the sky and a cold wind wove its way through my fleece jacket. The low gray sky silhouetted barren hillsides. Along the highway south toward Tahlequah, the Cherokee County seat, gray-shingled shacks settled into the muddy fields, and trash decorated the ditches.

To those who grow up in Cherokee County, Oklahoma, it's like an imperfect baby you love because it's yours. Those of us who come here from other places find it grows on us, sometimes in slow increments, sometimes in quick bursts. My first quick burst was the green street signs in Tahlequah. The small town is the capital of the western Cherokees, and the street names are printed in their graceful alphabet in addition to the English translation. Goingsnake, Muskogee, Choctaw.

Then there's the state flower, the mistletoe—a parasite that grows high in the treetops—and the license plates, which modestly claim "Oklahoma is OK." What's not to love?

Well, for starters, there's David Menckle, who had moved here last year from Little Rock with his Junior League wife to start up the *Green Country Journal*. Menckle talked in a soft southern drawl and worked hard to fit into the good-old-boy network. He was a member of the Chamber of Commerce, the Kiwanis Club, the Echota Springs Golf Club and the American Legion. He's one of those guys who look at home in a Stetson and tie and can say "paradigm shift" without winking.

Our Friday morning meetings were an exercise in one-upmanship. I saw myself as the defender of journalistic integrity, and Menckle claimed to be the voice of fiscal responsibility. He automatically won the first round just by being the boss.

Today a third person disturbed the uneasy balance.

Menckle hung up the phone and motioned to the pale woman who waited outside the door.

"Viv Powers," he said to me, "meet Lisabeth Ellis, our new managing editor and designer. Y'all will have fun working together."

Menckle had told me the week before that he had hired her and that I hadn't been considered for the position because I was, in his words, "already doing what you do best." Right. Living on microwave popcorn and hoping my boyfriend Charley Pack would find some high-paying gigs for his band before the credit cards were maxed out.

I wondered if the fact that Lisabeth Ellis looked so young and fragile had anything to do with Menckle's hiring decision. Her long, blond hair, gathered in an elegant chignon at the nape of her slender neck, echoed the sophistication of her black linen dress. I didn't even own a dress.

She walked in the room and sat in a chair opposite me, her back ramrod straight. She inclined her head toward me in what might have been a nod. She looked as serious as a heart attack.

"We're all about fun here," I said, slumping deeper into the imitation leather chair. All Menckle cared about was creating the proper showcase for his advertisers. All I cared about right now was paying my bills. Who knew what Lisabeth Ellis cared about.

Fun, right.

Menckle sat at his oversized walnut desk. A half-eaten glazed doughnut lay on a napkin near his elbow. We were probably the same age, but he seemed part of a different generation. He wore an expensive-looking gray suit, and the gel he used on his sandy hair left comb marks. His golfer's tan should have made him look healthy, but puffy eyes ruined the effect. Too much Johnny Walker Black Label on a daily basis.

He clutched my most recent offering, a story about adventure-canoeing on the nearby rain-swollen Illinois River. "Good stuff, Viv," he said. "Lisabeth will have fun putting this one on the page."

"I like this part." He settled his wire-rim glasses on his nose and read aloud. "Canoeing the flooded Illinois felt like riding the Screaming Eagle at Six Flags—full blast ahead, our skin stretched tight over our faces. I later learned we were traveling less than ten miles an hour."

He looked at me. "I like the way you set up the story, too. Tagging along after your friend Lucie Dreadfulwater. She's a bit of a celebrity around here."

Daredevil's apprentice, Charley had called me the morning Lucie and I canoed the flooded Illinois River. Lucie Dreadfulwater being, of course, the daredevil. In the few months we had known each other, Lucie and I had bonded while rappelling off the cliffs above Lake Tenkiller, making a tandem skydiving jump and bush-whacking on horseback in Arkansas.

Nevertheless, such actions should be undertaken by choice rather than for a magazine assignment. Choice somehow elevated risky behavior to a kind of heroism. At least it did in my own admittedly skewed ethical system.

"You'll have to get me life insurance before assigning another story like that," I said to Menckle. "I'll kill myself on my own time."

Menckle smiled as though I had made a joke. "I thought you were an outdoors girl."

"Woman."

He didn't get it. Or he ignored me. Same difference.

"Your next assignment won't be as strenuous," he said. "In fact, imagine yourself digging through the dusty archives of the university library and the county courthouse."

Menckle paused, and when he felt the suspense was at its proper level, he said in a dramatic voice: "Unsolved mysteries of Cherokee County! People who disappeared without a trace! Lost treasures! Girl Scouts slaughtered! Our readers will eat it up."

I hated to admit it, but Menckle had a hot idea. Of course, by the time he was finished with it, the story would get the tabloid treatment, but it beat writing about the top ten barbecue joints in eastern Oklahoma.

"So who are they? Your slaughtered innocents and lost treasures?"

He handed me a sheet of paper that listed the usual crimes: The Girl Scout Murders, the Dora Doe Murder, the Little League Murder. Ho hum. They had all been solved to the satisfaction of the law. Did Menckle expect me to rewrite history? One item on the list jumped out at me: the disappearance of John Dreadfulwater.

"John Dreadfulwater? Is he any relation to Lucie?"

Menckle looked at his watch. "I'm the idea man," he said. "It's up to you to dig up the details. You can start with your history professor buddy, Dr. J.P. Durant. He probably knows about every crime that was ever committed in these parts."

"I'll hop right on it, chief," I said. If he noticed my lack of enthusiasm, he didn't show it.

3

I can't remember the first time I saw Lucie Dreadfulwater. As is the case with most people we come to know, the transition from stranger to friend is an almost invisible process.

I probably noticed her at one of the Cherokee storytelling sessions. The Cherokee Nation works at keeping its culture alive by hosting a variety of events: ceremonial dances, corn stalk shoots, powwows and art exhibits. When I moved to Tahlequah, I was fascinated by this culture that seemed so foreign, even though it had flourished here long before my own ancestors had set foot on this continent.

At a journalism conference, I once heard politician Pat Schroeder say thank goodness there were some Native Americans with a very liberal immigration policy.

In any event, Lucie Dreadfulwater and her traditional Cherokee tales were in great demand. The Cherokee Nation had named her a "Cherokee National Treasure," an honor the tribe reserves for those who work to keep its culture alive.

My first clear memories of her began several months ago, when David Menckle assigned a story about her for the first issue of the magazine. After that, we had the occasional lunch, and then as we came to know one another, a bond grew between us that seemed like blood shared.

It's not surprising that I sought her advice before writing a story that might involve her family. I thought of my visit to Lucie as a courtesy. She was my friend, and if I was going to write about the disappearance of one of her relatives, she should be the first to know.

The Dreadfulwater house lay on the south side of Tahlequah at the foot of Park Hill Mountain. It was an imposing two-story Victorian, built of hand-quarried Arkansas limestone, painstakingly hauled by wagon and mule more than a hundred years ago. The arched windows were topped with carved keystones, and a wide veranda stretched around three sides of the house.

Lucie's parents had fled the old house for the central-heat-and-air comfort of a new split-level ranch down the road. But Lucie kept the family fires burning.

When I pulled into the circular driveway of the Southern Gothic Mausoleum, as I privately called it, Lucie's Explorer was parked in front of the house, and behind the Explorer was an unfamiliar blue pickup. A pang of disappointment hit me. I wanted to talk to her alone. Since I was here, I thought I would at least say hello and arrange for a time to come back.

When I rang the doorbell, feet pattered across the hardwood floor, and a barking dog hit the door. I peered through the lace curtains and saw Lucie's golden cocker spaniel, Custer.

Other than the dog, no one came to the door. I followed the porch around to the east side of the house and went down broad steps to a brick walk that wandered through the lawn.

Under the tall sugar maples and bur oaks that spread limb-to-limb across the large backyard, the light was like gun-metal gauze. The bricks led through an iron gate to a faded barn. When I entered the enclosure, a chestnut-colored horse whinnied nervously and trotted to the far side.

Lucie stood in the doorway of the barn, her hands gripping the doorjamb. As a storyteller, drama was her job, but I had never seen her like this. Her face was a changing tapestry of emotions: surprise, fear, indecision, anger.

"What is it?" Some extra sense drew me to the dark interior of the barn.

She grabbed my arm. "Don't go in there."

"What's wrong?" Images raced through my mind. The horses. Her daughters. Please, God, not Rachel or Anna.

"What the hell are you doing here? You shouldn't be here, dammit."

"Lucie, tell me what's going on."

She tried to pull me away from the barn, but I resisted, and we stood toe-to-toe, staring at one another.

The words came like small explosions. "I killed him."

"What?"

"I have to call the sheriff's office, but I..." She paused. "There's something I need you to do for me first."

"Is he in...in there?" I gestured to the dark throat of the barn. Even though it was midday, the interior seemed dim and sinister.

She nodded.

I now saw that blood was spattered like paint across the front of her denim shirt. An ugly gash puckered her left hand.

"Who is it?"

She hesitated so long I thought it must be Truman.

Women's friendship is rooted in confession, and Lucie and I had shared many confessions. Especially about men.

Lucie and her husband, Truman Gourd, for instance, fought constantly. Usually about money. Truman was poverty-conscious, Lucie said, while she had been raised in wealth in which the definition of poverty is cleaning your own house. But Lucie hadn't inherited the family fortune yet, and money was tight.

Not long after I met her, she told me she had decided to leave Truman. He had yelled at her once too often. She went to the bank, cashed in a CD and walked away with a thousand dollar bill. That night, while they shared a bottle of after-dinner wine, Lucie pulled out a cigarette lighter and lit the bill. It burned with a smoky cedar smell, and as it was consumed, the bill curled to cover Grover Cleveland's face. Truman went crazy, she said.

He tried to snatch it away, and failing that, he gave her a black eye.

For some reason they had stayed together, despite Truman's drinking and violence and despite Lucie's baiting.

So now I asked, "Truman?"

A ghost of a smile crossed her face. "Not this time," she said. "Someone you probably don't know—Dale Nowlin."

I had never heard the name. "But what happened?"

"He came to discuss a business deal and ended up attacking me." Lucie held out her slashed hand as evidence. "I'm lucky to be alive."

"Are you sure he's dead?" I almost whispered the question, as though he might hear me.

"He's dead."

I pushed past her restraining hand into the barn. Next to the hay manger, a man lay on his side, his knees pressed to his chest. He was very still.

It's strange what you notice in such situations. It's as though your brain can't deal with the whole picture so it just accepts small pieces. I focused on Dale Nowlin's hair. It was gray and had the synthetic texture of doll's hair. I had a crazy impulse to touch it.

Trails of blood led from his body like a medieval map of doom. A pair of flies landed on a red pool. I stopped before getting any closer, realizing I had already seen too much.

Lucie pulled me back to the light of the doorway. Her makeup was smudged under her eyes, giving her a bruised, vulnerable look. She spoke very fast, and I had trouble keeping up.

"You were sent here today for a reason," she said. "I tried to do it myself, but I can't. Truman took Rachel to a horse show in Wilburton. They won't be back until tomorrow. Who knows where Anna is. My father is too frail. You're the only one who can save me."

"You need a drink, Lucie. Let's go get a drink and figure this out."

She grabbed my shoulders and shook me. "You're not listening, Viv. I need your help."

"Anything," I said. I meant it in the raw emotion of the moment. The wind had picked up again, and it seemed like a creature that whispered secrets and pushed us toward its own blind ends.

"I may be arrested, and someone needs to make sure Custer and Cricket are fed tonight."

Cricket was the chestnut-colored horse. I had forgotten his name until Lucie reminded me. "I can do that."

"There's something else."

Lucie picked up a two-by-four from the ground. One end was wrapped in plastic. She handed it to me plastic end first, stared into my eyes and said, "Hit me."

Her eyes were dark pools. I said, "Christ, Lucie."

She thrust her injured hand toward me, forcing me to look. "How do you think it's going to look to the sheriff if I claim self-defense with this puny injury? Remember what happened when Sarah was raped?"

I stared at the massive bulk of Park Hill Mountain, not really seeing it. I was remembering how Sarah had been alone in her shop after dark when a man came in the back door, held a knife to her throat and raped her. The man who was arrested and charged with the crime said that Sarah had been a willing participant, and the defense attorney did his best to put her on trial. Because she had suffered no physical injuries and because there were no witnesses to the crime, the rapist had walked. Sarah closed her store, returned to her parents' home and withdrew from the world.

Oh, yes, I remembered Sarah.

The board was about the length of a baseball bat. I hefted it, looked at Lucie and dropped it on the ground.

"I can't."

Lucie picked it up, shoved it back at me and said, "There's no other way. My life is in your hands."

The legal repercussions of what we were doing didn't even register at that moment. All I could focus on was the image of wood striking flesh. I felt sick to my stomach.

Lucie's entire body grew tighter as though she were gathering herself. "Who joined you in that stupid canoeing stunt?" she shouted. "Who pulled you out when we were dumped in the river? Who tore you loose from that tree that was drowning you? Did that hurt?"

I nodded, conscious of the bruise in the middle of my back—the result of our wild ride on the river a few days earlier.

"Did I care? No. I just wanted to save your life. That's all I'm asking of you. Save my life!"

I had never seen Lucie so angry, and it triggered anger inside me. Fear, too. I tightened my grip on the board and slapped her upper arm with it.

Triumph flashed in her eyes. "Not there," she said. "Hit me on the back of the head."

I tapped her head, a knot of dread growing in me.

"Harder!"

I drew the board back and swung. The wood connected with a sickening thud. Lucie sprawled on the ground, and I dropped the board as though it had struck me.

She put one hand to her head and rose to her knees, then, slowly, to her feet. I should have helped her up, but I felt rooted in place.

"Thank you, Viv," she said in a suddenly calm voice. "Now go. Please."

I hesitated, unwilling to leave her alone with this disaster.

"Just go!"

4

Half an hour later I parked my Honda Civic in front of the small house Charley and I had built. I had driven as though pursued, squealing my tires on the ninety-degree turns south of Moodys, barreling down Long John Hill.

I was trying to escape those moments at Lucie's house, but they kept pace with me—the body on the barn floor, the pool of blood, the vibration of the board in my hand when it hit Lucie—and I knew I had made a huge mistake.

It was too late to undo it.

I was like a criminal escaping to my mountain hideout. Our small house perches on an oak-covered ridge above Spring Creek, fifteen miles north of Tahlequah. The thick growth of oaks and hickory and the rise and fall of this rugged land screen us from the nearest neighbors, who aren't that near anyway.

Us. Charley Pack and me. For a brief moment, I wished that Charley was here. I could have poured out the story to him, and he could have offered some brilliant advice that would make everything all right again. More likely, he would quote some obscure Tibetan master about the transitory nature of being, or he may given me a long look and then said, "Ever since you met Lucie Dreadfulwater, you've been on this path."

Which wasn't true—despite the evidence.

But Charley Pack, who shares this house and forty acres, wasn't here to dispense comfort or censure. He was on the road with his band, Powers That Be. Earlier that morning he had loaded his beat-up Gibson guitar case into his equally beat-up Chevy utility van. He brushed Mack the cat off the driver's seat and out the open door, pushed back his short, thinning hair, and looked at me with those deep-set eyes that after eight years of cohabitation still sometimes surprise me with their indigo blue. If it weren't for the eyes, his thin, ascetic face could be taken for that of a monk.

"Saturday night," he had said. "Late."

"Don't wake me."

"Hah."

We were gentle with one another these days, trying to skate on the ice that had formed a few months earlier when we had learned that our supposedly solid relationship wasn't any thicker than the glaze on a December pond. We were trying to rebuild the easy give-and-take we had once shared. But it couldn't look like we were trying. That was one of the unspoken rules.

He kissed the tip of my nose and reminded me about the benefit concert and birthday party we were throwing on Sunday for Randy Silvers, who was the bass player and newest member of his band.

Then he was gone.

I entered the deserted house—deserted except for Mack, that is, who rushed inside, crying as though he had been foraging for mice for weeks. I picked him up and he squirmed to be let down. Some cat.

I was more restless than Mack. I paced the floor between the Vermont Castings woodstove and the desk where my Macintosh computer sat. Then up the stairs to the loft where the bed was still unmade and back down through the kitchen, with its racks of cast-iron pots hanging from the ceiling beams. Then to the large windows. Now that the leaves had fallen off the trees, bright shards of creek water cut through the bare branches.

Coming home had been a mistake. I felt like I was in a prison. Unwelcome images kept popping into my head: Dale Nowlin's body curled on the floor, Lucie telling me to hit her. I dug into my pocket and pulled out the list of names David Menckle had given me earlier. Unsolved mysteries of Cherokee County. I had a hot story to add to the list. But it wouldn't exactly be in my best interests to tell it.

However, John Dreadfulwater's name was there. And given my recent encounter with the Dreadfulwater family, I wanted to know more. I grabbed my jacket and headed back to Tahlequah.

The Bertha Parker Bypass wound around the east side of Tahlequah and dumped me on a back road near Professor J.P. Durant's red brick house on Normal Street. A complex of Northeastern State University dormitories loomed to the north; Professor Durant's house was set back from the street, sheltered by tall maples and a bare hedge of bridal wreath spirea.

I pulled into the concrete driveway and saw his slight figure kneeling over a flower bed by the front steps. Always formal, even for yard work, the professor wore a black wool suit and one of his colorful trademark ties.

He straightened slowly, as though it were an effort, and walked toward me with his arms open for a hug. I kissed the top of his bald head, and said, "You're the only person I know who dresses up to dig in the dirt."

His laugh sounded like a cough. "They call me that nutty old professor around here. But eccentricity, you know, is nothing more than a difference made public. Of course, Emily would scold me for getting dirt on my trousers. But since she's not here to keep me in line, sometimes I'm like a little boy. I'm old enough to get away with it, too."

Back when I worked for the newspaper, I wrote a story about Emily Durant's work with a local women's shelter, and while interviewing her had met the professor. After Emily died, I stopped by occasionally to see Professor Durant. But it had been awhile.

He didn't seem surprised to see me. "I'll make us some tea," he said, leading the way into the house. "Why don't we adjourn to the library, and I'll tell you what your boss got me started on."

"He called you."

"Mr. Menckle. Nice magazine he has."

I couldn't tell if he was serious.

I followed him through the dim and dusty living room and the formal dining room. The house had a closed-up, musty odor.

The kitchen counter was stacked with dirty dishes. Spode china, tarnished silver and crystal goblets were mixed in with the everyday dishes.

He fumbled in the dishwasher for clean cups. I felt twitchy and impatient—I should have stayed home and gone running along the creek—but I forced myself to lean against the counter as though I had no cares. Pretend, and the rest will follow.

It wasn't working.

"Could you add a shot of something to that tea?"

He was pouring the tea from a china pot into delicate cups, and he paused to glance at me with eyes much younger than the drooping lids above them. "Is the idealism at low ebb to-day?"

"Something like that."

Professor Durant reached into a cabinet and handed me a bottle of Crown Royal. I added a generous splash to my tea, followed him into the library and sank into an overstuffed chair.

The upholstery was worn and comfortable, like everything else in the room. Except for the narrow windows on the east and south, the wall space was covered with bookshelves atop low cabinets. I scanned the titles. The books that crowded the shelves were mostly about Cherokee history and culture.

He sat across from me, and wagged his finger. "You want to

know about unsolved mysteries. You should have taken my Indian Territories class."

"I should have." I sipped the doctored tea and told myself to calm down. But against my will, my mind kept rushing back to the barn and to the board in my hands. Somewhere in the back of my head, a chant had begun. The words were very simple. Stupid, stupid, stupid. I forced my attention back to Professor Durant.

"Before statehood, Oklahoma was a wide open place, and outlaws such as Belle Starr, the Younger Brothers and the Daltons operated with little fear of reprisal. Eventually Belle Starr was murdered, but no one was ever charged. There are rumors that she hid her gold and jewels in the wall of a well that has since been covered by Lake Eufala."

Belle Starr, murder, gold. I pulled out my notebook but didn't write down the words.

"Later, during the Great Depression, Pretty Boy Floyd introduced the submachine gun to Oklahoma criminals. He died in 1934 in a hail of bullets."

I sensed that Professor Durant was about to launch into a lengthy off-topic dissertation that, once started, would not be easy to halt.

"I came to ask about an unsolved mystery closer to home."

I handed him my list, and he looked at the names on it. I couldn't tell what he thought. The Little League and Girl Scout murders were a long remove from Belle Starr and Pretty Boy Floyd. But they weren't my primary interest, either.

"John Dreadfulwater," I said.

"That name," he said slowly. "John Dreadfulwater. The Dreadfulwaters are still one of Cherokee County's leading families. The year was 1945. John Dreadfulwater, a judge and banker, disappeared. He took no money, no clothes. Left no note. His body was never found. In fact, no one ever proved a crime was committed."

"Lucie Dreadfulwater is my friend." I wasn't sure what the word "friend" meant at the moment.

"Ah, yes," Professor Durant said. "She would be John's grand-daughter. Then you no doubt know the family history."

Sudden anger washed over me. Lucie hadn't shared her family history with me, but she felt free to involve me when she killed someone. Lucie was so proud of her ancestry that she had kept her last name when she married—not uncommon—but in addition, the two daughters she and Truman Gourd bore carried the Dreadfulwater name. Lucie and I had talked of many things; she had never hinted at past scandal in her family.

I gulped the rest of my tea, felt the whiskey burn my stomach, leaned toward Professor Durant and said, "Tell me about it."

Professor Durant was warmed up to the subject now, and even had I proclaimed myself an expert on the Dreadfulwaters, he probably would have found himself unable to stop the lecture.

"By Cherokee County standards," the professor said, "the family is Old Money. Your friend's great-great grandfather, Samuel Dreadfulwater, was among 16,000 Cherokees forcibly relocated to eastern Oklahoma from Georgia and the Carolinas in 1838. Four thousand died along the Trail of Tears.

"When the white man first came to Georgia, the Cherokees quickly caught on that fighting the European invasion was the road to annihilation. So they adopted the civilization of their conquerors—completing in little more than a generation, as Grace Steele Woodward described it, a transformation from the war lords of the southern Appalachian Highlands to genteel farmers. They had their own alphabet—I'm sure you've heard of Sequoyah." He waited until I nodded, then resumed. "They had their own schools and newspaper, and they had a ruling hierarchy, with laws and judges."

He loosened his tie and noisily swallowed some tea. "Like

many other Cherokees, the Dreadfulwater family had a prosperous farm in Georgia. They even owned slaves. The American soldiers rounded them up and forced them west with the rest of their tribe.

"In Oklahoma, the Cherokees who had voluntarily moved to Indian Territory in the years before 1838 struggled against the newcomers for control of their government. Young Sam Dreadfulwater joined forces with the winning side, and when the nation built its Capitol and Supreme Court buildings in Tahlequah, he was ready to reap the benefits of power.

"Just what did that amount to? He eventually served as a judge for almost twenty years. During that time he accumulated enormous land holdings. When Dreadfulwater died at age ninety-three in 1899, he left a fortune to his family, including his grandson John Dreadfulwater.

"In recent years that dynasty has crumbled. In 1945 John Dreadfulwater disappeared, leaving behind one son. His son is an old man now just like me and in poor health. Johnny Dreadfulwater is the last male of his line."

"What do people say happened to Lucie's grandfather?"

"I had just moved here when it happened," he said, his eyes clouding with memory. "Ponds were dragged, bloodhounds scoured the family land. A skeleton was found, but Dreadfulwater had shrapnel in his skull from the Battle of Chateau-Thierry, he was an Army officer during World War I, and the skeleton had no shrapnel.

"Dozens of people were questioned. People speculated that he skipped town with a satchel full of money. And, as always in such cases, there were rumors of another woman. His wife was known as a rigid and God-fearing woman. Some say she did him in." He coughed his dry laugh again.

My anger toward Lucie had faded, leaving an empty feeling inside. And worry. What was happening to her now? Had she called the sheriff?

Professor Durant looked at me. "When you dig around in other people's pasts, you almost always wind up wishing you hadn't."

I half-heartedly quoted the sibyl's advice to Aeneas: "Yield not to disasters, but press onward the more bravely."

The old hag should have said run the other way.

5

When you want to know what's going on, ask a cop. If you can't ask a cop, ask a cop's girlfriend. If the cop's girlfriend also happens to be your sister, so much the better.

Maggie Power's white frame house lies at the north end of Bluff. It perches above the Tahlequah city park and Town Branch, the modest creek that cuts the town in half.

My sister is everything I'm not. Maggie has big hair—body-waved, bleached and gelled. She shops in Tulsa stores that issue their own charge cards. She's a bouncy, vibrant package of gab, and where some people are fortunate in marriage, Maggie was fortunate in divorce, still pulling in the proceeds of a short union with an oncologist.

I can't claim that Maggie followed me to Tahlequah. After mother and The Sergeant left Fort Sill in the dusty, red-earth part of Oklahoma, Maggie ended up in Tulsa with her doctor. I moved to Boulder to major in English at the University of Colorado and stayed to work for the *Daily Camera*. Eventually, I followed a singer/songwriter from Boulder back to his Oklahoma roots. After Maggie's divorce, she moved here, too. Funny how things work out. Sometimes it was nice to have her nearby; sometimes she was a pain in the butt. Maybe she felt the same way.

I tapped on her front door, which stood open despite the brisk wind, and she motioned me in through the screen. Her clumsy black lab, Jake, almost knocked me over in his zeal to plant slobbery kisses.

"Jake! Jake!" Maggie said. As usual, the phone was glued to her ear, but this time she was listening instead of talking. She showed me how hard it was by rolling her eyes while she waved me to a blue leather sofa.

"Uh-huh. Uh-huh," she said while she danced from one bare foot to the other. Suddenly she stood still, and looked at me.

"Get your ass over here. Now!"

I thought she was talking to me, but she squinted her eyes and said, "I don't care about Murray. You can handle him. I want to hear in person."

She slammed the phone down, shivering with excitement, a small smile on her magenta lips.

"I need to talk to your cop buddy." I leaned over and scratched Jake behind his ears. He groaned with pleasure and stretched out by my feet.

"You look like hell."

"I mean it. I need to see him."

"You're in a mood." She paced back and forth on the hardwood floor, lit a cigarette and inhaled deeply, closing her eyes with pleasure.

I knew how to deal with her. Act bored, lose interest. Maggie can't stand not being the center of attention.

"He won't want to talk to you," Maggie said. "When you were a reporter for the *Tahlequah Daily Tribune*, you probably pissed off every last member of the police department with your attack-dog journalism."

"The journalist's urge to wound and humiliate has been well-documented."

"He's on his way over here. That was him on the phone."

"Your boyfriend Rance Dawes? Now?" I didn't believe her.

She gave me a speculative look and headed to the kitchen.

"Rance Dawes?" I asked again, following her. Jake padded behind us. I watched her mix a pair of Scotch and waters.

Maggie's kitchen, like everything else in her house, reflected her attention to detail. The surfaces were black-and-white art deco, and on the wall an enormous red sign with an orange soda bottle on it said, "Get Kist Today." It was a room for looking more than cooking.

"You look like you need it," she said, handing me a glass.

The Scotch went down like smoke.

"Mom called," she said. "Why don't you ever call them?"

I set the glass on the countertop. "Remember how The Sergeant would roust us out of bed before dawn on Saturdays to play survival games, and The Saint would roust us out on Sundays to go to church and save our souls? Life's easier without them."

"Hah!" Maggie made it sound like an explosion. "Are you your father's daughter?" And she laughed.

In the late November afternoon, it was already dusk, and the police car that pulled into the driveway and parked beside the Civic had its headlights on.

Maggie was working her way through the police force one by one. Something about young men in uniforms. Our father had worn a uniform. I didn't want to think too much about the implications.

Maggie slipped on a pair of black heels. "Let me do the talking."

Until that moment, I hadn't really believed that the man I wanted to talk to was actually coming to Maggie's house. I decided to play it smart for once and keep my mouth shut until I learned what was going on.

Heavy boots clumped across the porch, and a deep voice said, "Maggie!" Jake jumped up and let out his heavy, hoarse bark, but his tail was wagging. Maggie met Rance Dawes at the door, and he grabbed her arms and bent down to kiss her. She struggled free, protecting her lipstick.

"Rance, you remember my sister, Viv Powers."

Dawes was a big man, with short blond hair and a smooth

face. His face was a walking advertisement for youth and inexperience, and when he looked at me, he caressed the holstered .44 at his hip.

"Let me make you a drink," Maggie said.

"I gotta get back. But a soda would be nice. None of that diet crap." Dawes followed Maggie into the kitchen.

"What's she doing here?" I heard him ask.

Maggie talked too low and fast for me to hear her reply. They came back into the living room, and Dawes sat awkwardly in one of Maggie's delicate armchairs, clasped and unclasped his hands and licked his thick lips. He glanced at me.

"Say again what you said on the phone," Maggie said.

Dawes looked at me. "Maggie says you won't talk. If word was to get out I blabbed about this, it could mean my job."

"This is a small town," I said. "Whatever it is, everyone will know soon enough."

"Not 'til tomorrow they won't."

"I can keep my mouth shut."

"Are you writing a story?"

"I don't work for the newspaper now."

Dawes leaned back, satisfied. "You know Lucie Dreadfulwater?"

Maggie shot me a warning look. I nodded, trying not to give away anything with my face. My lungs felt as though they couldn't suck in enough air.

"Well," Dawes said. "Primm and me were on patrol this afternoon. It was too quiet, like folks were resting up for a wild weekend. We did have a call over to Velma Tucker's. Her son was released from the prison at McAlester this week, and she says someone's been nosing around her place. She's worried he'll try to come back and live off her. Primm gave her the Ann Landers treatment. Said, 'Ma'am, can't no one sponge off you unless you let them.'"

My hands were clenched so tight the knuckles were white,

but I kept my mouth shut. Get to Lucie.

Dawes took another drink. I was beginning to hate the delicate way he put the glass down on the side table. Maggie caught my eye and winked. I looked away.

"Well." He made the word into a sentence. "We got back in the car and the radio squawked. Cindy said to get over to Park Hill on the double. To that big mansion the Dreadfulwaters own. The sheriff's office shoulda taken the call, but they were all up to Peggs busting up a meth lab."

He paused again. I knew the type. The cops and politicians and lawyers and journalists who want to think that what they do is more important than what other people do. They want the limelight. They think they deserve it.

"Well...," Maggie said, to jump-start him.

"Well. Ms. Dreadfulwater was in a state. She was beat up and bleeding and nearly in hysterics. It took awhile to get it out of her, but there was a dead man in the barn, Dale Nowlin. He don't have any family here to notify, so I guess it's okay to say his name.

"She said he attacked her with a club, and she accidentally stabbed him. She said it was self-defense. She was just a little too lucky with that knife, and he bled to death." Dawes folded his hands on his lap and leaned back in his chair.

Perhaps I should have told what I knew at that point. I sometimes wonder if it would have made any difference. But I remained silent. My loyalty to Lucie and my aversion to Dawes overcame any feelings of obligation to the law.

"What did you do with her?" The tightness in my chest took another twist, and I tried to take slow, deep breaths. I remembered the look on Lucie's face when she rose from the ground after I hit her.

"There's another story!" Dawes said. He finished his drink and fished out an ice cube. The crunching sound he made struck my nerves like small jolts of electricity.

"Well. We took her to the hospital to be examined and stitched up and then got her down to the station, and she said she wanted to make a phone call. Well. You won't believe, she called Judge Clark. I heard that the Judge and her old man were tight—he was down there in a New York minute. He wasn't happy about it, either. But I expect 'Miss Lucie' is home by now."

I let out a long breath I hadn't realized I had been holding, and clenched and unclenched my hands. I stood up and said with someone else's voice, "I have to leave."

I let the screen door slam shut behind me.

6

I pulled off beside the blacktop after I turned onto Park Hill Road. Lucie's house lay just around the bend, hidden under the shadow of Park Hill Mountain, and I was both drawn to and repelled by her and her mansion. I was a criminal drawn back to the scene of the crime. I climbed out of the car and drew in deep breaths of the crisp November air.

The wind had faded. It stirred the bare branches and brushed my hair with the stealth of a pickpocket.

The sky was black except for a sliver of moon that shone like light behind a rip in the fabric of the night. I imagined that another world could be glimpsed through that tear, as though I could peek through a window into a house party the size of the universe filled with gaiety and laughter. So different from this dark world.

In the distance, a dog barked and was answered by a coyote. I shivered in the cold night air.

When I pulled up to the Southern Gothic Mausoleum, I expected to find someone home, but the house was dark and Lucie's Explorer was gone. The blue pickup was gone, too. Perhaps Lucie had gone to her father's house down the road. I was grateful that her husband wasn't home.

Truman Gourd was a silent man, with a long ponytail, an acne-scarred face and unreadable black eyes. Lucie and Truman's stormy marriage had lasted long enough to raise twenty-one-year-old Anna and fourteen-year-old Rachel. Anna sometimes lived at home, depending on whether she was going to school or working. Rachel was a student at the Tahlequah High School.

I knocked on the door and Custer banged against it from the inside, barking frantically. I dug the hidden key out of the box behind a loose stone and let myself inside, and Custer rushed past me through the open door. He ran down the brick path toward the barn until the gate stopped him. Then he stood at the gate and barked.

I wondered if he could smell Dale Nowlin's blood or perhaps the leftover odors of Rance Dawes and his partner and the medical examiner who had come in response to Lucie's call.

I scooped up Custer and carried him back in the house. When he heard the rustle of dog food in the bag, he calmed down. One animal down, one to go.

The last thing I wanted to do was enter the dark barn and feed Lucie's horse. I slowly walked toward the barn where, hours earlier, a man had bled away his life on the floor. It seemed like a bad dream, but the yellow crime scene tape that sealed the double doors assured me that it was all too real.

The best way to deal with fear is to curse a lot. I don't know why, but it helps. So I kept up a running commentary under my breath while I ignored the warning to not cross into the crime scene. It is always better to beg forgiveness than to ask permission. I pushed the doors in, ducked under the tape and fumbled for the light switch.

The switch activated a pair of dim bulbs that hung from beams under the loft and lit a path across the center of the barn. The edges of the room disappeared in deep shadow. Above me, the loft was a black hole.

I looked at the place where Dale Nowlin's body had lain hours before. Looping strings of tape marked the spot. Not that further marking was necessary. A dark stain had soaked into the sawdust and straw.

I took a deep breath and forced myself to do the job I had come for.

Earlier in the day, Cricket had been loose in the corral, but now he was confined to a stall. He whickered when he saw me.

I reached through the steel bars to pat his neck. "Hey, boy. Hungry?" He was skittish, not sure whether he liked my hand on him. His coat was smooth and dry, and his velvety muzzle dripped with water from the tub in the corner of the stall.

I gave the horse a measure of feed and a section of alfalfa bale, and he forgot me and began to eat. It would have been a peaceful scene any other time.

Sometimes nothing changes except a shift in perception— and I had been living all day with a heightened sensitivity—but I felt a sudden prickle spread across my face. Against the far wall, the refrigerator door gaped open. Dim light fanned out of it. It must have been open the whole time I was inside the barn, but until now it hadn't registered.

I could imagine several reasons a refrigerator door might hang open, and I listed them one-by-one as though reciting magical incantations: Someone was defrosting the freezer; the refrigerator didn't work and the door was always open; someone had been interrupted and left it open.

Only the last possibility grabbed me. I glanced around the dim interior of the barn. Nothing was out of place. No movements in the shadows. I cautiously walked around the area that was cordoned off by the crime scene tape and looked inside the refrigerator. The interior bulb illuminated a six-pack of Diet Coke, a can of liniment and two small bottles of a clear liquid. I picked up one of the bottles. "Rompun," the label read, "sedative and analgesic for use in horses only. 100 mg/ml injectable. Not for use in horses intended for human consumption."

Perhaps it was the thought of horses as meat, or the memory of recent violence in this place; perhaps it was the small rustling sound in a dark corner of the barn. Whatever it was, a chill ran up my back. I looked around me and said, "Hello?"

The rustling noise could have been anything. Bat. Snake. Person.

I called myself a coward while I pushed the bottle of Rompun back in the refrigerator, switched off the barn lights and got out of there.

7

After a night of broken sleep and disturbing dreams, I awoke thinking of Lucie. Feeling the board in my hands again as it struck her head. Remembering the look of triumph on her face. The heavy weight of dread hung over me.

Most friendships are seldom tested. We float along on a cloud of good times—of parties and adventures and gifts and exchanged confidences—and it's not until something goes wrong that we realize that clouds are made of mist.

My friendship with Lucie had fallen to earth with a thud, and now I had to pick myself up and discover what was broken.

I listlessly ate a cold bagel and drank a pot of black coffee while Mack rubbed against my legs for attention.

I wondered if any of the Tulsa newspapers had picked up the story of Dale Nowlin and Lucie Dreadfulwater. The nearest newspaper stand was in Moodys. I'd have to drive six miles if I wanted an answer to my wondering.

It's a nuisance to drive that far for the smallest of conveniences, but it was a choice Charley and I had made. No one comes to our door hawking vacuum cleaners or booster-club candy; no one in black suits leaves pamphlets and asks if our sins are forgiven. If I pull off my top and work bare-breasted in the garden, no one calls the morality police.

On the other hand, the world could end, and we'd be the last to know.

It was afternoon before I mustered enough energy to call Lucie. No one answered, and once again, I was filled with a deep uneasiness. Only action could relieve my restlessness.

I threw a jacket in the back seat of the Civic and took off. The liquid, single-string runs on B.B. King's guitar accompanied me as I drove.

The day was sunny and bright, and the thick growth of oaks along the highway, which seem so dense and closed in during much of the year, opened to new vistas now that the trees had dropped their leaves.

I took the river road to Tahlequah. The miles slipped away— past the rugged faces of Hanging Rock and Eagle Bluff, past closed canoe rentals and glimpses of the Illinois River, still running high from the recent rains.

The Illinois River—which neither starts nor flows through Illinois, but in fact cuts a swath through eastern Oklahoma— gushes out of the spring-fed creeks of the Arkansas Ozarks. A week before, clouds had dumped six inches of rain in northwest Arkansas, swelling Flint Creek, Falls Creek, Luna Creek and nameless brooks and branches and forks, which in turn spewed into the Illinois.

Only days earlier, Lucie and I had defied death and ran the flooding river—all for the sake of a magazine story. There must have been more to it, though, or we would have taken one look at the churning water and scrubbed the idea. Perhaps Charley was right: We were the daredevil and the daredevil's apprentice. Now, the memory of that day ran through my mind like a movie in fast-forward.

I knew we were in trouble when the carcass of a Guernsey cow floated past. The cow, traveling at roughly the same speed as the white-water canoe that pitched and heaved under Lucie and me, pushed me over the edge of misgiving to outright apprehension. The side of the cow that was visible bloated grotesquely, like a worn tire on the verge of a blow out, and its tawny hide was slick with mud.

From the safety of shore, a river at flood stage is a thrilling experience; from the throat of the devil, its animal power is terrifying. The raw friction of elements grinding against each other creates the sound of thousands of voracious beasts feeding, akin to the roar of a rock slide or an avalanche. Death and decay wrap the frothing water in the odor of disaster.

The river narrowed and quickened, making the shore on either side a blur. Ahead of us, the river made an elbow macaroni turn to the west. All the flood's fury seemed to focus in that turn. My canoeing instruction, administered by Lucie earlier that morning, centered on one rule: The key to controlling the craft is to paddle faster than the current.

"Paddle faster," I yelled.

We had put in only half an hour before at Hanging Rock. In deference to the high water, it was to be a short trip in Lucie's new canoe: seven river miles to No Head Hollow. The name of our destination should have served as a warning.

The river was officially closed by the Oklahoma Scenic Rivers Commission. When the waters of the Illinois rise above 9 feet, 6 inches, the commission shuts down the float-trip operators. The normal level is 3 feet, 6 inches.

When Lucie had her brainstorm—about how to spice up my story on stay-at-home adventures—I had called the OSRC to find out what the penalty was when someone ignored their directive.

"Death," said the dour woman on the other end of the line. "If you have your own canoe, we can't stop you unless you're drunk." Her voice was hard with disapproval.

I was thinking about that phone call when the canoe sucked into an elbow-shaped bottleneck with a motion similar to being flushed down a toilet. The current whipped the canoe around so that we were sideways in the river. A low-lying branch scooped me from my seat and dangled my legs in the cold water. I yelled at Lucie while she and the canoe disappeared around the bend, Lucie mouthing something that the river snapped away before it reached me.

The branch teased me, dipped me up and down, then broke and dumped me in the river. The air temperature was seventy-eight degrees; the water felt like ice. The cold squeezed out my breath and left me gasping.

The river dragged me downstream behind Lucie, and I lost all sense of time and place. Nothing was real but the struggle to survive. Three times I went under while I tried to make the shore, and the third time my life jacket hooked on the roots of a submerged tree. Strainers, the river rats call them.

The roots grabbed me from behind and held me under while I struggled to free myself. I couldn't reach the hook that caught me in a deadly grip, and I couldn't think clearly enough to shuck the life jacket.

Just at the point where my lungs felt as though they would explode, something struck me hard from behind. I gulped in water and popped to the surface, my lungs convulsing. Lucie's voice finally got through, and I saw her scrambling along the bank, extending a long branch to me. I grabbed it, and she pulled me to her.

I owed her my life. Did yesterday pay my debt, or was the price yet to be determined?

When I arrived at the Southern Gothic Mausoleum, I half expected a replay of the night before: hysterical dog, skittish horse, absent people. But I knocked on the door, and Lucie opened it, with Custer close on her heels. Custer sniffed my shoes and trotted back inside.

Like survivors of a disaster, Lucie and I hugged each other. She looked good, despite the dark smudges under her eyes and the bruise on her cheek. Her hand was bandaged. Lucie wore tight denim jeans and a ribbon shirt, with a heavy silver and turquoise concha belt. Her long, black hair swung free. She looked like she was ready for a National Geographic photo shoot. Lives of the modern Cherokees.

"I hoped you'd come," Lucie said. "I kept you out of it. When I made a statement, I kept you out of it."

"It was stupid. We shouldn't have done it."

"It was the right thing. You have to believe that, Viv."

We were talking about the events of the day before in a weird kind of shorthand, which seemed appropriate somehow. As though our secret was too dangerous for words.

"I tried to call before I came over."

"We're not answering the phone."

By this time, we had walked into the living room. We sat across from one another in dainty armchairs that were upholstered in a diamond pattern of Dresden blue. A polished silver coffee service sat on an ornately carved walnut table that separated the chairs from a white-tufted sofa. Heavy oil paintings of a stern man and solemn woman in Victorian-era clothing hung above the stone fireplace. I wondered if the man was Lucie's great-great-grandfather, Samuel Dreadfulwater, and then I thought about what Lucie had said.

"You're not answering the phone? Are reporters bothering you?"

She poured me a cup of coffee before answering. "Not reporters. Someone called three times in a row this morning. When I answered, the person on the other end was silent. Just waiting. And breathing. Finally I unplugged the phone." Lucie leaned toward me. "My ancestors believed that the souls of murdered people can't pass into the next world until they are avenged. I had the weirdest thought when the phone rang the third time: What if it was Dale Nowlin?"

"It wasn't Dale Nowlin."

"I've thought about what happened yesterday from every

possible angle," Lucie said. "I shouldn't have killed him. I've shamed my family."

"You did what you had to do. Your family is lucky that you're still here."

She shook her head as though I were a child who couldn't possibly understand adult complexities.

By the time people reach middle age, their wrinkles sketch a map of their lives. Puffy bags under the eyes of the insomniacs and drinkers. Horizontal furrows across the foreheads of the worriers. Deep hatchet marks beside the mouths of the discontented. Lucie's face drew a picture of forty-five years of unhappiness.

"What happened yesterday?"

She looked away. "He wanted me to sell him some land. He didn't like my answer."

After awhile she spoke again. "This morning I realized I hadn't checked the mail yesterday so I went out to the mailbox. There was a rabbit head in the box."

"A real rabbit?"

"A real rabbit's head. Why would someone do that?"

"It was probably kids."

"I'm performing in Legends of the Five Civilized Tribes. We're supposed to open at the university next week."

I was confused by the sudden change of subject. "Yes, I remember you told me."

"In Legends, I tell a story about Rabbit. Rabbit is the trickster in Cherokee stories. But his tricks backfire, and he is often beaten at his own game by those he intended to victimize."

"It was probably kids," I said again. But I didn't believe it, and neither did she.

It wasn't until Lucie walked me to the car that I brought up the story I had been assigned the day before. After all that had happened, it seemed like a part of someone else's life.

I stood with one foot in the driver's side of the Honda; Lucie's hand rested on the top of the open door. I wasn't sure how to begin.

"I'm not sure how to begin," I said.

Her eyes were suddenly alert.

"Menckle assigned a story yesterday. Your grandfather is part of it. His disappearance."

Lucie's face became impassive, as though a mask had settled over it. "That happened so long ago," she said. "Why would anyone care about that?"

"It's part of Menckle's tabloid mentality. He thinks he can sell more magazines if he appeals to people's impulse to stare at train wreck victims."

"He wasn't in a train wreck."

"The story is about sensational crimes and unsolved mysteries in Cherokee County. People love that kind of stuff. I read once that it makes us feel giddy with relief because it happened to someone else and not to us."

"It happened to my grandfather," Lucie said. "I wish you wouldn't write about our family." Her lips thinned to a stubborn line.

"Wouldn't you like to know what happened?"

"As if you could solve a mystery that stumped the best legal minds in this county for more than half a century?"

Our voices were rising, and we stared at each other with an intensity that shut out everything else.

The question was never answered. Someone jerked Lucie away from the car.

She yelped in surprise or pain.

A tall, thin man gripped Lucie's arm, and she heaved away, falling to her knees.

"You're drunk, Truman."

"You shouldn't be talking to her," he said.

Oh, great, I thought, Truman Gourd in all his glory.

Truman was said to go on violent binges when he got drunk. He had been arrested for knifing a man outside a bar once, although the charges were later dropped. Rumor had it that a woman was involved.

We made an interesting tableau: Lucie on her knees, a threatening Truman towering over her, and me, not sure whether to rush to Lucie's defense or run.

"I'll talk to anyone I want to." Lucie rose to her feet as though she had been through this before, dusted off her jeans and faced Truman. "Where's Rachel?"

"She's with her people." The light reflected off Truman's face and made his acne-scarred cheeks look like hammered brass.

Lucie translated the cryptic statement. "She's at Oaks with your parents." She cradled the arm he had jerked.

Truman no longer looked threatening. He stumbled and half-fell against the Civic. "You think you're too good for real Cherokees," he said thickly.

Truman came from a family of Paint Clan Cherokees from Oaks. Oaks was just a few miles from Charley's and my land, but its culture was a world away. The Cherokees there cling to their traditions; some of them earn a bare living by selling buckbrush baskets, native dyes and herbs, and wild huckleberries. Truman's parents had not been happy, Lucie once told me, when he married a mixed-blood Cherokee.

"We're all real Cherokees, Truman." Lucie's voice held a weariness that said this was a repeat of an old fight.

It was ugly being in the midst of the domestic quarrel, as though I were seeing something that should be behind closed doors. I was afraid that if I left, though, Truman might get violent again. I faded into the background and waited.

Truman followed his own line of reasoning. "I told your father to call the police, and now look what happened." He shook his fist at her. "You going to kill me, too, someday?"

"Probably," Lucie said, her voice stripped of inflection. "If you don't kill me first."

"You're a crazy lady. Crazy!" Truman gave her one last stricken look and lurched off around the end of the house.

Lucie let out a mirthless laugh. "Welcome to my dysfunctional family."

I took her hand. It was trembling.

8

Sometime during the night, Charley made it home, and we lay close, his warmth spreading to me. He smelled like bar smoke and beer.

I awoke early, spooned against Charley's body, and I felt the urge to rub my body against his and slowly bring him to life. I rose on one elbow so I could see his face. One arm was thrown over his head as though he were warding off a blow. He looked so tired, even with his features relaxed in sleep, that I turned away and slipped out of bed.

Not much chance he would be up before noon. He lived on musician time. Downstairs, I brewed a pot of French Roast and carried a thermos down the hill to Spring Creek.

Sunday was a perfect autumn day. November can bring stinging, dusty winds, early snowstorms or late tornadoes to Oklahoma. Today it soothed us with sunshine and a soft breeze. I felt buoyant compared to the past two days. Nothing had changed; perhaps my capacity for guilt and fear had been exhausted.

I picked my way down the rocky path to a pool formed by a bend in the creek. It was just wide enough for skipping stones. I chose a flat rock and let it fly.

The breeze rustled the bare sycamore branches, playing accompaniment to the riffle of the water. Two buzzards glided on wind currents, and a gray squirrel crouched on a rock downstream. His bushy tail dipped into the water while he drank.

I wanted to sit along the creek forever, feeling the warm glow of the sun against my face. I wanted to be ignorant of friends in trouble, ignorant of Randy Silvers' birthday party scheduled for today. I wished I could slip down the winding stream to the Illinois River to the Arkansas to the Mississippi to the Gulf. I would simply disappear like John Dreadfulwater. No Lucie. No Maggie. No Charley. No guilt and no obligations.

When I returned to the house, Charley was up. He was wearing a pair of ragged cutoffs and a Pink Floyd T-shirt, reading the newspaper and digging into a plate piled high with fried potatoes, toast and eggs.

"That's last Sunday's paper," I said.

"It's still news to me." His wire-rimmed reading glasses made him look more like a professor than a rock musician. He was so thin that I could see his ribs through the T-shirt fabric, but he ate three huge meals a day, sometimes more, putting away food like a bear that had just emerged from hibernation.

I refilled my coffee cup and offered the pot to him.

"No thanks, no drugs."

"Don't be so goddamned superior."

He looked at me in mild surprise, his potato-laden fork suspended in midair.

"Toast?" he said finally. The potatoes disappeared into his mouth.

I took a deep breath and reached for the plate of toast. "Lucie killed a man Friday."

"Jesus! Who?"

I told a carefully edited version of Friday's events, leaving out the part I had played, and while Charley listened he pushed his plate aside and watched me with his indigo eyes.

"You know she'll be fine," he said. "If it even goes to trial, which it won't, there's not a jury in this town that would touch her family."

"I hope you're right." I breathed a little easier. I had told Lucie's story to the one person most likely to catch me in a lie, and he suspected nothing. After it happened, after I had struck Lucie with the board and recklessly involved myself in Dale Nowlin's death, I had wanted to tell Charley and to ask his advice, and now I realized that it didn't reflect well on my judgment. Better that he never know. Better that no one ever found out.

I bit into a slice of Charley's toast. "Nine-grain bread. Where'd you get it?"

"Randy bought it at a bakery in Kansas." A memory creased his forehead.

"Don't tell me Randy Silvers was the cause of another uproar."

Randy had moved to Tahlequah from Texas several months earlier to join the band just in time for its annual Spring Break gig in Tulsa. Her appeal went beyond the fact that she was gorgeous, with long, blond hair and a willowy, graceful figure. She also was feral; she moved with a cat-like self-involvement that was a powerful aphrodisiac.

Maybe it was the bass guitar that made her so macho and feminine at the same time. I had watched a fight break out in a local bar one night, with Randy egging on the fighters, striking her guitar while the men punched each other.

Charley shook his head. "I don't know how she does it. So we're in this little college bar in Lawrence, and the frat boys are crowding the stage. Randy starts doing a striptease while she's playing. The kids go wild. She'll get us all thrown in jail someday."

"This is the woman we're honoring today with a party?"

Charley laughed. "For the lack of a more appropriate ceremony."

"How about a gathering of the coven?"

Charley shot me a look. "Here's the bottom line. She's the best bass player I've ever had; maybe my route to a new recording contract. So I can overlook the other shit."

9

The Creekside Bar and Grill, the site of Randy Silvers' party, perched above Town Branch on the north side of town. The siding was unpainted barn wood, and the walls inside were covered with rusty tools and old advertising signs. Years of spilled beer had warped the wooden floor. The Creekside holds 150 if you count the three tables on the small deck out back.

Randy and the Powers That Be attracted, as usual, a standing-room-only crowd.

I was pleased to see the crowd. It was the band's tradition to play a benefit concert on each band member's birthday, with the proceeds going to the charity of the honored person's choice. I had heard that Randy was donating her money to the local women's shelter.

Hank and Betsy, the latest owners of the Creekside, prodded their staff to work at top speed serving the jostling, noisy crowd. The band had completed its sound check, and Randy Silvers stood at the bar, thronged by admirers.

I grudgingly admitted to myself that maybe I was a little jealous of Randy. Not only was she sexy and a gifted bass player, she had a dynamite whiskey voice. Everything seemed to come so easy to her.

I stood next to the band stand and watched her. Close behind me the voice of Neil Hannahan said cattily, "The blonde leading the blond."

"Leave it for one day," I said.

Neil was one of Randy's former blonds. He always seemed to be where she was, looking like a pathetic bloodhound, with his sad eyes and sagging jowls.

Neil moved to Oklahoma from Texas a couple years back. Although he showed promise as a sculptor, he was usually more interested in downing a six-pack than in working. He bummed beers the way some people bum cigarettes.

I once asked Neil how he had ended up in Tahlequah, and he told me he had come to visit a friend, got drunk and never sobered up enough to leave.

I escaped from Neil and joined Charley, who sat at a table nursing a bottle of mineral water while the band members waited for his signal. Crowded around the table were the rest of the band and its entourage: John Franklin, the drummer; his third wife, Corey; Badger, the keyboard player; and Badger's girlfriend, Janet-From-Another-Planet, who happened to be the first of John's ex-wives.

While waiting for the spirit to move him onto stage, Charley fanned away the cigarette smoke. "When I sign with a major label," he said in my ear, "I'll play smoke-free venues."

"Play some music."

Watching Charley transform himself from ordinary guy to rock musician is akin to watching mild-mannered Clark Kent turn into Superman. He turned to the other band members to make sure they were ready. When he was satisfied, he closed his eyes and took three deep breaths, seeming to take in electricity each time he inhaled. Then he stood and bounded onto the stage.

He broke into a guitar solo that silenced the audience with its first wailing blues note. The rest of the band filed onto the stage and one by one joined in Charley's flying guitar riffs with their instruments. It looked spontaneous, but I knew how often the Powers That Be had rehearsed their casual entrances.

I felt a pride that I really had no right to, and looked at the faces of the audience. They watched Charley and the rest of the band with a bemused wonder as though a pack of wild dogs had suddenly burst into song. Neil Hannahan gazed soulfully at Randy Silvers. Janet-From-Another-Planet rocked out. Corey went in search of a fresh drink.

I sipped a bottle of beer and wandered, letting the music surround me. After the intensity of the past two days, I felt relaxed and ready for whatever came. I had no reason to feel optimistic, but over the years, I've learned that sanity depends on laughing in the face of reality.

I must have been in a daze, because Neil Hannahan cornered me. Several beers into the evening, he was on a mission.

"I've been looking for you." He backed me up beside the silent jukebox.

"Oh?" I looked around for someone to palm him off on.

"I have a great idea for your magazine." He drained his can of beer, dug another out of his pocket, pulled the tab and took a drink, all in one practiced motion.

"The Neil Hannahan beer ballet," I said, trying to sidetrack him.

"A great idea," he said.

"It's not my magazine."

"I've just finished a trio of sculptures. I call them the Cherokee Legend series. Utlunta or Spear Finger, Raven Mocker and Tlánuwa, the great mythic hawk." He said the names as though he had carefully memorized them. "They're powerful figures. The *Green Country Journal* should cover my opening. It will be a cultural event."

"Heaven knows we could use more of those," I said with irony so light that it floated over Neil's head. Legends seemed to be sprouting all around: Lucie's storytelling; Neil's art. Fortunately, I didn't assign the stories, so I could sidestep publicity grabs.

"You need to pitch that to our new managing editor slash designer," I said. "Lisabeth Ellis."

There couldn't have been a more timely entrance. Lisabeth Ellis stepped through the door of the Creekside, and looked around as though she were a virgin entering a whorehouse.

I had met her only two days ago, when I learned that she had won the job I thought would be mine, and now here she was again.

Lisabeth was pale and thin like Randy Silvers, with fine, light hair. However, the resemblance ended there. Lisabeth had none of Randy's flamboyance. Tonight her hair was pulled back in a ponytail, and she wore khaki pants and a tailored blue Oxford shirt that gave her skin the bluish pallor of someone who spends most of their waking hours in front of a computer.

I turned to Neil to introduce him to Lisabeth, and then to make my escape. But Neil was gone.

I nodded at her, and she looked at me with a little frown as though she couldn't quite place me. I turned away, relieved of the responsibility of small talk, and made the rounds. By the time I'd said hello to the regulars, I was due for a trek to the bathroom. I was in one of the narrow stalls when two women entered the room.

The first woman's voice quavered, and I could hardly understand her. "Why did you make me come here, Randy? I just want to die."

I couldn't hear what Randy said.

Eavesdropping has its detractors, but overall, I think most people get a thrill from listening in on other people's conversations. I peeked through the crack in the stall door to see the speaker. Lisabeth Ellis.

"Let me find you a ride home, babe."

"No! I won't let anybody chase me away."

"Deal with it, Lisabeth." Randy's whiskey voice was harsh. "I have to get back."

I waited until they were gone to emerge from the bathroom.

Back in the bar proper, the band was taking a break, and Charley stood at the bar with a petite woman whose black braid hung almost to her waist. Lucie.

I joined them, and Lucie squeezed my hand.

"I'm glad Randy was able to reach you," Charley was saying. "She told me earlier today that she changed her mind and decided to donate the proceeds from the benefit to the Cherokee Heritage Center."

"We can use the money." Lucie looked around the bar. "Half the people in here have a significant amount of Cherokee or Creek or Chickasaw or Osage or some other Native American blood. But I wonder how many of them know any more about their culture than what they see on television."

I saw the faces in the bar with a sudden clarity that bordered on pain—or maybe I had downed too many beers. When you live in northeast Oklahoma, the home of 165,000 full- and mixed-blood Cherokees, the differences fade away. It seems normal to have neighbors and friends with last names like Drywater and Sixkiller and Moss. You forget where they came from; you forget that 900-mile winter trek in which one out of four of their ancestors died.

"Wow," I said, wordsmith that I am.

Lucie took my arm and pulled. "Let's go outside. It's too noisy to talk in here."

Charley's eyes met mine before he headed back to the stage. If there was a hidden message, I didn't receive it. Moments later, the band launched into one of my favorite songs. There's a line in it about "my fragile family tree." I let Lucie lead me out the door.

My car was parked nearby, and we climbed in it to escape the wind.

Clouds scudded across the night sky; the ghostly fingers of

bare trees reached toward a crescent moon. From the banks of Town Branch, the cry of an owl cut through the sound of the music from the bar. Lucie and I sat in silence for a minute, as though we had escaped from something and needed to catch our breaths.

"Beer?" I offered.

"You've got beer?" Lucie's eyes gleamed in the darkness.

"John Franklin loaded up a cooler with Pearls this afternoon before we left the house. He said it was a long trek to town."

"John's such a boy scout."

Pearl beer might not boast the prestige of an import, but it has something no other beer has: a rebus in the cap, a small puzzle of letters and pictures. Cheap entertainment.

I rummaged in the back and emerged with two beers, dripping with melted ice. I sighed with contentment. "This is the best time of year. If only winter didn't come next."

Lucie laughed. "There's always something worse that comes next."

The thought spread through the air like a virus. The optimism and peace I had felt earlier suddenly seemed naive, dangerous even. Something worse comes next. Time to change the subject.

"I almost forgot." I leaned over and dug in the glove box for a flashlight. "What does your bottle cap say?"

Lucie twisted the top off her Pearl and examined the cap, shining the light on it, turning it in her hand. Finally she said, "My glory was I had such friends."

"Yeats! Wait a minute, it can't possibly say that on a bottle cap."

Lucie laughed. "I had you going for a minute. And I gave you a chance to use your English degree."

"Finally, it's good for something."

She handed the cap to me. "How about 'Friends forever.' See? F-wren-Ds 4 + ever."

"The sentiment is appropriate, but that doesn't even look like a wren." The cap slipped from my hand and fell to the floor. I groped through the dust and discarded food wrappers, but it was lost.

"I didn't come out here to talk about dead white poets," Lucie said.

"Okay."

Lucie sipped her beer before she spoke. "I've trusted you with a lot—even though, as a journalist, it's your business to tell people's secrets."

"You think I'm going to tell anyone about coming to your house on Friday? We'd both end up in jail."

"We're not finished with that yet," she said. Sadness ran under her words like a dying river.

An uneasy silence settled over us, and I thought again about the vibration of the board in my hands. Of the dead body in the barn.

"I wasn't talking about that day," Lucie said. *That day.* "It's about my grandfather. John Dreadfulwater. Viv, don't write about him."

"You never even knew him. He disappeared in 1945."

"Yes. But he's part of my family's reputation. I've given them enough grief to deal with right now."

"It's a nothing story." I didn't like people telling me what to do. Even if they were friends. Especially if they were friends. "No one will pay any attention."

Lucie was silent for a minute. "I told my father," she said. "He became very angry. He said he would sue David Menckle and you."

"Jesus," I said. "Want another beer?"

The next wave of sidewalk drinkers and marijuana smokers poured out the front door, indicating the band was taking another break. It was an hour before midnight, and the familiar Sunday night melancholy settled over me.

I finished my beer and said to Lucie, "Ready to go in?"

She nodded. "I need to thank Randy and go home."

At least she had dropped the subject of my writing about her grandfather. Maybe we could work something out before it affected our friendship.

It was none of my business, but I asked anyway. "What's Truman up to?"

In the dim light, Lucie twisted the wedding band on her finger. "He's mostly bluff. I don't think he'd ever really hurt me."

"He scared me yesterday."

"He was just drunk."

"That's what Mary Jo Koepechne said when Ted Kennedy drove off Chappaquiddick Bridge."

"That's not funny, Viv."

"No. It's not."

I followed her into the bar.

Inside, we split up: Lucie to find Randy Silvers, me to find the bathroom again.

But Randy found me first. I was standing in the bathroom line when she spotted me. "Was Lisabeth outside?" Her face was pinched with worry.

"I didn't see her."

"She's been hitting the tequila a little hard." Randy looked at me beseechingly. "Could you find her and take her home?"

Hanging out at bars with a rock-and-roll band is not an uplifting way to spend your evenings. I sighed. "We met only the other day. I don't think she would go with me."

"She would if you asked, babe." Randy flashed her melting smile. "You're a real pal."

I didn't feel like anybody's pal but I agreed that if I saw Lisabeth, I'd offer her a ride.

I wandered around the bar, half-heartedly looking for

Lisabeth, and instead spotted Truman Gourd, pushing his way onto the deck. Worried that he might attack Lucie again, I followed him.

What happened next was confusing. The electricity flickered and went off. An excited buzz rushed through the crowd, and the air was split by a shrill scream.

When the lights came back on a few seconds later, the group in the bar surged toward the deck—the source of the scream. I couldn't make any headway through the closely packed people, so I ran out the front door of the bar and around to the back of the building, where the rickety fire escape steps rose above the creek to the deck.

I climbed the stairs and slipped through the gaping hole in the gate that was supposed to block the fire escape. The deck was crowded.

A circle formed around someone sitting on the deck. It was Lucie. I pushed through the onlookers and knelt beside her.

"What happened?"

She shook her head. "I was standing at the top of the stairs. Someone bumped me. Hard. The gate broke and I fell down a couple of steps before I caught myself."

"Are you all right?"

"I think so." She stood slowly. The crowd clapped, as though she were a football player walking off the field after an injury.

I looked around. I was sure I had seen Truman come out on the deck, and now I couldn't find him. By this time the band had joined the crowd. Betsy and Hank tried to clear the deck. It was like putting toothpaste back in the tube.

"Who screamed?"

"She did," a man said. He pointed at Lisabeth Ellis.

Lisabeth huddled by the rail, her face pasty. Randy's hand on her elbow seemed to be all that held her up. I joined them.

"She saw her fall," Randy said.

"Did someone push her?"

Lisabeth shook her head. "I didn't see anything. The lights went out."

Randy led her away. "Let's get you out of here, babe."

The show was over and the people on the deck went back inside. The night felt late as though we had been in suspended animation, transported to the hour where sleep hovers between dream and memory. Charley stood beside me, and he put a hand on my shoulder.

Lucie sat backward on one of the deck chairs while an amateur chiropractor worked his way down her vertebrae.

I crouched beside her. "What happened, Lucie?"

Her braid had come loose, and hair fell around her face like a shroud. "It was crowded; maybe someone just fell against me."

I stood to stretch, but Lucie misread my movements.

"Don't go yet." Her hand gripped mine. "Don't go."

Her touch was as cold as the night had suddenly become.

10

The morning Lucie's body was found, I slept in. Even now, that's what sticks in my mind. The memory points at me like an accusing finger. I drifted under a pile of quilts and fleece while a few miles away, Lucie's body grew cold on the bank of a rocky creek.

I should have sensed something, felt a passing shiver at least. After all, she was my friend. She was bound to me by ties stronger than blood. We had chosen one another.

There was a man, an old Cherokee named Roy Calico, who found her. Later he would tell me about that morning.

Roy Calico was thinking about the grape dumpling dinner his church was having Friday night when he found the body early Tuesday morning. He had been gathering wild grapes along Goodman Branch, a creek that cut through a back corner of Lucie Dreadfulwater's property. The hollow was deep, with rocky bluffs lining both sides of the creek. It was wild country; the highway was a quarter mile away and separated from the creek by underbrush-choked forest.

Calico's rheumatism was acting up in his right knee, and he hoped his wife, Audie, would appreciate the trouble he had taken to find the grapes.

Audie would take the wild grapes to the Park Hill Indian Baptist Church early in the afternoon, along with a crate of eggs. With the cooler weather, the hens had started laying again. She and the other women would begin preparing food for the large crowd that was expected.

The annual ritual brought back people who didn't bother to show up in church all year and old friends who had moved away. The Pigeon family was coming over from Welling, and the Fourkiller boys usually drove all the way from Spavinaw with their families piled in the backs of their pickups. Folks would fill their paper plates, sit at long, makeshift tables and chow down on eggs, grape dumplings, pinto beans, fry bread and soda.

Some of the men would go behind the church and pass around a bottle hidden in a paper sack. Later in the evening, the talk and laughter would get louder, and the women would exchange glances, call the little kids to the cars and pickups, and tell their men it was time to go home. It was the church's largest fund-raiser.

Calico rounded a bend in the creek, thinking he should pick up a pint of Wild Turkey on his way home. He was almost blinded by the sudden flash of early morning sunlight. He shaded his eyes and saw what looked like a pile of red rags maybe fifty yards downstream. He worked his way toward the pile, stepping on stones in the creek when the bank sloped up sharply.

The rags were half in the water, and the current tugged at them, pulling a banner of red downstream. Calico was uneasy. Something wasn't right. But his weak eyes didn't focus on the pile until he was close. When he realized an arm was sticking out, he jumped back and his heart rate went wild. He pushed hard against his chest with both hands, and he whispered, "Good Lord."

Calico looked at the bluffs and up and down the creek, looking for something, perhaps another person, perhaps a witch, although he didn't believe in witches. He knew who wore the red dress. He had seen her just the evening before, at dusk, when her vehicle had been parked at the metal gate that blocked casual access to her property.

She had been sitting in one of those big SUV things, with the door open and one leg stretched down toward the ground. Calico thought as long as she was here, he should ask her permission to gather wild grapes on her land. She jumped a little as though she were startled when he stopped his pickup, and she drew her leg back into the vehicle.

Calico took off his grimy black cap with the yellow McCullough logo and walked toward her. He stopped several paces away, giving her the same space he would a wary dog. "Ma'am? Ms. Dreadfulwater?"

She nodded in acknowledgment or recognition. It was hard to tell which.

"I'm Roy Calico, ma'am." he said in a gravelly voice. "Your neighbor up the road. I'd like your permission to pick some wild grapes along your creek."

"Yes. That would be fine," she said.

"Thank you ma'am. I'll be out here in the morning then."

His business taken care of, Calico should have left, but he paused, finding the woman's solitary presence in the darkening forest unnerving. Finally, he said softly, "Are you all right, ma'am?"

She laughed, but the sound held no humor. "I'm here to meet Utlunta. Do you think I'm all right?"

Calico was shocked. "Don't make jokes, Ms. Dreadfulwater," he said. "Let me stay here with you."

She frowned then, and said, "I'm sorry. I shouldn't have said that. Really, I'll be all right; you can go."

So he had left, and now here she was, at the bottom of a bluff, her body a sodden lump. Utlunta, she had said. Even Cherokee children know the legend of Utlunta, Spear-Finger, the witch who can take the shape of anyone she chooses. Then when her unsuspecting victim comes close, Utlunta stabs him with her sharp, bony finger. Utlunta, they say, rips out the liver and eats it. Utlunta cannot be killed.

Calico paused long enough to touch Lucie's skin and feel

the plastic-like rigor that indicated she had been dead for many hours. Then he bolted straight up the side of the hill, forgetting about the pain in his knee and the bag of grapes he had gathered, his workboots sliding for purchase on the steep slope.

11

Tuesday. The day I slept in. The wind pushed in a line of low gray clouds, and the temperature dropped ten degrees in an hour. November is the month of melancholy and decay.

After I finally rolled out of bed, I ran along the road to the east that follows Spring Creek. There's something about running in the morning and gasping for breath that gives me the illusion of being cleansed—as though the shock of fresh air hitting my lungs forces out all the crap I put into my body.

When I got home, I showered and then dashed, shivering, up the loft steps. Charley and I hadn't bothered to build a fire in the woodstove the night before, and now the house felt like a refrigerator.

"Why's it so cold?" I said to Charley.

"Because hell froze over?" he murmured from the cocoon of the bed. "Put some Stevie Ray Vaughn on the CD player and come back to bed."

"You can sing to me." My towel fell to the floor, and I slid between the sheets.

There were no phone calls to answer, no appointments to rush to, no band practices scheduled. Charley and I made slow, delicious love in the way that only two people who have devoted themselves to each other's pleasure can.

Charley and the Powers That Be were loading up later in the day to leave, this time for Texas, and wouldn't be back until late Sunday night. It was a proper sendoff. I felt hopeful, for the first time in months, that Charley and I could put past mistakes behind us and carve out something that was honest and lasting.

After Charley left, I spent the remainder of the morning in the garden. Fall cleanup time. Tear out the dead corn stalks and tomato vines; cover the strawberry plants with a thin layer of straw. Plant the apple trees that I had bought at a local nursery the week before.

The only way to garden in the Ozark Mountains is to subscribe to the build-up-your-body-by-tearing-it-down ethic. The rocks and roots tangle underground into a daunting thicket. If I am someday inducted into the National Masochism Hall of Fame, I will first thank my father, Randolph Gunter Powers, retired army sergeant and bona fide survival nut, for drilling that value into me. Second, I will thank our neighbor, Otis Choate, who sold Charley these 40 acres of rocky hillside. Then I will pull my rocking chair onto the porch and contemplate life from the cadence of its arc.

It was afternoon before I drove into Tahlequah. The wind blew steady and sharp, bending a line of pine trees in front of Northeastern State University on the north side of town, and hunching the shoulders of students as they ran between classes.

I had hoped to meet Lucie for lunch, but no one had answered the phone at her home or her studio. I parked the Civic in front of the *Green Country Journal* and sat for a minute, not yet ready to face the man inside. Instead, I studied the old Cherokee County courthouse, which dominates the square. A handsome two-story red brick structure, the building was originally the Capitol of the Cherokee Nation. After the Cherokee government dissolved in 1914, it fell into the hands of the county government. In recent years the county returned it to the Nation and built a new courthouse two blocks to the west. Now it's the courthouse again—but this time for the Nation and its system of justice.

I put off facing Menckle by walking across the courthouse square to the arts co-op where Lucie had a studio.

The glass door of the co-op was locked and the display room dark. I peered through the windows. In the dim light, the handwoven rugs, Trail of Tears paintings, buckbush baskets and beaded jewelry looked dusty and faded, as though no one with money would be coming by—ever.

I thought about the story Menckle had assigned me. Unsolved mysteries of Cherokee County. What had seemed like a good idea only days ago now sounded like the cheapest form of tabloid journalism. I shouldn't have told Lucie about it. Had I not needed the money, I would have turned around and gone home.

Instead I went to the office. I would talk to Menckle and see if he could be persuaded to accept a topic that was less sensational.

The conversation never took place.

Tanya Webster wasn't at the reception desk when I came in, but Lisabeth sat in front of her computer. Her face was pale, as though she had a hangover or hadn't slept well. There was something more, though, a kind of suppressed excitement that flushed her high cheekbones.

She looked at my face, then said, "You haven't heard, have you?"

"Is this a guessing game?" A feeling of dread swept over me. My first thought was that something had happened to Charley.

"God, Viv," she said, "I shouldn't be the one to tell you." Her voice was anguished, but there was a second when she paused that I saw in her eyes the glee of the town gossip, the power of breaking news.

It came out in a rush. "Lucie Dreadfulwater is dead. They're saying it may be suicide."

I couldn't take it in. "That's not possible," I said in someone else's voice. "I saw her on Sunday. You saw her on Sunday."

"Someone found her body this morning on Park Hill Mountain."

I just stared at her, as if I could prevent reality by not believing.

"I'm sorry, Viv; I heard you were close."

Do you know that your heart is a muscle, and when something hurts, you can clench your heart tight like a fist? Sometimes it feels so tight that it might collapse in on itself.

Somehow I made it to the Civic, and after I had fumbled the key into the ignition, I looked up to see Menckle's face staring at me through the windows of the *Green Country Journal*. Our eyes locked. His face was expressionless, but something about his eyes made me think, *he's afraid*.

I managed the two blocks to Maggie's without wrecking the Civic. I didn't know where else to go or what to do. It's funny how we seek out family when we're most vulnerable.

I don't know what I would have done if Maggie wasn't home, but she was. Wearing a silky flowered dressing gown and without her makeup on, she looked like a child.

Jake greeted me with his usual bark of welcome, but I ignored him. Maggie took one look at my face and said, "God, Viv."

"I heard Lucie Dreadfulwater's dead." I tried to sound matter-of-fact.

"Jesus." Maggie put a cigarette to her lips. "What happened?"

"I don't know," I said, my voice rising. "I need to know. That's why I'm here. Call your buddy Rance Dawes and get some information."

"He wouldn't know anything about it," she said. "He's on nights now. He just left here to get some sleep."

"Look, dammit! Call him."

Maggie sucked on the cigarette until a halo of smoke billowed around her head. Then she went to the phone and punched in the numbers. I paced back and forth, and Jake matched my steps, as though we were playing a game.

"Hey, baby." Maggie had Rance on the line, and her voice was as silky as her gown. "Sorry to wake you, but I need something."

She bit her lip while she listened. "I know. I know," she said. "I wouldn't be calling if it wasn't important. I heard Lucie Dreadfulwater is dead, and I want to know what happened."

She paused a minute, then said, "Call me back, okay?"

Maggie and I sat in grim silence in her living room, waiting for word from Dawes. It was a macabre reenactment of Friday afternoon when Maggie and I had waited for Dawes to come by.

I tried to picture Lucie's face. It flashed past like fading photographs of moments we had shared. Already she was slipping away from me.

I summoned an incident from a week earlier. I had gone by Lucie's studio at the crafts co-op. The studio seemed less a necessity and more a way for her to get out of the house and away from Truman. Why would a storyteller need a studio? However, she decorated the room with props and books and the work of other artists and filled the space with inspiration.

Her door was ajar, so I tapped on it and walked in. Lucie was on the phone. "You son of a bitch," she had said, "you've already put us through too much!" She slammed the receiver in its cradle.

The usually bright studio was dim—the heavy drapes drawn over the tall windows—and I saw what Lucie's face would look like when she became an old woman. The lines around her mouth were deep slashes, her eyes hooded, her jaw shaded and heavy. She was middle-aged, and I had never before realized it.

She started when she saw me, then smiled. Her face became the youthful Lucie I knew. We didn't talk about her phone conversation that day, but now I wondered who she had been talking to.

Maggie drew my attention back to the present. "May I get you a drink?" Her formal manner fit the occasion.

"Water. Water would be good."

The phone rang, and I started to answer it, but Maggie already had it in the kitchen. I went in and stood beside her. For my benefit, she repeated everything Dawes said.

"So her body was discovered about 7:30 a.m. on her Park Hill property by a neighbor. From the preliminary investigation at the scene, it looks like suicide. She may have injected herself with a tranquilizer and fallen off a bluff."

I shook my head. "She wouldn't do that!"

Maggie put her hand over the mouthpiece. "What?"

"She wouldn't kill herself!" I was angry and anguished at the same time.

Maggie spoke into the phone again. "Rance, why are they saying suicide?"

Once again she acted as translator. "Traces of a drug and the empty syringe were found in her purse on top of the bluff. And there was a note. What did the note say?" I could hear Dawes' voice rise, but I couldn't hear what he was saying.

"I know, baby," Maggie said smoothly. "If I knew someone at the sheriff's department like I know you, I would have called him instead."

She hung up and turned to me, a look of triumph on her face. "There was a note, but the sheriff's department is handling this case, and they won't say what was in it. I expect this one will get handed to OSBI; it's too hot for our sheriff to hang on to."

OSBI is the Oklahoma State Bureau of Investigation. It steps in whenever there's a major felony. I felt a small surge of hope; at least I knew someone in that department who might talk to me. But first I would see what the sheriff had to say.

I headed toward the door.

"Where are you going?" Maggie blocked my way.

"Sheriff's office."

"I've seen this look on your face before. Something goes wrong, and you think you have to set it right again. Nothing can get in your way."

I was barely listening. "What's wrong with that?"

"Nothing," Maggie said. "It's just that you get tunnel vision. If a train was going to hit you from the side, you'd never see it coming. I'm going with you."

"I don't want you."

"Tough."

She shrugged out of her robe and into a tight dress while she talked. "Just give me a minute to put some makeup on."

"I'm leaving."

"Viv, puh-leeze!" Her voice rose in the little-girl wheedle that had annoyed me ever since she had been old enough to tag along. But it worked. It had always worked.

I glanced at my watch. "Five minutes."

On West Delaware, the gray walls of the Cherokee County Courthouse rose behind the more friendly facade of the public library. The sheriff's office was located in the basement of the courthouse. Sheriff Wes Turner would not be happy to see me of all people when he was busy with a major case, but I had to talk to him.

One of my last acts as a newspaper reporter was to uncover a fraud scheme involving two of Turner's deputies. Turner had been angry about the unflattering publicity the story shed on his office; however, he had narrowly won re-election.

Maggie and I parked on the south side of the building and walked down a dozen concrete steps and through a heavy metal door. The hallway was brightly lit with fluorescent lights. At the far end, metal doors barred the county jail. The warm air was heavy with the acrid stench of burned coffee and unwashed bodies.

The Sheriff's Department lay through a gray metal doorway. A woman in a brown deputy's uniform talked on a phone at a desk in the outer office. She eyed us as we came in. I could see Turner's white hair through the glass windows in his office. He was talking to a man. Even though I could only see his back, Truman Gourd's long, black braid made him immediately recognizable.

Turner shook Truman's hand and put a hand his shoulder, and then Truman came into the outer office. He looked the way someone who had just lost his wife should look. The acne scars stood out on his face, and grief had twisted his face. I don't think he would have noticed me if I hadn't stepped in front of him. He stopped like a robot who has sensed an obstacle and must change direction to get around it.

"Truman," I said, taking his arm. He brushed my hand off and walked around me. His hand felt like ice.

Turner was watching through his window. He stuck a match stick in his mouth and started working it. His round face was impassive, but when he hitched his brown polyester pants up under his belly and came through the door, the dislike in his voice was unmistakable.

"Whatever you and your buddy want, Powers, I'm busy," he said. He turned to the woman at the desk. He got as far as, "Sharon, dammit..." before he saw that she was on the phone. She looked at him helplessly, and he looked at me again. The match stick was moving quick and furious in his mouth.

"I need to talk to you about Lucie Dreadfulwater." I talked fast so he couldn't cut me off. "There's been talk about suicide. That's not possible."

Turner gave me a disgusted look, then he wheeled on his polished black cowboy boots and motioned us in. Maggie fluffed her hair, hitched her dress higher on her thighs, and followed me. Once we were in his office, he closed the door and leaned against it.

"Okay," he said, "Are you coming to me as the press or as an individual?"

"Individual."

"And you would be?" He glared at Maggie.

"I'm Viv's sister, Maggie Powers," Maggie said sweetly, extending her hand. "It's a pleasure to meet you."

Turner grunted and took her hand. "Your sister's a pain in the ass," he said.

"Isn't that the truth." They exchanged a look as though they shared a private burden.

Turner took a deep breath, shook his head as if trying to clear it and turned to me again. "So what makes this any of your business?" He pulled off his horn-rimmed glasses and wiped them on the tail of his khaki shirt.

I could tell he enjoyed having me at his mercy, and it pissed me off. But I couldn't afford the luxury of anger right now. I took a deep breath and let it out slowly.

"I know Lucie Dreadfulwater." I corrected myself and felt my heart tighten again. "I knew Lucie. I spent some time with her on Saturday and Sunday." I didn't mention the time we spent together on Friday when Dale Nowlin's body lay in the barn, and she was screaming at me to strike her with the board. I lost my train of thought and hesitated before I remembered what I wanted to tell Turner.

"She was not in a suicidal frame of mind," I said. "She's not that kind of person."

"You're a psychologist now?"

"Look, Turner, I'm begging for information. Anything. Does that please you?"

Maggie put her hand on my arm to remind me to stay calm.

"It's a change; that's for sure." Turner replaced his glasses and spat out the match stick. His eyes were watchful. He wasn't bad as law enforcement officials go; he wasn't stupid. But he did have an enormous ego, and I had made his administration look bad in public. I waited him out.

"Okay, Ms. Cronkite," he finally said. "What was her frame of mind?"

I ticked off the items on my fingers. "First, she didn't expect to go to jail for Dale Nowlin's death. Second, she was rehearsing for a storytelling event at the university this week. Most important, she loved her daughters; she wouldn't do that to them."

"I'm not going to stand here and debate you on things you don't know nothing about," Turner said. "But I will tell you this. You saw her husband here. He identified the body earlier, and he came by to make a statement. She was depressed. She felt like she had shamed her family; that's a big deal in some cultures. They found a note near her body. It's going to take an autopsy to determine the cause of death. That's all. I'm busy. Get out of here."

"She was my friend."

"I know, and I'm sorry," Turner said. "Go."

12

Over Maggie's protests, I dropped her off at her house, and then I sat in the Civic for a long time, the wind rocking it. I thought about Lucie. About the things we had done together. About the turbulent final days. The longer I sat, the more possible it seemed that Lucie had killed herself. There was the note. And I remembered the bottle of Rompun I had picked up in the barn refrigerator on Friday. Some kind of tranquilizer, Rance Dawes had said. I thought about the terrible emotional burden she surely had been dealing with: her husband's alcoholism and violence, Dale Nowlin's death, the pain she felt she had caused her family. What was it she had said in the car the last night I saw her? "There's always something worse that comes next."

I hit the dash with my palm. I should have told her I would back off when she asked me not to write about her grandfather. I should have been there for her.

I wanted to go home. I wanted to burrow in and lick my wounds. I started the Civic and headed north.

The wind let up as I was driving, and a fine drizzle settled over the hills, making them feel low and cramped. The gray of the sky and rain was reflected in the farm ponds and on the roofs of the chicken houses. The soggy gray fur of an opossum lay in the road near Moodys.

I made excuses for Lucie as I drove. What person of intelligence hasn't considered, at one time or another, suicide as a possible solution? Don't we have the right to check out of this life whenever we decide it's time? Most of us pull away from the edge, though, and decide that living is the lesser of two evils.

I pulled into the muddy driveway and automatically stopped to get the mail. A gust of wind shook the cedar tree that sheltered the farm-sized box and showered me with scented rain. The box was crammed with catalogs, magazines and junk mail. I scooped it into the canvas bag that I keep in the Civic and skidded up the slick driveway to the house.

The house was chilly and filled with the heavy acrid smell of damp wood ashes. Mack followed me in, demanding food. I dropped the bag of mail on the table, fed the cat and built a fire. Then I pulled the rocking chair up close to the stove and watched the flames spit and sputter through the open door. Mack leaped into my lap, purring, and I stroked his soft fur. I rocked back and forth, felt the heat on my face and listened to the rain dripping from the eaves. My body felt as heavy as a rain-soaked quilt.

Eventually I dragged myself from the chair to find some food. I washed down a peanut butter sandwich with a glass of well water and sat at the kitchen table to sort through the mail.

It's important to go through the motions.

I have a system for mail. Magazines go in one pile—receiving *Utne Reader*, *Outside Magazine* and *Organic Gardening* all in the same day ordinarily would have thrilled me, but I tossed them aside. Catalogs and junk mail go in a second pile, bills in a third, and any personal correspondence goes in a final group.

At the bottom of the bag was a large manila envelope, hand-addressed to me. It had no return address. It was the only unidentifiable piece of mail, so I opened it. Inside was a smaller manila envelope with a note taped to it. My hands started shaking when I recognized Lucie's graceful scrawl.

Dear Viv,

This is really silly, embarrassing even, but could you please, please bring this packet to me on Wednesday morning? If there's some reason that you can't (and you will know what I mean), I'm entrusting the contents to you. This is definite proof that I've watched too many late-night movies. Ha, ha. I owe you one.

                                              Lucie

Slowly the meaning filtered through. "You will know what I mean." I lifted the metal clasp of the second envelope and pulled out a sheaf of papers. The top paper said "Real Estate Purchase Contract." I read the legal description several times before it made any sense. Part of Lucie's Park Hill tract. I had a county plat book somewhere. I tore through the stacks of books and folders on the cluttered desk in front of the bookshelves, found the Park Hill area in the plat book and confirmed it.

Someone had been trying to buy eighty acres of Lucie's land. That much was apparent. The same land on which she had died. It lay to the southeast of the property the family mansion stood on. On the contract, someone had marked an X next to a line at the bottom to indicate where Lucie should sign her name. The line was blank.

The buyer was listed as M&M Investments, Inc., and the purchase price was $400,000. I did some quick division in my head. That was a generous offer for Cherokee County land—even though it was close to the Cherokee Nation Headquarters.

I put the document aside and examined the second sheet. It was a letter on watermarked bond, thanking Lucie for agreeing to visit Hot Springs, Arkansas, as a guest of M&M Investments, Inc. The embossed image of a thoroughbred race horse on the corporate logo alerted me to the business M&M Investments was in. Hot Springs was the home of the Oaklawn Jockey Club, the region's best-known horse racing track.

"We're certain," the letter ended, "that once you meet us and see our plans, you will agree that the property is well-suited to our purposes."

It was dated on Monday and signed by Jonathan Marlin. The name meant nothing to me.

Paper-clipped to the letter was an itinerary. Lucie was to meet Michael Probst, a pilot, at the Tahlequah airport at 10 a.m. Wednesday. Someone would be waiting at the Hot Springs airport to take her to the Arlington Hotel. She and Jonathan Marlin would meet at Oaklawn; post time was 1:30. She would return home the following day.

The realization of what the packet meant hit me like a blow: Lucie had not killed herself. There was no way. She was wheeling and dealing and covering her bases. And I had almost bought into it. I sank into a chair, clutching the papers. I read for the second time the note Lucie had taped to the envelope. The words had taken on a sinister meaning:

"If there's some reason that you can't (and you will know what I mean), I'm entrusting the contents to you."

My first thought was to head back to town and give the packet to Sheriff Turner. But from out of a deeper place, a voice told me to wait. The packet had come to me for a reason, and this time I couldn't let Lucie down. I wasn't sure at which point I had let her down, but I knew that I had. When I struck her with the board? When I stayed silent these past days while she dealt with the fallout from Dale Nowlin's death? When I accepted Lucie's suicide as fact?

I needed to clear my head. I walked out on the porch and from its shelter watched the wind whip gusts of rain across the valley below. The air around was gray and thick as though the sky was gathering me in.

Lucie had been afraid of something. And her fear had prompted her to send the packet to me. Saturday she had told me about the rabbit head in her mailbox and the phone calls.

Sunday night she had almost been pushed from the deck of the Creekside. On Monday... what had happened on Monday?

I suddenly realized that I had never told Lucie about the open refrigerator door in the barn. I had gone to her barn that night to feed her horse, the door stood open, and I had picked up the bottle of Rompun. Had someone been there in the barn while I was there, watching from the dark shadows? There had been too many other distractions, and somehow, I had forgotten to say anything to Lucie about it. A sound like a growl began in the back of my throat, but it came out as a moan.

Why had Lucie gone to a remote area of her land on Monday night? Had she left a will, and if so, who would own the property now? What other factors came into play? Dale Nowlin's death? What had her "suicide" note said?

How could I have bought into the notion of suicide?

I needed to talk to someone. I tried the number Charley had left, even though it was unlikely he had reached Austin already. A surly bartender answered, and I left a message for Charley to call me.

I knew what a proper, law-abiding citizen would do: Take the papers into the sheriff's office. I would do it first thing in the morning. To reinforce my decision, I took the manila envelope to the Civic.

The last light was fading from the forest. I paused beside the open door of the Civic and listened. The rain had stopped. No birds called or dogs barked. Even the hum from the faraway highway was silent. Only the hypnotic sound of water dripping from the eaves to the porch steps punctuated the silence. This is what it would feel like to be all alone in the world.

On the Civic's floorboard, the faint dash light glinted off a piece of metal. It was the Pearl bottle cap Lucie had handed to me Sunday night. I picked it up and read the rebus: "F-wren-Ds 4 + ever." It seemed like a talisman, and I held it in my hand, rubbing the smooth top, as though a genie might appear and tell me what to do next.

Sometime in the night I dreamed about Lucie. Dogs were chasing her. Huge, snarling dogs. With the omniscience of a dreamer, I knew these were the hounds of hell. I awoke to the distant cry of baying hounds.

I slipped on a long robe and a jacket and stood shivering on the front porch. The rain had stopped and the sky was clear. There might be frost by morning. A fine sliver of moon caught on the treetops, and a fire flickered on the ridge across Spring Creek. Someone was running their dogs.

There are plenty of animals to chase in these hills: whitetails, raccoons, coyotes, fox. Once I saw a bobcat. A few bear live deep in the hollows, recent immigrants from the Arkansas Ozarks.

As I stood barefoot on the porch, I remembered a long-ago hunting trip to Colorado with The Sergeant. Perhaps I had been squeamish, perhaps I felt the contest was unfair; whatever the reason, I wanted the hunt to fail. I had gathered all the power of my mind to broadcast a warning. *Someone is after you. Go away.* It was probably a coincidence, but for the first time in his hunting career, The Sergeant didn't take a trophy home.

It was the last hunting trip we took together.

I turned back into the dark house and climbed up the loft steps to the bed, but sleep eluded me. When the gray light of dawn fanned through the windows, the first thing I saw was a large double-walled basket hanging on the loft wall. Lucie had given it to me. The seven strands of reed that formed the skeleton of the basket represented the seven clans of the Cherokee. It was delicately tinted, with the acorn color forming a zigzag pattern of lightning against the darker walnut.

The thought that I'd never see her again hit me full force. I had never lost a friend before, and an unexpected tangle of emotions engulfed me. I was left with a feeling of things unsaid, conversations forever unfinished, favors never granted. I felt angry at Lucie for leaving me, and then I felt guilt for the anger.

We are fortunate to have a few good friends in our lives—friends we share an unspoken understanding with, friends who accept our foibles and failings and nevertheless see something of value in us. We can't afford the loss of a friend.

I knew what I had to do. I would go to Hot Springs in Lucie's place and meet this Jonathan Marlin. Maybe it wasn't a brilliant idea, but it was the only one that made sense to me.

13

I showed up at the Tahlequah airport a few minutes before ten in my one dress-for-success suit. I thought it might pass for something Lucie would wear to a business meeting. The navy skirt and jacket were subdued, but the relaxed cut allowed me to push the jacket sleeves back.

My lips were red, thanks to the tube of lipstick Maggie had dropped in my Christmas stocking months before. I wasn't accustomed to wearing lipstick, and I kept wanting to lick my lips. A cream-colored silk blouse and my only pair of heels, freshly polished, completed my professional masquerade.

The sky was overcast, but the air had warmed, and the humidity settled on Cherokee County like a clammy blanket.

I didn't have a plan of action other than presenting myself to Michael Probst, pilot, and seeing what happened. Play it as it lays.

A redbone hound greeted me when I walked into the airport office. He lifted his head from the concrete floor and thumped his tail.

"That's Leon," a man's voice said from behind the counter. "Leon Redbone. Get it?" The man was young, with thick brown hair and a matching mustache. He was wearing a brown leather flight jacket, even though the morning was warm.

"Leon Redbone and Frank Zappa," I said. "Twins separated at birth."

He looked at me approvingly and said, "Michael Probst."

I faced my first test, but skirted it by shaking his hand and showing him Lucie's itinerary with my free hand. "Can we make it on time?"

If he knew Lucie or if he had read about her death in the newspaper, I would have to switch to plan B. I didn't have a plan B.

"No problem. The ceiling has lifted enough for us to fly VFR." Probst made it sound like he had arranged the altitude of the clouds. "I just called the weather station, and we'll have a tailwind this morning. Are you ready?"

"VFR?"

"Visual Flight Regs."

"What if the clouds come back down?"

"I'm instrument-rated."

Except for the one time Lucie and I had gone skydiving, I hadn't flown in a single-engine plane. I preferred my adventures to be land-based, and without Lucie to cheer me on, I felt as confident as if I were embarking on a trip across the Pacific in a raft.

"Grab your luggage, and we'll be off into the wild, blue yonder."

"I'm traveling light," I said, indicating my shoulder bag. "What you see is what you get."

"I wasn't going to mention this," Probst said, "but since you brought it up—you're not quite what I expected."

"Which way to the plane?" And then, casually, I hoped, "Exactly what were you expecting?"

Probst led the way to the runway. "I don't know. It's just that with a name like Dreadfulwater you expect someone who looks a little more, you know, ethnic."

We stopped in front of a white Piper Arrow with a navy blue stripe. Probst leaped up on the low wing and opened the door.

"I have to get in first," he said.

I could tell the heels and I would not get along for an entire day. I had already twisted my ankle once, and I almost caught my left heel in the narrow step onto the wing.

"Probst," I said, trying to not show too much leg while I settled into the co-pilot's seat, "You must be new around here."

He nodded. "Six months now. Moved here from San Diego."

"You need a quick history lesson. "

Probst tore the pre-flight checklist off the velcro on the door and studied it while he chewed the end of his mustache.

I plowed ahead, ignoring my first rule of successful lying— never explain.

"The Cherokees have been intermarrying with whites for more than 200 years now. Many of the Cherokees on the tribal rolls have less than fifty-percent Cherokee blood. I know Cherokees who have blond hair and blue eyes."

Probst was only half-listening. He frowned and moved his lips while he read as though he were a little boy making out the words in his first reader. I hoped he flew better than he read.

Probst handed me a headset—"ear protection and communication," he said—and we were off.

I waited until we reached cruising altitude before asking any questions. In the meantime, I watched the receding landscape of eastern Oklahoma unfold beneath us like a colorful tapestry. Except for Lake Tenkiller to the south and the Illinois River behind us now, the view was of wooded hills and farms with eroded fields and small ponds round like gemstones. And everywhere were rows of white chicken houses, those 100-foot-long pollution factories.

I spoke into the small microphone dangling in front of my mouth. "So, Probst, you work for M&M Investments?"

He spoke without turning his head. "I'm strictly free-lance. Have plane, will travel."

"That reminds me," he said. "Do you know why there are more men pilots than women?"

I shook my head.

"Because if God meant for women to fly, the sky would be pink!"

I groaned as though I thought that was funny. Have to keep the communication channels open. "Is Jonathan Marlin footing the bill for this entertainment?"

"Jonathan Marlin? Oh! Jonathan Marlin. He signed the check, but I'm throwing in the entertainment."

I tapped my fingers against my leg in frustration. I never went into a situation cold if I could help it, and I had hoped Probst could fill in a few pieces before we reached Hot Springs. "What can you tell me about M&M Investments?"

"Nada," he said. "This Marlin guy called Monday to book a flight. Gave me a name and a time."

We arrived in Hot Springs forty minutes later, circling around a pine-crowned mountain and coming into the airport from the south. From the air, the town looked prosperous, with large houses and a resort-lined lake. There were swimming pools, golf courses and manicured lawns.

As I stepped out onto the pavement, I wished for my comfortable Levis and running shoes. The sun was trying to break through the high clouds, and the air was thick with humidity.

A skinny, colorless man in a golf shirt and slacks stood in front of the terminal, anxiously watching me as I crossed the pavement. I waved at him, and he started my way.

I turned to Probst. "I may not stick to the program," I said. "Where can I find you if I want to leave tonight?"

Probst groaned. "Wouldn't you know? Just when I've got something going." He opened his hands in resignation. "Mama Teresa's. It's in the phone book."

I turned my attention to the skinny man. His humorless smile revealed crooked teeth, and long strands of grayish-brown hair were combed over the bald spot on top.

"You looking for me?"

"You're the only Piper Arrow this morning." His voice was

gravelly.

I doubted that this little man was Jonathan Marlin. However, I had found in my years as a reporter that acting dumb usually opens up people more than acting smart. So I extended my hand, and said, "Mr. Marlin?"

"Oh no, ma'am." He shook his head so hard one of the strands of hair fell out of place. He smoothed it back. "I'm Mr. Marlin's assistant. Albert."

"Well, Albert, what's on the agenda?"

"We get your bags, get you settled into your hotel, get you some lunch, I take you out to the track." He looked at his watch. "Post time is two hours from now."

I gestured at my shoulder bag, and thought to myself, I'll be damned if I explain my lack of luggage again.

He raised his eyebrows and motioned me toward a black Buick in the parking lot. I didn't wait for him to open my door. When I slid in the front seat, I earned another lifted eyebrow. The interior reeked of closed-in heat and stale cigarette smoke.

"D'ya mind?" Albert asked, simultaneously lighting a Camel and turning on the air conditioner. He didn't wait for an answer.

We drove past the Wal-Mart store that anchors the edge of nearly every Arkansas and Oklahoma town, and turned onto a broad tree-lined street. I drew in a deep breath of second-hand smoke.

"Tell me a little about Mr. Marlin," I said, trying to sound young and uncertain. "It makes me nervous to meet people."

"Oh, you don't need to be nervous about Mr. Marlin," Albert said, resting his arm along the top of the seat. He talked around the Camel hanging from his lips. "He knows how to treat people. He wanted to meet you himself at the airport, but he had business to attend to."

I waited, knowing that most people will say anything to fill the hole created by silence.

"I don't mean to make him out to be a saint 'cause he ain't,"

Albert said after a short pause. "But you treat him right, he'll do okay by you. Y'know?"

I nodded encouragingly. "He likes horses, I guess?"

Albert laughed, a short, choking bark. "He don't like horses as much as he likes tracks. World-class parimutuel racing. It ain't about the horses anyways. They don't even have real horses here this time of year. You watch 'em on a screen while they race at Santa Anita or Aqueduct. Places like that."

"No horses? You just watch TV screens?" What a rip-off. If I were a betting person, I'd at least want the sounds and excitement of the real thing before losing my dollars.

"It's live via satellite," Albert said as if he had read my thoughts.

I let the silence build again, but he didn't speak. I tried another direction, putting together the scanty information I had along with my best guess. "What makes Mr. Marlin think a race track in Cherokee County would be a good investment?"

"The fans at Oaklawn wager more than $50 mil a year," Albert said. "Wouldn't you like a piece of that?"

I breathed a little easier. At least I wouldn't be going in cold to the meeting with Marlin.

Albert turned west onto Central Avenue and turned garrulous again. "This here's the historic district," he said. "Mr. Marlin said you might like a little sightseeing tour since you hadn't been here before."

"Great." Perhaps Lucie hadn't been here before, but I had.

Albert launched into an enthusiastic recital of the history of the ornate Victorian-era bathhouses that lined Central Avenue. They looked like once-grand ladies who had fallen on hard times. Many were boarded up; paint peeled on the scrolls and gargoyles, and dust muted the stained glass windows.

"If you have time," Albert said, "visit the Fordyce Bathhouse. Part of downtown is a national park, and the Fordyce is the first bathhouse that's been fixed nice like it used to be. The only reason Hot Springs is here is because of the thermal springs under the town. The hot water is good for whatever ails you, and folks come here from all over the world to take baths. Mr. Marlin thinks people come for the horses. This stuff was here way longer."

He pulled into the driveway of a tall, white hotel that rose out of the hillsides like a sultan's palace. "This here's the Arlington. It's the best in Hot Springs. Al Capone used to hang out here in the thirties."

I got out of the car before Albert could help me. "So," I said. "You'll pick me up here in an hour?"

He started to get out of the car.

"I'll be all right on my own."

He frowned. "One of them modern ladies, huh?"

I flashed what I hoped was a disarming smile. "I'll be watching for you in an hour."

Albert reluctantly drove away. A red-coated bellhop walked toward me, and I waved him off. I watched while Albert disappeared down the street, and then I turned and walked the other way. I needed to pull my thoughts together before I met Jonathan Marlin.

I bought a gyro from a sidewalk vendor and carried it up to the Promenade, the broad brick walkway above the downtown area. A stone bench under a cherry tree served as a hard but aesthetically pleasing vantage point for watching the noon-time crowd while I ate.

I thought about Marlin's offer for Lucie's land. Cherokee County already had a small horse track, but it was more akin to a county fairground than to the resort-like facility at Hot Springs.

I knew how important Lucie's land was to her. I wondered if the $400,000 had been enough inducement to change her mind.

I couldn't see how murder fit into that picture. Marlin was expecting Lucie, which seemed to absolve him of any knowledge of her death. Still, he might know something that would point me to her killer. All I had to go on was the note Lucie sent me and her unnamed fear.

14

I was in the lobby of the Arlington when Albert came back. I spotted him first and tottered out to the Buick on my ankle-breaking heels. Albert opened the back door for me, and I slid in.

Grim silence replaced his earlier tour-guide spirit. We headed south on Central Avenue to the Oaklawn Jockey Club. His silence suited me. My hands were clammy in anticipation of the meeting with Jonathan Marlin.

Albert pulled into the huge parking lot at the race track and drove past rows of cars, minivans and pickups and finally behind a line of blue charter buses. A row of dilapidated stables stood at the edge of the lot, and he turned down a deeply rutted road beside them.

An uneasy feeling gripped me. "I thought we were going to the track."

"Mr. Marlin's waiting for you here." Albert's voice was cold.

Be cool, Viv, I told myself. Be tough. But my hands were shaking. I clenched and unclenched them and took slow, deep breaths. What's the worst that could happen? They might try to scare me? Who was I kidding? They already had done that. They might beat me up? Rape me? That line of thought didn't help. Once my father, The Sergeant, told me a technique he used when all hell broke loose. "Stand outside yourself," he had said. "Observe as though it's happening to someone else, and when your time to move comes, you'll be ready." I thought of standing outside myself and imagined I was a hawk riding the drafts above the race track.

The road turned at the far end of the stables; the developed land ended abruptly against a tangled forest. In front of the feral backdrop, another black Buick, newer than Albert's, was parked with both front doors open.

A fat man in a gray suit sat behind the wheel, fanning himself with a newspaper. He waited until Albert pulled up beside him before he got out of his car. I nervously tugged my skirt over my knees.

Jonathan Marlin's face was pink and round. He wore small gold-rimmed sunglasses and a Panama hat that left a red stripe on his forehead when he took it off. He shook out a white handkerchief and wiped his face. He reminded me of Orson Welles after he gained all that weight.

Marlin gestured to Albert, who jumped out of the car and opened my door. I grabbed my shoulder bag, got out with as much dignity as I could muster and stood face-to-face with Marlin. I thought of Lucie and why I was here. The possibility that Marlin might know something about her death gave me courage.

Marlin looked at me like I was a lobster in a tank, and he was selecting one for dinner. "You're not Lucie Dreadfulwater," he said.

"Mr. Marlin, I presume."

He ignored the hand I had extended and nodded to Albert.

Albert was both quicker and stronger than I expected. He grabbed my shoulders and backed me up against the wall of the stable. His face pushed close against mine, and I could smell the rotten teeth in his mouth. In the distance, the crowd inside the track walls roared. Big excitement on the TV screens.

My heart pounded as fast as the horses' hooves, but I pushed against Albert's weight. He kicked my right leg so it crossed over my left and stepped on my right foot to keep me in place. I was pinned against the wall as securely as the tail on a donkey. Marlin took off his sunglasses and looked over Albert's shoulder and into my eyes. His eyes were like the bright, red-rimmed orbs of a game rooster.

"The lady's dead," Marlin said. "What the hell are you doing here?"

I tried to match the menace in his voice. "Lucie Dreadfulwater was murdered. You wanted to buy her land to develop a racetrack. What's the connection?"

"You're not a cop," Marlin said. "Are you a lawyer?"

"You're going to need a lawyer if you don't let me go."

"Maybe you're the one who will need a lawyer," Marlin said, backing off a step and wiping his face again with his handkerchief. "You're impersonating a dead woman. You've come to Hot Springs at my expense." He looked at the sky as though answers might be written in the clouds, then bored into me with his hard eyes. "What's his game?"

"His?"

He watched me squirm under Albert's grasp.

I countered with another question. "Who killed her?"

He raised his almost invisible brows. "How should I know? I only wish she would have signed the damned papers before she went and did such a stupid thing." He took a step toward me. "You haven't answered my questions."

"I followed your advice and went to the Fordyce," I said, focusing my attention on Albert. I pulled on memories of a past visit. "My favorite room is the one with the Greek statues in the pool under the stained glass skylight."

Albert's expression didn't change, but confused by my sudden change of focus, his hands on my shoulders loosened slightly. I wiggled my toes. The extra space in my ankle-twisting heels provided me enough room to slip my right foot out. I kneed Albert in the crotch. He let out a hoarse cry and doubled over. I kicked off the other shoe and ran.

"Bitch," Albert croaked.

"Stop her!" Marlin said. He sounded like the evil overlord in a bad movie. I would have laughed, but I was busy.

They both started after me, Albert still half doubled over and Marlin too large to move fast.

I glanced back before I ducked around the end of the stable. Albert was headed for his car.

Another long row of stables paralleled the one I was beside. I paused for a second, assessing my options. It was pay-off time for the survival training The Sergeant had tried to pound into me. This time it wasn't a game. If I went between the two buildings, I could be boxed in. The windows were boarded, and it wouldn't be easy to scale the walls. If I went around the far side of the stables, I would be in the open, unarmed against two men. I judged the distance to the parking lot—about 150 yards. The ground underfoot was cushioned with grass emerging through layers of old hay and rotted horse manure—passable for a barefoot sprint.

I had already spent too much time thinking. I peeked around the end of the far building. It was clear. I pulled my shoulder strap over my head to secure the bag, hiked my skirt over my thighs and ran. The bag bumped against my leg as I ran. I was about halfway to the lot when a black Buick pulled in front of me around the end of the building. Marlin was driving, and Albert sat in the passenger side. Had they stopped the car and waited for me, I wouldn't have had a chance. Instead, Marlin tried to corral me, or maybe he planned to run me down.

In the back of my mind, I heard The Sergeant's voice: "Never turn your back on the enemy." I played chicken with the Buick, running directly toward it, feeling the soft earth under my feet and hearing the roar of the crowd at the track. I felt like one of the horses straining for the finish line. I was close enough to see Marlin's widened eyes and to gauge to the split second when the car would hit me. At the last moment, I dove to the right.

The shoulder bag pulled me off-balance, and the Buick barely missed me. I smelled the exhaust and heard the swish of tires on grass as it swept past.

I rolled once, felt the shoulder of my jacket rip, and was on my feet running. The Buick turned around and headed for me again, but I had reached the relative safety of the parking lot. I could dodge among the vehicles, and the Buick had to go down long rows before it could turn.

Unfortunately, the ground was no longer soft. A piece of gravel ground into my foot. I cried out in pain and hopped a few yards before I took off again in a limping run.

The guards at the gate of the track watched as I limped toward the line of idle taxis. I must have looked like an apparition—shoeless, ripped jacket, frantic expression. I jumped in the first taxi I came to and looked behind me. No black Buick was in sight.

The driver had been napping with his cap over his face. He started when I opened the door, and when he saw me, his eyes opened even wider.

"Mama Teresa's," I said. "Now!"

He radioed his dispatcher and pulled onto Central Avenue before he looked at me again in the mirror. "Tough day?" he asked.

"You could say that."

"I've got two rules for the road," said the Hot Springs cabbie. "First. Don't sweat the small stuff. Second. It's all small stuff."

But it didn't feel like small stuff until we picked up Michael Probst and headed back to the airport. At Mama Teresa's, Probst had taken in my dirty, torn clothes and my shoeless feet.

I said, "Don't ask."

The black Buick wasn't at the airport, and we took off into the mid-afternoon sky. I had the uneasy feeling that the escape from Marlin was just a temporary reprieve. A man like that didn't like to lose.

Probst and I were silent on the flight back to Tahlequah. I had a headache after the adrenaline high at the track, and I wondered just how much useful information I had gained. Not much. Probst watched me out of the corner of his eyes. He probably wondered what crazy thing I was going to do next.

He began the descent into Tahlequah before he spoke.

"Guys who mistreat women are scum," he said.

"The worst kind."

He looked at me, sizing me up, and then gave me a gift. "You know the guy around here who really likes the horses? I fly him to Hot Springs a lot. David Menckle."

15

It suddenly seemed that my day hadn't been wasted. Probst told me that he had flown Menckle to Hot Springs two or three times—most recently a week earlier.

"Poor bastard," Probst said, shaking his head, "he was really sick on the way back. I thought we would run out of sick sacks. I felt sorry for the chick with him."

"The chick?"

"Yeah. I never did catch her name. She was good-looking, with long blond hair and Tina Turner legs."

David Menckle and friend. Unless his wife had recently grown out her hair and changed its color, it wasn't her. I tried to think. Jonathan Marlin. David Menckle. I wondered if a welcoming committee was waiting at the Tahlequah airport.

"Can you land this plane on that little strip at the lake?"

"Down at Chickenhawk Landing? That's just a grass strip!"

"You seem like a man who likes a challenge." I gestured at my shredded nylons. "Someone might be waiting for me at the Tahlequah airport."

"You're not Lucie Dreadfulwater."

"No."

He turned the airplane south and cursed his way down the bumpy runway at Chickenhawk Landing. To the south, regiments of oaks splintered the view of Lake Tenkiller. A lone gull rode the waves that crested and broke against the rocky shore.

I climbed out of the plane, limped down the runway, and

turned to thank Probst again. He was already turning the plane, eager to return to the sky. I gave him a little wave and headed toward the marina down the hill. Adversity builds character. That was my new mantra. Yep, I could already feel the character building in me, swelling like sourdough, bubbling up like champagne.

John and Corey lived nearby. With any luck, Corey could give me a ride to town. Of course, I would have to swear her to secrecy. If she told John, he would tell Charley. I didn't know if I would ever be in the mood to explain this day to Charley.

I called Corey, and she sounded delighted to be able to do me a favor. While I waited for her, I pulled off the nylons and threw them in a trash can, and sat on a rickety bench in front of the marina and drank a Diet Coke. I thought about what Probst had told me. It tied together.

Menckle was from Little Rock, which was just a short drive from Hot Springs. Menckle liked to play the horses. Perhaps he wanted in on the ground floor of a high-class track closer to home—a track that would allow him to rake in the profits.

I wanted to bang my head against the plywood wall of the marina. If I weren't so damned impulsive and if I were a better reporter, I would have done my homework before I took off for Hot Springs. I had probably just wasted a day on a wild-goose chase. A phone call or two would have given me the names of the corporate officers in M&M Investments. The basic information I should have started with should be filed at the county recorder's office. Face it, I preferred footwork to paperwork. Barefoot work in this case.

Corey arrived in a cloud of dust, her two children in the back seat of the station wagon.

She took one look at me and whistled. "Honey, you look like you been chewed up and spit out."

"What happened to Viv, mommy?" said Dylan, her four-year old.

I climbed in beside Corey and twisted around to face the back seat.

"I was fishing in Lake Tenkiller and a giant catfish grabbed hold of my line and pulled me in," I said to Dylan. "Ate my shoes before I could get loose."

Twila, his older sister, looked at me like she had heard that one before. I've noticed that there's not too much the children of rock musicians haven't seen or heard. Maybe that's one reason I've resisted Charley's desire to add another child to the world.

"Oh, forevermore. You can tell me," Corey said as she pulled onto the highway.

"It's not that exciting."

Corey rolled her eyes. "Excitement. Tell me about it. You know what I dreamed last night? I dreamed I opened the dishwasher after it ran and some of the plates were still dirty. It totally depressed me that I would dream about something so boring. I need to get back on the road with the band."

I deflected Corey's questions while she drove me to the Tahlequah airport to retrieve the Civic. If a welcoming committee had been awaiting my return, I hoped it was gone by now.

Corey drove slowly past the airport parking lot, and seeing no one at all, much less anyone who looked suspicious, dropped me off at the Civic. We went through the question-and-answer ritual:

"Are you sure you'll be okay, honey?"

"I'm sure. "

"I can wait."

"No, that's not necessary."

"Well, if you're sure…"

"Don't go fishing anymore," Dylan said solemnly. Twila rolled her eyes.

I watched them leave then threw my shoulder bag in the Civic. A piece of paper was wedged under the windshield wiper.

I pulled it out and unfolded it.

"Dear Mystery Lady," the note said, "Mr. Menkel (sp.) was here when I landed. He asked about my passenger. I played dumb. Keep me in mind if you want to take another trip. Have plane, will travel. M.P."

I pulled onto Highway 51 and headed back east into Tahlequah. The day was still early enough to get some answers.

I topped the hill opposite the brick ruins of the old Tahlequah train station before I realized that walking into the courthouse in my present disheveled, barefoot condition would be akin to advertising the train station as a "fixer-upper." If I drove home to change I couldn't get back to town before the courthouse closed. I cursed and headed to Maggie's house.

Maggie's little red Miata was in the driveway. I let myself in the front door, and Jake jumped off the sofa, planted his huge paws on my shoulders and slobbered on me.

Maggie came out of her bedroom. "Viv? That better be you." She wore a slinky red dress with ruffles at the throat and the price tag hanging from a sleeve. Two more dresses were draped over her arm. "Where the hell have you been? I've been trying to reach you all day."

"I've been out."

She looked at the dresses on her arm. "It is damn near impossible to find a nice dress in Tahlequah. I've got to make a trip to Tulsa. You didn't answer my question."

She put the dresses down and looked me over. "What happened to your shoes?"

I told Maggie about the past twenty-four hours, beginning with the packet from Lucie and concluding with David Menckle.

She looked deep in thought. "I learned a little trick when I was going through my divorce," she said. "Hang on a minute."

I checked my watch. The courthouse would close in half an hour. "I need to borrow some clothes. I have to leave."

"It'll just take a minute," she said in her little-sister whine.

She punched some numbers in the phone. It took four calls, but she had a look of triumph on her face when she hung up the phone.

"As you may know," she said, "corporations register with the secretary of state's office. Oklahoma City had no record of M&M Investments, but when I called Little Rock, I hit pay dirt."

"Well?" When Maggie gloated, I had to fight the urge to choke her.

"M&M Investments was incorporated six months ago. Its address is a post office box in Hot Springs, and…" Maggie paused and made a dramatic flourish. "It's officers are as follows: president, Jonathan Marlin; vice president, David Menckle; secretary-treasurer, David Menckle."

"Good work," I said grudgingly. "Now I need to borrow some clothes."

"For what?"

"To go to the courthouse."

"I'm going, too."

"Of course." I sighed.

Between Maggie's petite size and my plain taste, there wasn't much we could share. I ended up wearing a pair of black shorts and a sweatshirt with "Hilton Head" emblazoned across the chest. Since my feet were larger than Maggie's, shoes were a problem. I cleansed and bandaged the gash on the bottom of my foot, then settled for toeless black sandals with adjustable straps.

It was a few minutes before closing when we got to the courthouse. The county clerk's office was upstairs, and we took the stairs two at a time. The deed index, a heavy leather-bound book, was open on the counter. I flipped through the pages looking for M&M Investments, Maggie peering over my shoulder.

"You went right past it," Maggie said.

"Deed book number 23, page 201," I said. "Thank God for public records."

"God has little to do with public records." Maggie took the deed book from the shelf and flipped through the pages. She ran her finger down page 201. "I'll be damned," she said.

M&M Investments held title to a thirty-acre parcel of land previously owned by Dale Nowlin.

"Jesus Christ. Dale Nowlin." My voice was louder than I intended. The woman behind the counter with the permed brown hair and the "Shirley" nameplate on her polyester chest frowned at us.

There were no mortgages recorded. Apparently Menckle and Marlin's group had paid Nowlin cash for the land about five months ago—shortly after the time M&M incorporated.

"What now?" I asked.

"The plat book," Maggie said. "We want to know where that land is."

When we matched the legal description with the proper page in the plat book, I let out a low whistle. A piece of Lucie Dreadfulwater's checkerboard-shaped property adjoined the parcel M&M had purchased from Nowlin. Another fact became obvious: Lucie's land lay between M&M and the highway. There was a section line road on the east side of M&M's land, but it was a long way around to the highway.

"We're closing," Shirley informed us as she bustled around the counter, slamming books shut.

"Can you tell me something first?" Maggie asked.

She put her hands on her hips. "What?"

"Easements. If I were to buy a piece of land and needed easement to a highway, how would I go about getting it?"

"Get a lawyer." Shirley slammed another book closed.

"What would improve my chance of success?"

Shirley tiredly turned to Maggie and said, "Look. D'ya mind? I got three teenagers at home, and they're probably blasting out the neighbors with the stereo and eating everything in the re-frigerator. If I'm lucky, that's all they're doing."

Maggie took a barrette out of her purse and pinned up her hair. She looked like she had all the time in the world. "Just answer my question, so we can all get out of here."

Shirley gave her a poisonous look and ticked three points off on her fingers. "Easement is easier to gain if there is no other access, if you're situated along a section line and on good-old-boy terms with a county commissioner, or if you can prove adverse financial impact through lack of easement."

"But you would have to pay for the use of the land you gained easement through?"

"Depends on the landowner."

"What if the landowner is dead?" I said.

Shirley looked at me. "Good Lord, lady. You need to talk to a lawyer."

Maggie decided to walk home so she could stop at a shop on Muskogee.

I sat in the Civic in the courthouse parking lot for a long time, massaging the aching shoulder I had landed on when I rolled to avoid the Buick. A flock of Canada geese flew north in a ragged V, uttering hoarse cries. The gray sky made the day feel late. It had been almost forty-eight hours now since Lucie had been killed, and her murderer was free.

I went back into the courthouse to the sheriff's office. The gray hall still smelled of unwashed bodies and stale smoke, and the deputy who had been on the phone when I was there the day before was still sitting at her desk.

She looked at me, allowing her penciled eyebrows to ask what I wanted.

"Turner in?"

"No."

"Back soon?"

"No."

"I feel like we're talking in shorthand," I said.

She looked at me.

"Anything new on the Dreadfulwater case?"

Silence.

I remembered Maggie's assumption that the Oklahoma State Bureau of Investigation would be asked to step in. "OSBI on this yet?"

Her expressive eyebrows gave her away.

"I hope you don't play poker," I said as I headed out the door.

Still, I'd rather have stayed and talked to her than to make the phone call I knew I had to make next. I had one source at OSBI. Unfortunately, we had once been lovers.

16

It's nobody's business, but I feel the need to defend myself. I met "Hutch" Hutcheson when I was a news reporter, and he was a detective assigned to the Tulsa OSBI office. It wasn't until later, after covering a particularly brutal murder, that he and I came together as lovers for a short time.

He wasn't involved with another person at the time; I can't claim that ethical distinction. In fact, the only excuse that even halfway absolves me in my little shades-of-gray world is that it was during a spell in my relationship with Charley where we were drifting apart and not sure that we would drift back together.

I had heard Hutch was now assigned to the Muskogee office. I stopped at a phone booth on Water Street and got the number from information. Someday I would have to join the rest of the world and get a cell phone. While the phone rang, I watched the late afternoon traffic. Mud-crusted pickups with gun racks, rusty station wagons with small children bouncing around in the back, shiny new four-wheelers with roll bars. On the seventh ring, a man's voice said, "Hutcheson here."

"Hutch? Viv Powers."

There was a short silence. "It's been awhile."

"I'm looking for a favor. I have some information about Lucie Dreadfulwater, but I need something in return."

"What makes you think I can help?" He tried to sound bored, but I could hear the hunter's eagerness.

"I'm assuming you talk to your colleagues, Hutch." I leaned against the side of the booth and closed my eyes. "And, I'm grasping at straws."

Another silence. Then: "Have you had anything to eat? I was getting ready to go find some dinner. Can you meet me at the Hayden House in Fort Gibson?"

Fort Gibson is fifteen miles away, between Tahlequah and Muskogee. I looked down at the black shorts and Hilton Head sweatshirt. "I can be there in fifteen minutes."

What's over is over, I told myself fifteen minutes later. Even so, I ran my fingers through my hair before going inside. The Hayden House was an ornate, Victorian-era home that someone had renovated into a decent Italian restaurant. Hutch was not in sight, so I waited in the bar, resplendent with mirrors and brass light fixtures. I sat on a stool at the carved walnut bar and rested my feet on the brass rail. A ceiling fan stirred the air overhead and distributed the smoke of the other lone early evening patron.

Moments later, Hutch paused in the doorway of the bar. He was tall and thin and dark, wearing gray twill pants and a navy sport coat that hung on him like a scarecrow. He leaned slightly forward as he surveyed the room, taking in everything, his eyes coming back to me. His thin lips pulled sideways in what passed for a smile as he crossed the floor in long strides.

I shook his hand and said, "Hey, Hutch." His hand was hard and cool.

His hawk-like eyes took me in, and he said, "You look good, Viv."

"And you haven't changed." I had felt tired and discouraged; now energy flowed through me.

He pulled out a chair and sat on the edge of it, leaning toward me. "So," he said.

"So. I don't know where to begin."

Hutch raised his hand and signaled the bartender. While we waited for our drinks, we caught up on the lives of shared friends and acquaintances, like any old friends who meet after a long separation.

There were new lines etched on his thin cheeks; his blue chambray shirt needed ironing. His life was none of my business.

Our drinks arrived, and when we touched glasses our eyes met. "To sudden death," Hutch said.

"To vengeance."

The watchful hawk in Hutch's eyes flickered.

I rolled the smooth Scotch on my tongue and let it slide down my throat.

"Vengeance," Hutch said, savoring the word. "You knew Lucie Dreadfulwater."

"She was my friend." I pushed back the sudden tide of emotion.

"You said you had information."

"I said I wanted to trade information."

"You think OSBI cuts deals?" Hutch sliced the words. "If you have information, it's ours." His jacket hung open, revealing the hard corner of a shoulder holster.

I had a sudden urge to break down and tell him everything. About going to Lucie's house and seeing the dead man in the barn, about striking her with the board. Maybe I was some kind of criminal. I didn't know. Maybe telling would ease the burden of guilt that I carried like a ball and chain.

I forced a laugh. "Hell, Hutch. I thought the OSBI cut deals all the time."

He looked at me appraisingly while I wiped the condensation off my glass. Then he polished off his drink and gestured to the bartender for refills, even though my glass was half full.

There was a long silence that Hutch finally broke. "I'm not assigned to the Dreadfulwater case, so there's not a lot I can tell you."

I let out a slow breath and made my hands stop fidgeting. "All I'm asking for is basic info. What was the cause of death? Time of death? What did the so-called suicide note say?"

Hutch stretched his long legs out in front of him. "We had a briefing this afternoon, which probably means all this will come out in the papers tomorrow. But you know how that works. Her body was sent to Tulsa for an autopsy, and preliminary results indicate the time of death between 8 p.m. and midnight. The cause of death was probably a horse tranquilizer. Apparently she stumbled and fell over the bluff, but the drug might have killed her anyway." Hutch consulted a notebook in his pocket. "Rompun, it's called. Very potent stuff."

I remembered the bottle I had picked up in the barn refrigerator at Lucie's house.

"What?"

"Rompun," I said reluctantly. "There was some in the refrigerator in Lucie's barn."

"It's a controlled substance. It shouldn't have been there."

Another thought occurred to him. "How much was there, and how long ago?"

I told him, and he made a note.

"You're sure there were two bottles?"

"I'm sure."

"Tell me what else you've got," he said.

I told him about Lucie's land and M&M's adjoining land, and the offer to buy. I gave him the names of the corporate officers. I didn't tell him Dale Nowlin had once owned the land; OSBI could do a little legwork. Hutch made some more notes and killed his second drink.

"We're going to want those documents she sent you," he said.

"So is suicide still the pet theory?"

He shrugged. "There's a lot that doesn't hang together."

He watched me long enough to make me fidget.

"You still brush your hair back when you're nervous."

I waited him out.

After a minute, his lips pulled sideways. "And you still clam up when someone's got your number."

I tried to divert his attention. "Someone tried to push Lucie off the deck of the Creekside Sunday night."

He straightened in his chair and looked away as though I'd said the wrong thing. "I heard about that, but my witness said it looked like an accident. Crowd. Alcohol. You know."

"Sunday night she almost gets pushed off a deck, and the next night…"

"Quite a coincidence. But of course, there's always loose ends in a violent death. You can't expect a neat package."

"There's the note, for instance," I said.

"Yes. The note."

"What did it say?" I swirled the amber liquid in my glass and watched the light reflect off it. Someone turned on the TV over the bar. On the evening news, images of armed soldiers and tanks filled the screen. Somewhere in the world people were dying.

I felt Hutch's eyes on me, and I turned to meet them. "So. The note?"

He let his breath out as though he had made a decision and then leafed through his notebook until he found it. "Quote: 'As her body burned up, her spirit began to rise and she was still singing as she ascended. She had created evil and then sacrificed herself to save the people from the evil she had made.' End quote."

I repeated the words. "That's bizarre," I said. "Like mentally ill bizarre. That wasn't Lucie."

"Or artist bizarre. You wouldn't expect a mundane, everyday suicide note from someone like her."

"Where was the note found?"

"A few feet from the top of the cliff. It was in her purse, along with the empty Rompun bottle and the syringe."

"What did the note look like?"

"Look like?"

"Was it printed or typed? Written in ink, pencil or crayon? On notebook paper, stationery, torn newspaper?" My voice rose along with the length of the list.

Hutch's eyebrows lifted. "I can guess what you're thinking," he said, "but her family identified the handwriting as hers. Our expert's looking at it, of course, along with samples of her writing."

"So what else?"

"Hmm? Oh. It was written in ink on a sheet of lined paper that had been torn out of a daytimer."

"Was there a date on the sheet?"

"It was dated about a week before her death."

"Where's the rest of the daytimer?"

"We don't know."

"But you want it, don't you?"

Hutch's eyes sharpened. "Oh yes."

"Why don't you ask David Menckle?"

"Tell me how her death would benefit someone trying to buy her land."

"I have no idea," I said. "It's just that the land is where everything leads. Something frightened her, or she wouldn't have mailed the contract to me. And I knew her. She wasn't suicidal."

He gestured at my drink. "Are you through?"

It was obvious that I wasn't; my glass was still half full of Scotch. I stood and pushed my chair back in. "I'm through."

"Shall we get something to eat?"

I was hungry, but I wanted to get away from the lingering, sour taste of old love. "I can't stay any longer," I said.

Hutch looked relieved.

He followed me out to the parking lot to get the packet Lucie had sent me.

"I'll pass it along to the officer in charge," he said. "He may want to talk to you. In the meantime, go home, mourn your friend, let us do the investigating."

"Fine. I'm going home," I said. I felt like a little girl crossing her fingers behind her back. I had no intention of leaving the investigation to the experts. They had no emotional investment in this murder. Tomorrow there would be some other crime that demanded an instant solution, and the trail to Lucie's killer would grow cold.

Hutch caught my arm and pulled me against him. "I mean it," he said in my ear. "If Lucie Dreadfulwater was murdered, we're looking for a dangerous and clever killer."

I pulled away. "I'm glad to hear you're not convinced it was suicide."

"There are questions."

"Thanks, Hutch."

"Call me if you think of anything else."

I touched my fingers to my head in a mock salute.

Instead of going back into the restaurant, Hutch got in his white Chevy pickup and headed south toward Muskogee. I sat in the Civic and tried to remember the words of Lucie's note. I wrote them down and turned north on Highway 62, back to Tahlequah.

17

By the time I reached downtown, it was early evening. Against the western horizon, the sinking sun suffused the ragged clouds with a smoky glow, as though a firestorm was straining to burst through.

I had a stop to make, but first, I had to find some food. My body was rebelling against the Scotch on an empty stomach. I felt light-headed and my stomach burned.

I went to Safeway and bought smoked turkey slices, two whole wheat rolls, Boston lettuce, stone-ground mustard with horseradish and a bottle of Mountain Valley Spring Water. The irony of drinking water that was bottled in Hot Springs was not lost on me.

I washed the lettuce in the supermarket bathroom and picked up a newspaper in the vending machine in front of the building. Then I drove up the street to the city park and parked beside Town Branch. The banks of the murky creek were the final resting place of crumpled McDonald's sacks and soiled Pampers. The rusting green trash barrel overflowed. I ate my sandwich and read the newspaper account of Lucie's death.

The official story was accidental death due to a fall from a bluff on her land. There was nothing about Rompun, a syringe or a note. The reporter had interviewed Roy Calico, who found her body and had perhaps been the last person to see her alive the night before. I tore out the story and threw the rest of the paper in the trash.

From where I was parked, I could see the front of the *Green Country Journal* office. Menckle's white Oldsmobile was parked in front. Tanya's VW bug, painted pink and white like an over-size cheerleader's oxford shoe, was parked next to it. The slot reserved for the managing editor was empty. Lisabeth Ellis was apparently gone. Just after the last light left the sky, Tanya came out the front door, checked to make sure it was locked, and drove away.

That was my cue. I waited a few minutes longer, brushed the bread crumbs off my lap and walked to the office. I still had a key to the door. I let myself in as quietly as possible. Surprise is a potent equalizer. The Sergeant had drummed that into me long before I was old enough to understand what he meant.

The light was off in Menckle's office, and he wasn't sitting at his desk. I stood in the doorway while my eyes adjusted to the dim room. He was sprawled in a chair, facing the window. He started when I flipped on the light switch.

"Leave the light off, babe," he said, without turning around.

"I want to see your face," I said.

He jumped to his feet and whirled to face me. "You! What the hell have you been doing?" His face twisted in anger. His white shirt was unbuttoned, and the sparse hairs on his chest were gray.

"Who were you expecting, babe?" I took two steps into the room and stopped. I wanted a clear path between me and the door. It occurred to me that if Menckle was involved in Lucie's murder, I was an idiot for being here. I looked around for a weapon, but the only thing close at hand was an unabridged dictionary. The thought of Lucie gave me courage.

"Get out before I call the police," Menckle said. His hands were clenched.

"Go ahead. Call them. I'd like to hear what they'd say about M&M Investments and a $400,000 land offer."

The golf-course tan on his face paled, but he opened his hands in a gesture of innocence. "I haven't done anything wrong. My group made an offer for some land. The owner of that land killed herself. Perhaps I should have notified my partners a little sooner, but I wanted to find the best way to break the news. There's nothing like an untimely death to give investors cold feet." His voice rose. "Then someone impersonating Lucie Dreadfulwater shows up in Hot Springs. Stupid move, Powers."

"Lucie didn't commit suicide. She was murdered. You know it, and I know it."

"Now wait a minute." Menckle held up his hands to ward me off. "I don't know anything of the kind. I hardly even knew the woman. We met once. That was it."

"You wanted her land. I haven't figured out how killing her would help you, but I'm working on it."

"You don't have jack shit." he said, sounding more confident.

Unfortunately, he was right. I shifted my weight and realized my sandal was caught on something. I reached down and picked up the something. It was a lacy cotton blouse. I wondered if "babe" was in a nearby room, listening.

Menckle crossed the room and snatched the blouse from me. He held onto it with one hand, grabbed my arm with the other and propelled me toward the door.

"Give me your keys." We were at the front door.

"Like hell!"

"Your office key. Now!"

While I wrestled with my key ring, I thought of one last question. "Had any luck at Hot Springs lately?"

The effect was startling. He pushed me against the door, knocking the breath out of me. "What the hell is that supposed to mean?"

I wrenched free. "Don't touch me." My voice was a raspy gasp. I clenched my fists, ready to break my right one on his jaw if it came to that.

Menckle seemed as surprised as I was by his reaction. He

looked at his hands and then at my face. I reached behind me, opened the door and tossed him the key. After I slipped through the door, the lock clicked behind me.

I stood on the street in front of the office, angry and humiliated. A shadowy Menckle watched me through the glass, so I turned and slunk away to the Civic, still parked beside Town Branch.

I sat in the darkness for awhile, breathing deeply and willing my racing pulse to slow. The night sounds of the town surrounded me: the trickle of the creek, cars passing above me on Bluff Avenue. The whine of a siren rose a few blocks to the west and faded into the distance.

I wondered whose lacy blouse I had held in my hand. Randy Silvers had worn something similar at her birthday party. But Randy was in Austin with Powers That Be. As far as I knew, she didn't even know Menckle. But Tahlequah is a small town.

I left the Civic once again, and headed for the alley behind Menckle's office. Two boys cruising Water Street whistled at me, and I waited until they turned onto Downing before I ducked into the alley. The trees cast grotesque shadows on the brick walls. In the woods the darkness is friendly, but here in town, danger seemed to lurk in the shadows of every metal dumpster and discarded cardboard box.

The high windows in the back wall of Menckle's office were a good eight feet off the ground. I tried pushing the nearest dumpster under the window, but it was too heavy to budge. My other option was to climb the drainpipe a couple of feet to the side of the windows and to inch along the gutter until I could see inside.

On my third attempt to climb the pipe, I finally made it by hooking the toe of my sandal into the metal support that secured the pipe to the concrete wall. I lunged for the gutter and clung to it. The galvanized metal sagged with my weight, but I struggled hand over hand to the windows. My hands hurt like hell.

I had time for one quick glimpse through a window before my aching hands gave out, and I crashed to the ground, banging my ankle against something. The one glimpse had been just enough to make me want to see more: a slender woman with long blond hair and Tina Turner legs had been silhouetted in the doorway. It could have been Lisabeth. Or Randy. Or someone I had never met.

I cried out in pain when I stood. There would be no more climbing for me tonight. I sank to the ground and massaged the ankle until I could stand on it. By the time I limped around to the front of the office, the lights were off, and Menckle's car was gone.

Back at the Civic, I slumped into the driver's seat. My body ached, and I was exhausted. The day had been long; the shots of adrenaline frequent.

While I sat in the Civic, gathering enough energy to drive myself home, a black Buick stopped in front of Menckle's office. From the driver's side, a figure emerged. Albert scuttled toward Menckle's doorway under the spectral glow of the street light. Someone—Marlin, I guessed—stuck his head out the passenger-side window of the Buick and said something. Albert straightened up and looked more like he had a right to loiter on the sidewalk.

Albert bent over the door lock for a few minutes. It was after 10 p.m., and the traffic had eased on Muskogee Avenue. No one turned onto the side street where Menckle's office was located.

My fatigue forgotten, I watched with a mixture of apprehension and fascination. Had Marlin and Albert followed me from Hot Springs? Why was Marlin breaking into his partner's office?

It took Albert about five minutes to get past the lock. He disappeared inside for a long time and finally emerged to consult with Marlin. Both men went inside. By the set of their shoulders when they came out later, I guessed they hadn't found what they came for.

I waited until they turned south onto Muskogee before I headed north for home.

When I staggered in the door, the phone was ringing. I hesitated, reluctant to talk to anyone, but the insistent ringing won out.

"Yes," I said.

"Is 'yes' any way to answer the phone when I'm nearly 500 miles away?" The voice was teasing.

"Charley," I said.

"There's something in your voice that says not all is well," he said. Trust a musician to pick up on tonal qualities. Or maybe Corey had talked to him.

I kicked off Maggie's sandals and stretched out on the couch with the telephone. Mack jumped on my stomach, meowing accusingly. I said, "Hang on," to Charley and poured some cat food into a dish. It seemed important to take care of the little things.

Then I picked up the phone again and told Charley about Lucie's murder.

There was a shocked silence on the other end.

"Has anyone been charged?" he asked.

"The law wanted to pass it off as suicide." The exhaustion must have been evident in my voice.

"Viv," Charley said, "Why don't you come down here for a few days? It'll do you good to get away from there."

"I can't."

"I think you need to."

"I can't miss Lucie's funeral." If I told him the truth, he would worry. I couldn't deal with that right now.

"Of course. You need to say goodbye to her," Charley said. There was a slight pause, and then: "I called for another reason.

Could you try to reach Randy for me?"

"I thought Randy was with you."

"She called John the morning we left. Said she was sick. She gave us the name of a bass player down here, and I've been trying to call her to let her know that he's working out fine. She felt bad about letting us down."

After Charley hung up, I sat on the couch, stroking Mack's soft fur. The owner of the blouse in Menckle's office wasn't my business except as a wedge with which to pry information out of Menckle. The more of his dirty little secrets I knew, the stronger my wedge.

I dialed Randy's number.

A woman's voice answered, but it wasn't Randy.

"Randy can't come to the phone right now," said the oddly familiar voice. "Can I take a message?"

"Tell her Charley said the bass player is working out fine."

"Working out fine," the voice echoed. I recognized it now. Lisabeth Ellis.

"Is Randy there now?" I asked. "Lisabeth?"

But she had hung up.

I wondered if Menckle's wife knew about his affair. I wondered if she would care.

Such a long day and so few answers. I needed company; I needed someone to watch over me. I turned on the CD player, and John Lee Hooker sang me to sleep.

18

The Sergeant wanted a son. But he had me instead. I knew from the time I was big enough to tag along after him that I didn't fit the bill. But I tried to be what he wanted, tried to divert him so he wouldn't realize he had been gypped. I was his willing student during survival treks in the woods, and he taught me about tracking and stalking and killing. The animals had no chance, and I felt guilty being a part of their betrayal. After I grew beyond the age where I wanted to please him, I asked him to teach me other skills. Rock climbing, for instance.

The Sergeant grew up in northern Idaho in Elk City, a small town surrounded by three million acres of rivers and forests and craggy peaks. Once, when he was on leave, he took me there, and we went into the Selway-Bitterroot on horseback. An old man named Bill Younger owned the horses, and he went along to watch over the animals, to secure the Decker packs on their backs and to hobble them at night so they wouldn't wander too far.

The Sergeant's destination was the Selway Crags, a ridge of sharp granite monoliths above timberline that punctured the blue Idaho sky. They were a two-day pack trip from the end of the Forest Service road. While Bill Younger fished the high mountain lakes, we climbed the crags.

It was my fourteenth birthday the day The Sergeant decided it was time for me to lead. It was my turn to climb above the protection and set chocks and stoppers and cams into the cracks.

If I fell, the rope would catch me—eventually—if the protection I set didn't zipper out. I thought I was tough, and I thought I was good. The Sergeant helped me select a rack of climbing hardware and draped it over my shoulder. I tied into the sharp end of the rope and started up.

To the east, the rugged Bitterroot range cut a rocky outline that marked the Montana state line. Below me, a creek strung together the South Three Links Lakes like blue gems on a chain. Bill Younger's horses grazed in a meadow. From where I clung to the rock, they looked like little plastic toys.

What I didn't anticipate was how different it would feel to be on the rock above the security of the anchor. Everything was magnified; I was playing for keeps. The rock, whose rough grit had felt familiar and friendly, now seemed to be trying to push me off. In retrospect, The Sergeant selected a beginner's route, but it didn't feel that way at the time. There were plenty of cracks to sink protection into, and I used them all. The rope unfurled beneath me in a crazy zigzag pattern, and before I was even halfway up the pitch, I had used the last piece of hardware on my rack.

The crack I was following disappeared. I couldn't go up, and I couldn't go down. One foot was wedged into the crack; the other smeared the rock face. My left fingers clutched a granite knob in a death grip, and my right hand searched up and down the face, trying to find a hold.

"What do I do?" My panic must have been evident.

"Failing to plan is planning to fail," The Sergeant shouted back.

I hated him then, and I started crying. My muscles were trembling, and I knew I was going to fall. Knew that if I hadn't planted that last cam firmly that I could plummet to the earth.

"You're a stupid son-of-a-bitch," I yelled, and I lost my hold on the rock.

I woke early, with the memory of that day in my mind. I felt that I was wasting valuable time. But the flannel sheets were warm and soft against my skin, and I lay awhile longer, tracing the grain in the red oak beams above me and listening to the blue jays and squirrels scold each other outside the window.

Finally, I sat on the edge of the bed and took stock of my injuries. I rotated the shoulder I had landed on when I dived away from Marlin's black Buick. The stiffness had crept up my neck, and when I turned my head, pain shot through it. My foot had fared no better: The rock cut on my instep was tender; there was an angry purple bruise on the ankle I had banged while falling from the gutter above Menckle's office window.

The wounds seemed evidence—in a masochistic way—that I had accomplished something. I had thrown myself against a brick wall and knocked some of the mortar loose. If I kept battering the wall, it might come crashing down.

Failing to plan is planning to fail. I pulled on a worn cotton robe and brewed coffee. While the pot gurgled and steamed, I made a list in my notebook of people to talk to: Truman Gourd; Anna and Rachel, Lucie's daughters; Roy Calico, the man who found her body. After that, I would see where events led. One thing was certain, I had been too eager in my approach to Menckle. I wouldn't go back to him until I had something solid.

I flipped back the pages in the notebook and found the text of Lucie's "suicide" note. "As her body burned up, her spirit began to rise and she was still singing as she ascended. She had created evil and then sacrificed herself to save the people from the evil she had made." It made no sense. Who had created evil?

I carried my coffee out the back door and through the fallen leaves to the garden. The sun slanted through the thorny branches of the honey locust on the east border, casting a subtle mosaic of light and dark. A covey of quail scattered through the dense underbrush beyond. I roamed up and down the raised beds, constructing elaborate theories about how and why Lucie had been killed. None of them made sense.

Underlying every thought and every movement, though, was guilt. Had my silence that day—after Lucie killed Dale Nowlin—in some way contributed to her death? It ate at me and made me long to go back and try another way. Go back to when, though? Try what?

I showered and pulled on Levis and a faded red sweatshirt. The Pearl Beer cap lay on the bedside table, turned to the "F-wren-Ds 4 + ever" side. I stuck it in my pocket like a talisman.

I was headed out the front door, a toasted whole-wheat bagel in one hand, a cup of coffee in the other, when Randy Silvers' rusty maroon Datsun chugged up the driveway.

She waved at me and parked behind the Civic. I bit into the bagel and sat on the porch steps. Randy wore India imports, a white crinkly cotton top and long skirt, raffia sandals. Her hair was in a simple braid. She walked to the porch demurely, looking like an acolyte on her way to a Hindu shrine.

"Coffee?" I asked.

"Thanks, babe," she said in her whiskey voice. There were dark circles under her eyes.

"Cream? Sugar?" The pilgrimage feeling gave way to that of a kaffeeklatsch.

"Black." Randy sank into the porch swing and gently rocked herself.

I had just turned off the pot, and the coffee was still hot. Inside the front door, I set my cup on the cherry table, and the leg gave way, spilling the coffee and shattering the cup.

Randy pushed through the door behind me. "Are you okay?"

When I finished cursing, I said, "I picked up this piece of junk at an auction and never got around to fixing it. That was my favorite cup, too." I picked up the table and moved it to the end of the sofa so I wouldn't absentmindedly set anything on it again.

Randy picked up the broken pieces while I mopped up the coffee. Then I poured fresh cups and led the way back to the porch.

We sipped our coffee and peeked at each other over the rims of our cups.

Randy broke the silence. "I heard you tried to call me last night."

"Yeah?"

She pushed the swing with her toe. It creaked in a hypnotic rhythm. She looked down at her feet as though she were embarrassed. This was a side of Randy I hadn't seen before.

Her confession came out in a rush. "I told John and Charley I was sick, but I wasn't. I had things to take care of." She looked up through long lashes. "You do things your own way, too, you know."

I laughed. "Charley said the bass player is working out, so I don't think you have anything to worry about. Unless he wants to move to Tahlequah."

She leaned forward, stopping the swing with a delicately pointed foot. "I might move on myself one of these days. My love life is too damned messy. I should enter a convent."

We both laughed then, but her smile stopped at her mouth.

"You were with David Menckle last night?" She had brought up the subject of her love life; the question was fair.

The creak of the swing began again. "You already knew that, babe," she said.

"Has he ever mentioned Lucie Dreadfulwater?"

The swing slowed. "I heard she killed herself."

"She didn't kill herself. She was murdered."

Randy's sultry eyes were startled wide. "God, Viv. How do

you know that?"

I didn't want to go into the details. "Lots of reasons."

"Do you think David had something to do with it?"

"Maybe." When asked outright, I found I couldn't give an unequivocal answer.

"Well, anyway, he never talked about her," Randy said.

"He's certainly on edge about something. Do you know what?"

"He's just a good-time guy when he's with me." Randy twisted her braid. "We don't talk about business—his or mine."

I gave up on Menckle and stood up. "I don't want to run you off, Randy, but I was on my way to town."

She stood and set the coffee cup on the seat of the porch swing. "Job hunting? I guess you're not working for David anymore."

"Until I find out who killed Lucie, nothing else seems important."

Her eyes widened again. "Be careful, Viv. Cherokee County is suddenly a dangerous place."

19

The Southern Gothic Mausoleum brooded over its domain of field and forest like a stern manor lord. From the western approach, the limestone was dark, with the morning sun backlighting it. I slowed when the slate roof came into view, remembering conflicting images of Truman: the grief on his face when I met him in the sheriff's office and his anger a few days earlier when he had attacked Lucie in front of their house. Perhaps the grief had been an act. The husband is usually the first to need an alibi when a woman is murdered.

I parked in the circle driveway under a maple. The sight of Lucie's Explorer stabbed me like a knife. The house was silent, and the drapes drawn. I took a deep breath, straightened my shoulders and walked up the wide veranda steps, nervously rubbing the bottle cap in my pocket.

No one answered the doorbell. I rang a second time. From far inside the house came the sound of Custer barking. I had decided no one was home when the door swung open.

Truman stood in the doorway, blinking in the sunlight. He was wearing baggy gray corduroys and a dirty white shirt with the tail out, and his uncombed hair hung loose. Ash dropped from a cigarette that hung out of his mouth. He looked shrunken, as though from a long illness, and he moved with the deliberation of an old man.

"I thought it was my mother."

"Truman," I said, "I know this isn't a good time, but I have to talk to you."

He said nothing but turned and shuffled toward the living room. I followed him.

The room looked just like it had when I last saw it, and I half-expected Lucie to come through the door.

"Her ghost is here," Truman said.

"Yes."

Truman clasped his hands and hunched over, staring at the Oriental carpet, seeming uninterested in anything I had to say.

"Lucie was murdered," I said finally. I watched him for any small reaction that said he was involved.

He didn't look up. "She killed herself."

"No. Someone made it look that way." There was something in his hopelessness that made me trust him. I ran my fingers through my hair. "You knew her. Do you think she would kill herself?"

Truman looked at me for the first time. Some of the dullness left his eyes.

"The day I saw you in the sheriff's office," I said, "he almost had me convinced. She was facing possible charges for Nowlin's death. She felt she had dishonored her family." I paused, and he nodded agreement. "When I got home that day, there was a letter in the mail from her. Do you know anything about it?"

"What letter? I didn't see any letter." For the first time there was interest in his voice.

"I'll tell you about the letter in a minute," I said, "but there are things we need to talk about." I heard the coldness in my voice.

I began with the land. "Lucie owned an eighty-acre tract next to this one. Who inherits it?"

He gripped the arms of his chair and shot me an angry look. "It was a gift from her father, and it will go back to him."

"Why not to you or the girls?"

This time the answer was long in coming, and when it came, the words poured out like bitter tears. "She knew her daughters would have it someday—after Johnny dies. She just wanted to make sure I couldn't get my hands on it."

We sat in another long silence, and then my questions took a new direction. "The last time I was here, you said something to Lucie I didn't understand." I remembered the way their faces had looked: Lucie on her knees, her anger deep inside like a rabbit gone to ground, the drunken Truman swaying over her.

"You said you told her father to call the police and now look what happened. What was that about?"

"That's family business," Truman said.

I let it go for the time being. "Did you and Lucie discuss the offer M&M Investments made to buy her land?"

"I don't like your questions."

"I'm just trying to understand."

Truman scowled at me. "We talked about it."

"What did you say?"

"It's not like Lucie listened to me."

"Did you think she should sell?"

"You don't know me." The acne scars on his face stood out like angry gouges in a piece of finely polished mahogany. He bit off the words. "Do you think I would sell even one more acre to white men to exploit?"

Silence again settled over us. His passion gave birth to a new thought: What if Truman had believed Lucie was going to sell the land? How far would he have gone to stop her?

I took a deep breath and glanced at my list in the notebook. "What did Lucie do on Monday?"

"All I know is she planned work in her studio," Truman said in a more subdued voice. "I got up early and went to Oaks to help my father build fence. I stayed there for supper, and when I got home about nine that night, Lucie wasn't home. Rachel was here by herself. It was nearly midnight when I called the police."

He spread his hands in a helpless gesture. "They couldn't do anything, they said. People go missing all the time, and then they show up again. Anna left Monday morning for a ski trip to Colorado; we're still trying to reach her. She doesn't know about her mother." His voice broke, and he covered his face with his hands.

After a few minutes, he regained control. He pulled his tangled hair back and fastened it with an elastic band.

"I'm no good, you know," he said. "I drink too much; I get in fights. I don't have what you think of as a job. I farm some; I find artifacts and sell them to collectors. But Lucie was good for me. If someone killed her, I will kill him."

It seemed like the time to ask. "What were you doing at the Creekside Sunday night?"

He shrugged, staring at the floor. "Don't you listen? I get a little crazy when I drink. I don't always know why I do things."

"Were you on the deck when Lucie was pushed?"

His face twisted. "I didn't know it was her. So many people, so much noise. I thought I would be arrested again—you know they like to arrest full bloods in this town—so I took off."

I let it go. "What do you know about the rabbit head in your mailbox and the phone calls last Saturday?"

He shrugged. "Hell, it could have been kids. You know how they are."

"On a Saturday morning? Don't kids sleep in then?"

Again, a shrug.

"Tell me about the Rompun, Truman," I said. "When I was here Friday night, there were two bottles in the barn. Are they both gone?"

"The police came. I don't know what they took."

"They left a list, didn't they?"

"A list." Truman dug in his pocket, pulled out a wadded sheet of paper and handed it to me.

I scanned the short list. Rompun wasn't on it. Nor was a daytimer.

"Isn't Rompun a controlled substance?"

"We transport the horses a lot. If you're careful, it's not dangerous." He paused and added bitterly: "To horses."

I was thinking out loud. "Lucie's daytimer. Have you seen it?"

"I told the police. She kept it in her purse."

"Did she use it as an appointment book?"

"I don't know. She used it for everything, I think. Notes to herself, appointments. Grocery lists, maybe."

I sighed and turned to another subject. "Why were Dale Nowlin and Lucie fighting?"

His eyes blazed, and he shook his fist. "I would have killed him myself! Damn that Lucie! God, she was a good woman."

He stood up and shuffled to the fireplace, hunched over like an old man. "I don't want to talk about him. I don't know why Lucie's old man had anything to do with him. He was scum."

The man in the portrait over the fireplace stared at me with cold eyes. Perhaps at one time he had cared passionately about his land, his house, his family. Now all that was left of him was brush strokes on a rotting canvas.

Before I left, Truman gave me directions to Roy Calico's house. He also gave me permission to talk to Rachel if I didn't bring up Nowlin's name. In return, I told him about the packet and letter I had turned over to Hutch.

"Why didn't she come to me if she was frightened?" He sounded angry again.

I didn't tell him what I thought, that maybe Lucie didn't trust him. And with only his parents as an alibi on Monday evening, I wasn't sure that I trusted him either.

As I let myself out the front door, Truman was still standing by the fireplace, shaking his head.

Rachel was probably in the barn, Truman had said. I followed the brick walk under the sugar maples and bur oaks to the barn. I paused inside the double doors, remembering the last time I was here. Dust motes floated in the shafts of light, and the fragrance of old hay and grain saturated the air.

Only one of the horses was in its stall. Rachel's slight figure stood beside it, brushing the paint's shiny back as though she would wear a hole through its hide.

I said her name, and she turned toward me. I had never before noticed how much she looked like Lucie. Her dark eyes were almond-shaped, and she had Lucie's small rosebud mouth.

In the awkwardness of her adolescence, she reminded me of Charley's stepdaughter, Iris. Iris was now in a magnet school for gifted students in Tulsa. She was finding a way to live with her losses. I hoped Rachel could be as resilient.

"He's a beautiful horse," I said.

Rachel shrugged and went back to brushing him. "He's spoiled rotten."

"Where's your other horse?"

She pointed with her chin, her mother's gesture, to the corral on the far side of the barn.

I rubbed the comforting smoothness of the bottle cap in my pocket. "I've been talking with your father," I said, choosing the words carefully. "He thinks you might be able to help me."

She looked at me out of the corners of her eyes.

I felt like the wrong word would make her leap away from me as quickly as one of her horses. "Can you tell me about Monday evening?"

"What about it?" she said warily.

"Did your mother say where she was going when she left?"

"No."

"Do you know why she went out?"

"About dinner time, there was a phone call," Rachel said. She shook herself, as though ghostly fingers had run down her back. "Someone asked for her."

"Man or woman?"

Rachel faltered. "I don't know. It was such a strange, whispery voice."

"What happened next?"

"Mom talked on the phone a few minutes, then she said she was going out."

"Was she upset?"

Rachel shrugged.

"And then?"

Rachel thought a minute. "After she hung up, she said she had to mail something. She couldn't find the stamps, so I helped her look."

I asked more questions, but Rachel had told me all she was going to tell. She went back to brushing the horse's coat. Her hand slowed, and she buried her face in the horse's mane. "I didn't even tell her goodbye," she said.

20

It was late morning by the time I spotted the gravel road at the base of Park Hill. Truman had told me to follow the road for a mile until it took a ninety-degree turn. The next house on the left was Roy Calico's. However, I made another stop first.

I pulled off the side of the deserted road and studied the plat book I had brought along. One corner of Lucie's land was defined by the 90-degree turn. The sheriff's office and OSBI would have gone over the area with a fine-toothed comb, but I needed to see the place where Lucie had died.

The steel gate was padlocked. I parked and followed a faint track back into the property, treading on the rotted humus of the forest. A bright red cardinal shot across the path like a bloody arrow, but other than the chitter of distant birds, the woods were silent.

The track led to a rocky bluff, where the oaks and pignut hickories gave way to a handsome stand of smooth-barked white pines. The breeze whispered through their feathery needles. I sat on a solid piece of flint rock at the edge of the bluff before I looked down.

Sharp rocks jutted from the vertical wall. Twisted pine saplings clung to pockets of earth in the rock cracks. A creek trickled through a rocky bed far below. Above the bluff in the autumn blue sky, turkey vultures caught wind drafts and floated like black ghosts.

I retraced my steps, searching for anything that may have

been overlooked. Shadowy trails were trampled through the thick layer of fallen leaves. Like all hilltop land in the Ozarks, it was strewn with rocks of all sizes, jagged shards of flint rock and chert.

Through the trees to the east, a vertical shape caught my eye. I walked toward it, trying to make it out. About the time I ran into the rusty remains of a barbed-wire fence, I realized the shape was a chimney.

The fence meant that I had reached the edge of Lucie's land and was looking at the land M&M now owned. The land that had once belonged to Dale Nowlin. I had thought of this land as undeveloped. But someone had lived here in the past, some poor homesteader trying to wrest a living from the unforgiving soil.

I stepped over the fence and fought my way through the underbrush to the remains of a foundation. A stone chimney stood on a sturdy concrete base, and on the remaining stones, the black scars of fire hinted at long-ago disaster. The chimney had withstood the elements better than the rest of the foundation, which was crumbling back into the rocky earth. Crudely engraved into the concrete was the date, July 4, 1945.

This land reclaims its wildness quickly. Oak sprouts grew in the center of what had been a small house. Blackberry briars and wild rose brambles formed a hostile barrier.

There was nothing here but ghosts and their memories. I went in search of Roy Calico.

Calico's wife, a small bird-like woman in a faded housedress, told me I could find Calico at his sawmill up the road. A child peeked at me through the curtains, and ducked out of sight when I looked toward the window.

The sawmill was little more than a rough shed in a clearing. A flatbed truck was parked in front of the building, half-loaded

with green lumber. At one end of the shed, a young man pushed
a log through the high-pitched whine of a saw blade. An older
man heaved the new-made lumber to one side. A diesel engine
chugged in a corner of the shed.

I watched for a minute from the Civic. The sharp smell of
diesel and fresh sawdust drifted through the open windows. The
older man spotted me and signaled the other to stop the saw.

I stepped out to meet him.

Under a grimy McCullough cap, the old man's face was a
fine web of leathery wrinkles. His greasy workboots and pant
legs were covered with sawdust.

"Hep you?" he asked in a gravelly voice.

"Mr. Calico?" I asked, extending my hand.

He turned his head and spat. "You ain't another one of them
danged reporters, are you, come to waste my time?"

"No. I'm not. This will only take a minute. I've been asked by
a member of the Dreadfulwater family to look into Mrs.
Dreadfulwater's death." I thought it best not to mention that the
family member had been Lucie herself.

His manner changed instantly. "That's different," he said. "Miz
Dreadfulwater was a fine woman. The police been here, a reporter from Tahlequah, one from Tulsa, even a TV crew. I can't
get my work done." He turned to his assistant and yelled. "Clear
out them slabs, Tommy!" Then he turned to me again and gestured to a pile of logs. "Ain't much of a seat," he said.

"It's fine."

Calico took off his cap and wiped his forehead on his shirt
sleeve. Then he fished a Prince Albert can out of his pocket,
shook some tobacco onto a paper, and deftly rolled a cigarette
with one hand. He saw me watching and offered the can to me.

I shook my head and waited until he lit up and drew in the
smoke. "I understand you may have been the last person to see
Mrs. Dreadfulwater alive."

He nodded and blew out a thin stream of smoke. "I reckon

so. Next to last, anyways."

"Did you speak to her?"

"We talked." He looked at the ground as though the memory made him uncomfortable.

"Tell me what you remember."

"She was in her car down the road. I'd just been talkin' with her about gathering grapes down in the bottoms, and I asked her did she want me to stay. I didn't like to see her out in the woods by herself with dark comin' on." He paused and took another drag on his cigarette.

"And..."

Calico hesitated, then said reluctantly, "She said she was meetin' Utlunta."

"Utlunta." The word hung between us. Calico took another careful drag from his hand-rolled cigarette. I watched the ash lengthen and drop. "Who is Utlunta?"

"She was jokin' me," Calico said. "Utlunta is a made-up person, a witch; someone you scare the little ones with when they ain't behavin'."

"Why do you think she said that then?"

"She probably meant she was meetin' someone and it wasn't none of my business." He stamped out the cigarette and stood up.

I stood up too, afraid that he was going to conclude the interview. "Mr. Calico, tell me about Utlunta."

He spat again in disgust. "There's some Cherokees in these hills that believe just about anything. They say there's medicine men who can heal you with ceremonies. They say they can turn into owls and fly in the night. It's nothin' but a buncha foolishness.

"The same with this Utlunta. They say she's a witch that can take others' shapes and she has this sharp stone finger that she kills you with. Foolishness!" He ground the cigarette butt into the dirt.

I remembered now where I had heard the name before. Utlunta

was one of the sculptures Neil Hannahan had told me he was working on.

"One more question," I said.

Calico had half-turned to go, and he paused.

"There's the remains of a house on the property next to Mrs. Dreadfulwater's. Do you know anything about it?"

He scratched his head with the bill of his cap. "Sis, that's old Mrs. Nowlin's place."

"Mrs. Nowlin?"

"Alma Nowlin."

The name made my heart beat faster.

"She related to Dale Nowlin?"

"Just his mama is all." Calico lowered his voice. "She had a hard row to hoe, and she passed on last year about this time."

"Did you know her?"

He looked at me. "She was our neighbor. She kept to herself, though, after her old man drank himself to death. I don't know how she got along. Why, she added onto that house all by herself. Even hauled the rocks for the chimney. That boy of hers wasn't much help. Course, he was just a sprout when his daddy died."

"Tell me about Dale Nowlin."

"Well," Calico glanced at the sawmill as though it were calling him back to work. "He was younger than me, and I didn't see him much. Somehow his mama scratched and saved and sent him to medical school somewheres in Texas. But that didn't work out, so he became a nurse. I do remember one time when he come home to visit with his wife and baby."

"What happened to his family?"

He gave me a sad smile. "I don't know. I kinda lost track of Dale. Now he's dead."

"One last question, Mr. Calico. When did the house burn down?"

Calico was already headed back to his work, and he said

over his shoulder, "Years ago, just after Mrs. Nowlin went to a nursing home."

It seemed like the more questions I asked, the less relevance everything had. I was overstuffed with bits and pieces of seemingly random information. If I shook my head, it would fall out like drifts of autumn leaves.

21

When I got back to town, I wasn't sure what to do next. The digital sign on the top of the First National Cherokee Bank said it was seventy-four degrees at 11:45. I scanned the late-morning traffic for a black Buick. I hoped Marlin and his side-kick had gone home to Hot Springs.

I spotted an empty parking space in front of the crafts co-op and made a U-turn. Lucie's studio was the only logical place left to look for her daytimer. In addition I wanted to question any-one there who may have talked to her on Monday.

From where I parked, I could see the offices of the *Green Country Journal* across the square. Menckle's car was parked in front. "Asshole," I muttered. My frustration level was about as low as Spring Creek in August.

I opened the glass door of the co-op, and a bell jingled in the back. The handwoven rugs and buckbush baskets that lay on the countertops seemed faded. I ran my finger along one of the glass cases and left a trail in the dust.

A doorway at the back of the room, curtained with glass beads, parted to allow Neil Hannahan through. He tossed his blond hair out of his eyes. When he saw who his customer was, he took the beer from behind his back and raised it to me in a toast before he drank.

"Finally! Company!" he said in his rich baritone. A cheerful smile replaced the kicked-dog look he had worn since Randy Silvers had dumped him. "This place is as dead as a tomb."

"I didn't know you were a member of the co-op, Neil." I hadn't seen Neil since Randy's party on Sunday, and that hadn't been nearly long enough.

"No point in sculpting if I don't have an outlet. Unfortunately they expect a donation of my time here in return."

"So business isn't exactly brisk?"

"Exactly not, my dear."

"I'm sorry to disappoint you, Neil, but I'm not here to shop."

His eyes lit up. "Working on a story for the magazine?"

"No." No point in getting into my current employment status. "But I'm curious about those sculptures you're working on. What got you started on Cherokee legends?"

He tilted back his head and shook the last drops from the beer can into his mouth. "I don't remember. However, we live in the midst of the Cherokee Nation. It should surprise no one that their legends would kindle my creative juices."

The thought of Neil and his creative juices was about as appealing as David Menckle and his marketing brainstorms. I changed the subject.

"Were you here on Monday, Neil?"

He frowned up at the ceiling. "I came in after lunch, I think."

"Did you see Lucie?"

He laughed nervously and twisted the can in his hand. "To be honest, I wasn't sure what to say to her. Should I pretend I hadn't heard about her killing that guy? Should I express sympathy maybe? It was too much. Now I feel bad I didn't say anything."

"Did she talk to anyone?"

"It was pretty dead here Monday." He frowned at the ceiling, not noticing the irony of his words. "Tammy Fishinghawk brought in some baskets right after I got here. She may have talked to Lucie. It was after two when the shit hit the fan, though." His eyes were bright with the memory. "I heard the phone ring in Lucie's studio; about ten minutes later, she comes marching out, steam rising from her head.

"I asked her what the problem was, and she was so mad she could hardly talk. She sure didn't talk to me."

I walked to the back of the shop and tried Lucie's studio door. It was locked.

"The police said no one was to go in there," Neil said. Then he winked. "But since it's you..."

He went to the back room and returned with a ring of keys and a fresh beer. He unlocked the door and started to follow me in, but I closed the door in his face.

The retail area of the co-op had been renovated, but the rest of the building showed its age. Lucie's studio had tall, narrow windows and high, pressed-tin ceilings. The plaster was peeling on the walls, and the hardwood floor was worn and uneven.

I checked her desk first. The top was bare except for a deskpad calendar, a phone and a standing file for folders. The files, if there had ever been any, were gone. I pulled the drawers open, looking for her daytimer. Lucie had been much neater than I, and it didn't take long to convince me that her daytimer wasn't in the studio.

I watched the pigeons on the window ledge and listened to the ghosts of the hours Lucie and I had spent in this room. Her presence still lingered, like the whisper of a half-forgotten song.

On my way out of the building, Neil revealed the reason for his exuberance.

"Randy and I..." He paused, savoring the words. "Randy and I would like to have you and Charley over for dinner soon."

"You and Randy?"

"You don't have to act so surprised," he said.

"Is this a recent development?" The question was nosy, but it was obvious he wanted to talk about it.

"Just this morning." The words were confident, but his voice wasn't.

It appeared that Randy wasn't headed for a convent anytime soon.

I stepped out into the sunlight. The neon arrow pointing to Jerry's Steakhouse was blinking, and my stomach growled.

Just behind me, a car honked, and I jumped. Maggie waved at me from the wheel of her red Miata.

"We have to talk!"

"Food first."

We ordered lunch at the counter in Jerry's then found a booth.

"So," Maggie said. "This morning, I went to the courthouse." She didn't continue; she just smiled an infuriating Cheshire cat smile.

"Tell me, dammit."

"It was an amazing feat of research," she said, casting her eyes down with false modesty. She pulled out a sheaf of papers. "I went back to the courthouse to visit Shirley with the permed brown hair and polyester chest. She was quite civil today, possibly remembering that she is a civil servant. While I was there, I looked up Dale Nowlin's name in the deed index. There were two entries under his name. The first was a Tahlequah residence. I followed the trail of the second and found that Nowlin inherited the land from his mother who died last year."

"Alma," I said.

Maggie looked at me in surprise. "How'd you know that?"

"Later," I said, waving my hand for her to continue.

"Here's the good part. One of the good parts," she amended. "There were two names on the deed: Dale Nowlin and Alexandra Nowlin."

"Alexandra?"

"Ha!" Maggie stabbed the air between us with a fork. "I've surprised you!"

"I found out today that Dale was married. Maybe Alexandra

is his wife."

"No idea. But I'm not finished. I kept working my way back in time with this piece of land. I looked up Alma's name in the deed book. The county clerk in the 1940s had a fondness for curlicues. I ran my finger down the yellowed page."

"Get to it, Maggie."

She raised her eyebrows and continued unperturbed. "Nowlin was halfway down. The index referred me to another heavy deed book and to a curious entry."

"Well?"

Maggie had to have her moment of drama. "We suddenly jumped from thirty acres to one-hundred-and-ten. It took me awhile to track down. Alma transferred eighty acres to John Dreadfulwater in 1953."

It took me a minute to absorb it. "She owned Lucie's land at one time?"

"Wait! Wait. This land's history reaches back even further in the courthouse records." Maggie took a bite of her sandwich and delicately wiped her mouth with a napkin.

She knew she was driving me crazy. She finally put down her napkin. "The year is 1935, the year Dale Nowlin is born. Alma Nowlin becomes the owner of 110 acres. The former owner was John Dreadfulwater." She smiled at me triumphantly.

I sat in stunned silence for a minute. "Lucie's father."

"No, dunce. Lucie's grandfather. Lucie's father is also John Dreadfulwater, but he's only ten years older than Dale Nowlin. I don't think he was selling land back then."

"Since you've got all this figured out, why don't you explain it to me?" Calling me dunce was going too far.

She raised one eyebrow. "I don't know yet. I just find it interesting that the land began as a 110-acre tract that passed from the Dreadfulwaters to the Nowlins, then eighty acres went back to the Dreadfulwaters."

It was my turn now. "John Dreadfulwater disappeared in

1945. So when the land went back to the family, it went to Johnny in 1953. Now that Lucie is dead, it returns to him again."

"Weird," was all Maggie had to say. I agreed. The land shuffle seemed to form a twisted circle.

I filled her in on my visit to Truman Gourd and Roy Calico.

Her eyes narrowed when I reported Calico's claim that Nowlin had once brought a wife and baby to his mother's home.

"Alexandra."

"The wife?"

"Or the baby."

"Hard to say."

Maggie had polished off her sandwich by now and was eating my fries. "I tried to find out who Alexandra Nowlin is. I called a friend at the police department. Computers are great, but they have their limitations. He said no driver's license in Oklahoma is issued to a person by that name. So then I called the Vital Records Department at the State Department of Health. No birth records. I didn't check death records because we know she was alive six months ago when she and Dale sold their thirty acres to M&M. Marriage records are kept at each county seat. And," she concluded, "Cherokee County does not have a marriage certificate on file for Alexandra Nowlin."

"You've been thorough."

"Yes. But I have no idea where to go from here."

"I do."

22

West Keetoowah is a short course in the architectural his tory of Tahlequah. Once-fine Victorian mansions with turrets, parapets and ornately carved cornices sit on large downtown lots. Some have been renovated into office buildings; others are termite-eaten, weathered relics, waiting for gravity or a big wind to pull them down.

The next few blocks feature small lots and wood-framed bungalows from the '20s and '30s. As the street climbs the long slope that makes up the west side of town, the houses transform into the boxier, cedar shingle-sided houses of the '40s and '50s. On top of the hill, where the road levels out, brick ranches with large lots and half-grown trees represent the '60s. That was where progress halted in this part of town.

Nowlin's house was one of the larger of the '50s era. A broad porch stretched across the front, flanked by two dying arborvitae. The house and yard looked neglected. I parked on the street, and Maggie and I walked up the decaying front steps and knocked on the door. There were dark scars on the wood near the knob, as though someone had tried to force the door.

Maggie hugged her bare arms. "This is spooky," she whispered.

"It's broad daylight."

I knocked again, and when no one answered, we walked around the house to the back. The ground on the side of the house, shaded by overgrown bushes, was slick and barren. Trash scattered across the backyard from an overturned barrel.

At the back of the house was a small screened-in porch. The screen door sagged on its rusty hinges, so I walked in and tried the back door.

"Viv!" Maggie shrank against the side of the house. "You're going to get us arrested!"

The door was secured with a deadbolt. I peered through the uncurtained window into the kitchen. Nothing but dirty dishes and a greasy floor.

I turned to Maggie. "I see two options here. We can break and enter to learn more about Nowlin, or we can visit the neighbors."

"The neighbors," Maggie said. "Who may be calling the police as we speak."

We tried the houses on either side of Nowlin's. The first one had a "For Sale" sign in the yard, and there was no answer at the door. We had better luck at the house to the east when a young man with a scraggly beard came to the door. He was wearing nothing but a ragged pair of cutoffs and the vacant look of a person who has just awakened.

"Yeah?" he said, blinking in the bright light of the sun.

"About the house next door…" I said.

"Looking for a rental?" He shook his head to clear it, and his eyes took us in and lingered on Maggie. "Pinch me."

"We're not looking for a house," I said. "We're looking for information about Dale Nowlin."

"You sound like a schoolteacher." He mimicked my tone in a falsetto voice: "'We're looking for information… 'C'mon, I was just kidding. Lighten up. Okay. Nowlin. Hell. I didn't even know the guy's name until he was dead. We don't exactly get together for block parties in this neighborhood." He thought for a minute, pulling at his sparse beard. "The old bird across the street is who you need to talk to. She's got her nose in everybody's business." He pointed across the street. "See that house with all the shit in the front yard? That's hers."

The "shit" was a collection of concrete lawn ornaments be-hind a white picket fence. As Maggie and I drew closer, the forms took shape: a pale shepherdess, deer, rabbits, a giant frog and a gnome, all frozen in poses of Disney-like cuteness. Plastic flow-ers lined gravel paths.

It was Marianne Moore who said poets should present for our inspection "imaginary gardens with real toads in them." I wondered what she would have said about this.

A blue-and-white stenciled plaque that said "God Bless This Mess" hung on the front door. The sound of a TV came through it, so I knocked loudly. The canned conversation was cut off, replaced with the thump of heavy steps. The door opened an inch, stayed by a chain. Maggie and I must have passed inspec-tion because a voice said, "Just a minute, dears." The door opened to reveal a white-haired woman who stood about five-feet-tall and was almost as wide. Her plump face was as grand-motherly as a Norman Rockwell painting, but her eyes behind bifocals were avid with curiosity.

I introduced myself and Maggie and told her why we were there.

"Oh, honey," she said, "you all come in. You can call me Granny Hillyard. Everyone does." She peered over the top of her glasses. "Don't I know you girls?"

"I don't think so. We're here about Dale Nowlin."

Granny Hillyard stood back from the door. "Come in, girls. I knew that poor man for nearly thirty years."

We crossed the threshold and entered a memorial to road-side stands and craft shops. Maggie sucked her breath in. She always claimed that just driving by a tourist stop made her nau-seated.

Knickknack shelves sagged with the weight of painted plas-ter figures of animals and impossibly large-eyed children. A bat-talion of rag dolls lay on a wildly flowered sofa. Painted glass bells lined the mantel, and cheap, framed prints of picturesque landscapes covered the walls. It was a flea market on steroids.

She saw us looking around, and smiled proudly. "You like crafts?"

I stepped in front of Maggie. "This is an amazing collection."

Maggie made a choking sound.

"Thank you." Granny Hillyard sank into a worn rocker covered with a multi-colored afghan. It clashed with her lime green stretch pants. "My late husband and I traveled all over this state and Arkansas, too, buying whatever took our fancy."

She waved at the sofa. "Have a seat, girls."

Maggie took a straight-back chair by the door. I scooted some cloth dolls aside on the flowered sofa. They stared ahead with unfriendly button eyes.

Granny Hillyard dabbed her chubby cheeks and chins with a white handkerchief. "I just can't take the heat," she said. "Are you with the newspaper?"

I used an old trick. Make them think you're answering their question. No lies needed. Smile big and say just enough. "We're gathering background information," I said. "We've been told that you've lived in the neighborhood a long time."

"Oh my yes." She laughed and her body shook again. "I've lived in this house nearly fifty years. My William and I bought this place when it was brand new. It was in 1947, just two years after he got back from the war. We never were able to have children, you know—the tragedy of our lives—and now he's gone. Five years ago he passed on, but it seems like yesterday.

"How old do you think I am, girls?" She looked back and forth from Maggie to me. This woman had the same effect on me as my grandmother: I was drawn into the suffocating loneliness of her world, helpless to escape.

I lied on the kind side. "Upper sixties?"

She laughed again, or maybe she was having an asthma attack. "Oh no, honey. I'm eighty-three years old."

"When did you meet Dale Nowlin?"

"I can tell you the exact date," she said. "It was Sept. 12, 1977, our thirty-fifth wedding anniversary. We had a reception and set up tables and chairs in the front yard. We were cutting the cake…" Her voice broke off, and she hoisted herself to her feet. "That's what I was going to do. I just couldn't remember." She wagged a finger at us. "You stay right there, girls. I'm going to get us a treat."

"Oh, that's not necessary."

But for all the attention she paid, she could have been Grandmother Powers reincarnated. She waddled off to the kitchen and returned a minute later with a tray laden with dessert plates and huge slabs of cake.

"Try it, girls," she said, handing out the plates. "This is my own recipe for pear cake, made with pears from the backyard."

It was already obvious that if we wanted to learn anything from Granny Hillyard, we had to play by her rules.

Maggie had recovered her equilibrium. "Delicious," she said, digging in.

And it was. The cake dissolved like sugar on my tongue. I tried bringing up the subject of Dale Nowlin again. "Mr. Nowlin moved across the street on your thirty-fifth wedding anniversary…"

"Oh yes, honey. He and his little family had everything they owned in the back of a pickup truck."

"His family?"

Maggie and I exchanged glances.

Granny Hillyard talked around a large bite of cake. "He had the sweetest wife and a pretty little golden-haired girl. She must have been about three at the time."

"Where are they now?" I hardly dared ask, afraid she would be off on some other tangent.

"Why, I don't know, honey. Mrs. Nowlin packed up and took off with that little girl. She wasn't more than five or six then. As far as I know, Dale Nowlin never heard from them again."

"Why did they leave?" Maggie had inhaled the cake, and now she set her plate and fork down beside a wooden gumball dispenser shaped like an outhouse.

Granny Hillyard spoke in a hushed voice. "Honey, it's not right to speak ill of the dead, but Mr. Nowlin was not an easy man to live with. Anytime I went over there to visit, he would stay right in the room with us, frowning and growling to himself. I'd say to him, 'Now, Dale, we're just two women talking over coffee; we're not going to get into any mischief.' He never laughed."

Granny Hillyard waved her fork at Maggie. "I have to say this for him, though. He doted on that little girl, and she worshipped him. It tore him up when they left. He wouldn't even so much as nod at me for years."

"What were his wife's and daughter's names?"

"His wife was Diane. She was a lovely woman; she studied history or something like that at the university here. Wanted to be a teacher." Granny Hillyard leaned toward us and lowered her voice. "Dale thought she was playing around with one of her professors. He went so far as to go down to the school and beat the man up. I think that was the last straw for Diane.

"She graduated a few weeks after that and left with her little girl the next day. Before she left, she took her scissors and cut up all the family pictures with the three of them together and threw them out in the yard. They blew all over the neighborhood. Those pictures were so pitiful, like the pictures of missing children on the backs of milk cartons."

Granny Hillyard stopped abruptly, and then she said in a raspy whisper. "One of them landed in my iris bed. I probably should have given it to Mr. Nowlin, but I kept it."

"Do you still have it?" I wanted to be able to put my hands on something tangible; I wanted to feel that I was getting somewhere.

Granny Hillyard nodded. "I have it somewhere. I wouldn't throw out something like that." She groaned as she got up from her chair. She picked up her empty plate and headed toward mine, but Maggie jumped to her feet.

"I'll take these to the kitchen while you look for that picture," Maggie said.

"That's nice of you, dear," Granny Hillyard said. "I'll just rummage in this cupboard. That's where I keep most of my pictures." She opened the bottom doors of a pine china cabinet. Photos cascaded around her feet. I knelt to help pick them up, and she paused to tell a story about each. I listened enough to make noises at appropriate times while I sorted through the pile, looking for any odd-size photo that may have been the victim of an angry woman with scissors. Maggie returned from the kitchen and joined the search.

Granny Hillyard was the one who found it. "I told you," she crowed, waving it in my face. "She was a lovely woman, and they had such a pretty little girl."

I took the photo and studied the two faces while Maggie looked over my shoulder. The picture was black and white, and the woman was smiling, holding up a large perch on the end of a cane pole. Her face shone with embarrassed pride. A scarf covered her hair so I couldn't tell if it was light or dark. A small girl stood beside her, solemnly staring at the camera.

"What was the girl's name?" I asked Granny Hillyard.

"I should be able to tell you, but I can't recall it right now." She sighed. "It's been so many years. She was an odd little duck though. So quiet and serious about everything."

"Alexandra?" Maggie said.

Granny Hillyard thought a minute then shook her head. "No, it was something everyone was naming their little girls at that time. Melissa? Cindy? It'll come to me."

It was another 20 minutes before we were able to extricate ourselves—with the photo. In the meantime, Granny Hillyard gave us each a granola bar to take along ("They give them to us at the senior center. They're not for resale; they're for distribution, but they are granola bars."), related the history of her lawn ornaments, and invited us to visit the Baptist church she attended.

Once we were out in the street, I took a deep breath. Maggie looked at me and laughed. "This was your idea," she said.

Maggie and I divided the rest of the street—she took the north side, and I took the south—but either the neighbors weren't home, were unwilling to talk or they knew nothing about Nowlin.

When Maggie and I met again, her mouth was set in an expression I knew all too well: the "I-can't-take-this-anymore" look.

"I need to talk to some people," I said. "Alone."

She looked relieved. "I have a hair appointment."

I looked at my watch. "Could you do something for me when you're finished?"

"Maybe."

"Find out about Dale Nowlin's funeral arrangements. Perhaps we can get a lead on Alexandra Nowlin. And try to find out who's handling his estate. He must have heirs."

We agreed to meet at the Creekside later to compare notes.

23

Johnny Dreadfulwater had passed the seventy-year mark, but he hadn't yet outlived the nickname his father, John Dreadfulwater, had given him. The youthful name contrasted oddly with the old man's personality. Even his daughter, Lucie, had called him "sir."

His sprawling ranch house was just down the road from the family mansion where Lucie had lived. Her parents built it when Lucie married. Her mother, Lucie once told me, had never liked the cavernous spaces in the older house and was glad for an excuse to pass it on to her daughter. I had never met Lucie's mother; she had died five years earlier.

Under the circumstances, I dreaded calling on Johnny Dreadfulwater. I had interviewed people in the midst of all kinds of trauma in the years I worked for the newspaper, but some things still felt like an intrusion.

The pale sun bathed Johnny Dreadfulwater's brick house in a soft light. Nothing disturbed the sterile surroundings: no barking dogs, no muddy farm trucks parked beside what looked like a brand new barn, no scraps of trash in the ditch. Dreadfulwater had a concrete driveway, a novelty in rural Cherokee County, and there were no trees in his yard, no oaks to drop their leaves in the fall and make an untidy mess on the perfect expanse of Bermuda that stretched for an acre or more.

I looked down at my Levis and sweatshirt, seeing myself through Johnny Dreadfulwater's eyes. Just another bad credit risk, despite my friendship with his daughter.

I rubbed the Pearl bottle cap in my pocket, my new talisman, and said, "You're procrastinating." It was enough to make me climb out of the Civic, march up the concrete walk and ring the bell.

The door was black walnut, worn and weathered, out of character with the new house. Carved into the wood was a map that traced the route from New Echota, Georgia, to Tahlequah. The inscription underneath was in the Cherokee alphabet and then a year, "1839."

The one other time I had visited this house with Lucie, she had translated the words: Trail of Tears. Samuel Dreadfulwater himself had carved the door for the Southern Gothic Mausoleum, and the map marked the long walk he and his family had made on the Trail. When Lucie's father built his new house, the door was the only part of the old house that Johnny Dreadfulwater took with him.

The door opened almost immediately. A middle-aged woman wearing an apron studied me. Her hair was a thick mink rope down her back, and her eyes were almond-shaped. I remembered Lucie telling me that her father's cousin had been staying with him since her mother's death.

"I'm Viv Powers, Lucie's friend," I said. "Could I speak with Mr. Dreadfulwater?"

The woman pursed her lips. "He's not receiving company."

"It's important."

A querulous voice from inside the house said, "For God's sake, Faith, what is it now?"

Faith's eyes darted over her shoulder and back to me. "Wait here," she said. She disappeared inside the house, but she didn't close the door.

I could hear their voices rising and falling. I stood on the porch and ran my finger along the trail carved into the wooden door. Georgia to Tennessee to a corner of Kentucky and Illinois, through Missouri and a small wedge of Arkansas to Tahlequah.

Nine hundred miles one step at a time.

Faith returned, and her eyes flickered from my hand to the door to my face, as though I had touched a museum exhibit. "Follow me," she said.

The entrance hall was dim, and the hall Faith led me through even dimmer. She stopped at the door of a room that looked like a study, although it was as sterile as the rest of the house. No papers on the desk, a matched set of law books on the bookshelves. The heavy drapes were drawn, and in the faint light, Johnny Dreadfulwater turned toward me in his wheelchair.

I hesitated in the doorway.

"Come in, Ms. Powers," he said impatiently. His voice was harsh but weak, as though he had been cursing until his vocals chords were slack.

I sat in the leather chair he pointed to. Faith hovered in the doorway.

"That will be all, Faith," Dreadfulwater said. He watched her leave then turned his attention to me. "Things have changed," he finally said.

His face was as worn and fissured as the oak door. The poor lighting masked his complexion, but the way he sat, defeated and tired, told me he was a sick man.

I told Johnny Dreadfulwater about the packet of papers his daughter had sent me.

"She shouldn't have brought you into it."

"Into what?"

He looked at me, an inscrutable look on his face. My usual tactic, silence, had no effect on him. I tried a different direction.

"Can you think of anyone who might have had a reason to murder her?"

Dreadfulwater stirred, and his hooded eyes took me in.

"I've been over this with the police. She had no enemies."

We sat in silence again; he studied his knotted and blue-veined hands, and my eyes fastened on a chessboard. It was set up for a game, and a black bishop lay on its side at the edge of the table while the white queen threatened the black king.

"Do you play?" Johnny Dreadfulwater asked.

"I don't have the patience."

"I play against myself these days," he said, "which defeats the purpose." He straightened as if he had an important point to make. "The key to winning is predicting the next series of moves your opponent will make and blocking them while executing a strategy of your own."

I hadn't come here to discuss games. "Did Lucie talk to you about the offer on her land?"

"We talked."

"Was she going to sell to M&M, Menckle's investment group?"

He turned his face toward the window as though the answer could be found in his sterile yard. "She didn't say."

I stood and paced the floor. "What I can't figure is how Dale Nowlin fits into all this."

Dreadfulwater jerked as though a hot poker had gouged him.

I sat down again. "He owned thirty acres next to Lucie's land, which he sold to M&M. Do you have any idea what he and Lucie were arguing about on Friday?"

"Why are you asking all these questions?"

"I want to find out who killed your daughter. That's all."

"The police are investigating." Dreadfulwater opened a desk drawer and pulled out a heavy ledger. "I have work to do."

"The police have other crimes to investigate," I said, moving my chair closer to the desk. "I have time to find things out. For instance, you bought Lucie's eighty acres from Alma Nowlin in 1953, who obtained the entire one-hundred-and-ten acres from your father in 1935. What's that all about?"

"Faith!" Dreadfulwater yelled. His voice suddenly sounded strong. "Faith!"

She appeared so quickly that I suspected she had been waiting outside the door.

"Show Ms. Powers out," Dreadfulwater said. His hands were shaking.

There was no choice but to follow Faith. I thanked Johnny Dreadfulwater for his time, but his head was bent over his books, and he made no sign that he heard me.

I expected Faith to herd me out the front door, but instead she put her fingers to her lips to caution silence and led me to the kitchen.

"Mr. Dreadfulwater's not himself right now," she said, after she closed the door.

The kitchen was friendlier than the rest of the house. Faith's room, obviously. Bright yellow curtains framed the windows, and bundles of dried herbs hung from a beam. A shelf held a row of dog-eared cookbooks. A pot of stew simmered on the stove. I leaned against the granite countertop and waited to hear what Faith had to say.

She pushed her hair out of her eyes and looked at me. "I've been in this house for five years now," she said, "and Lucie told me about you. She trusted you, so I do, too. I don't know what else to do." Her voice was like a cello, rich and warm, inviting intimacy.

For just a minute I felt a wild hope that Faith was going to tell me everything I needed to fit the pieces together.

"I'm worried about Mr. Dreadfulwater," she said, turning away from me and looking out the kitchen window.

Her skin was the rich gold of October oak leaves. I wondered exactly what her relationship was to Johnny Dreadfulwater.

"He's a very proud man," Faith said. "I try to anticipate when he needs help because he's not very good at asking for it." She turned to me, and her dark eyes were bright with tears. "He needs help now. There's more to it than the death of his daughter. I think someone is threatening him."

"What makes you think that?"

"Promise me you won't talk to him about this." It was a demand rather than a request. Faith had her own reservoir of pride.

"I'll do my best to keep you out of it."

She chewed on her lower lip and finally made up her mind. "Someone called today. The voice was so raspy I couldn't tell if it was a man or a woman. But there was something—scary—about it. When Mr. Dreadfulwater got off the phone, he was furious. I could hear him muttering in his study and banging things around.

"Any idea what the conversation was about?"

A guilty flush lit her cheeks. "I'm not an eavesdropper."

"Is that all?"

"Except when I went in his study later to take him his pain pills, he said, 'Not today, Faith, they dull my mind.'"

"He kicked me out when I asked about Dale Nowlin."

"I think Mr. Dreadfulwater was glad his daughter killed that man."

"Why? Did they have a business relationship of some kind?"

"I don't know."

I left by the kitchen door at Faith's request.

"He'll hear my vehicle," I said. "He'll know we talked."

"I'll tell him you asked to use the bathroom."

I gave Faith my phone number and asked her to call me if she thought of anything else. When I asked her if she had told the police about the phone call, she made a contemptuous sound.

"That chooch Ernie Terrapin came out to question us yesterday. I remember when he used to torment my little sister when they were in school. I wouldn't tell him anything."

"There's a man who works for the OSBI. It might help if you tell him what you told me."

She looked toward the study as though Johnny Dreadfulwater

might come roaring out in his wheelchair.

"Please," I said. "This goes beyond one man's pride."

She finally nodded her head in assent.

Then I crept out the back door of the house of Lucie's father as though I were a thief, or a lover.

24

I headed back downtown, thinking as I drove about what to do next. My subconscious must have had a better handle on things than the conscious part of my mind because without quite knowing why, I ended up in Professor Durant's driveway.

It was a balmy November afternoon, and across the street at the high-rise dorms, shirtless college boys sailed Frisbees across the parking lot. A single-engine plane flew low overhead, and I wondered if Michael Probst was flying gamblers to the races in Hot Springs.

Professor Durant didn't act surprised to see me when he answered the door. Perhaps he had seen enough in his long life that nothing could now surprise him. We enacted our usual greeting—the hug, my kiss on his bald head—and he held the door open to allow me in.

"You're just in time, Viv," he said, leading the way to the kitchen. "I can't open these darned olives. It's no good growing old. Your body is always letting you down, and people treat you as though your mind were going, too. But," he winked at me, "I always say it beats the alternative."

I popped the lid off the olives and handed the jar back. I was in a funky, morbid mood. "So what about artificially prolonging life through massive medical intervention—respirators, tubes— where does that fit in?"

He made a motion of dismissal. "That's not life. That's the result of a society that is so bent on immortality and youth that it

can't accept the inevitable. Eventually the medical establish-
ment ends up with your life savings and a hefty insurance pay-
ment, and you're just as dead."

We moved into the library, and I gave him an abridged version of what I had learned in the past two days. Professor Durant
patted my hand.

"I know Mooney's telling of the Utlunta tale," he said, "but it
might be better if you read his text."

He pulled a book from a shelf, thumbed through it and
handed it to me.

I used my finger for a bookmark while I closed the book to
look at the cover. *Myths of the Cherokee* and *Sacred Formulas of
the Cherokees* by James Mooney. Then I opened it again and
read.

The story of the magical Utlunta, or Spear-Finger, was bloody
and terrible. "Long, long ago—h'lahi'yu—there dwelt in the
mountains a terrible ogress, a woman monster, whose food was
human livers," the story began. Utlunta could take any form or
appearance to suit her purpose, and on her right hand she had
a long stony forefinger of bone that she stabbed people with.
She had powers over stone and could easily lift immense rocks.
A shiver ran down my back. Why would Lucie tell Roy Calico
she was meeting Utlunta?

I held the book up and shook it at Professor Durant. "Does
anyone believe this stuff?"

Professor Durant linked his fingers in front of him, eager to
deliver a history lesson. "I assume," he said, "that you are asking
if there are still Cherokees who observe the old ways, and the
answer is yes.

"More than 10,000 Cherokees, mostly full-blood, in eastern
Oklahoma speak the language, maintain the old beliefs and cus-
toms of their tribe, and don't take kindly to mixing with the as-
similated Cherokees. You," he pointed a bony finger, "probably
know Cherokees who are much like you except for their ances-

try.

"Back during the Civil War, a secret society of full bloods was formed by Evan Jones and his son John—ostensibly to perpetuate tribal traditions. But the group's real purpose was to fight slavery. They called themselves Keetoowahs. They fought against General Stand Watie's group, the "Knights of the Golden Circle," who supported southern rights.

"The bitter factionalism did not end after the war, and when the government tried to force the Cherokees to sign the tribal rolls for individual land allotments, the full-blood Keetoowahs retreated to the Ozark Hills and refused to cooperate.

"The old men and women of these seventy-some settlements of full-bloods have kept the traditions alive. When the American Indian Movement came along in the '60s, the Keetoowah Society was rekindled, and the young people were eager to learn the medicine and ceremonies. So, yes, there are people who still tell these stories."

I let out a long breath. "Why would anyone call himself or herself Utlunta?"

Professor Durant rubbed his forehead. "She is a frightening and a powerful myth. I suppose someone either needs or is attracted to the extra power that a myth bestows."

"That sounds sick to me."

"Sick? Maybe. It might just as easily be a red herring; while you focus on the exotic, the commonplace occurs under your nose."

"This has always been a violent place, hasn't it?" I said. "Cherokee County, the domestic violence capital of the world."

"That can't be blamed on the Cherokees," Professor Durant said.

"I wasn't even suggesting that."

"Well, I get feisty about it. There have probably been more murders here per capita than in many of our large cities."

The late afternoon sun slanted through the open windows in

Professor Durant's library. The yellow light in the dim room echoed the light in the painting on the wall—one of Karl Bodmer's interiors of a Mandan lodge. Dust motes danced in the air and settled on the table tops. After awhile, the professor stirred. "I'm not much help, am I?"

"Perhaps you can help me with this. Dale Nowlin was married to a woman named Diane. She was a student at the university in the early 1970s, perhaps a history major. Did you know her?"

Professor Durant looked at his shelves of books. "I've had so many students over the years..."

"This one may have stood out. There was a scandal connected to her. Dale Nowlin went to the university and assaulted a professor because he suspected they were having an affair."

"I really can't help you, Viv." His voice sounded far away.

"It was a long time ago, but sometimes those years seem most vivid to me—when I was young and the world was brand new."

He smiled. "I wasn't so young even then."

"You'll always be young to me." I kissed him on my way out. That was one lesson I had learned in the past week. Kiss your friends when you have the chance.

25

I parked in front of The Woodshop on Muskogee Avenue and sat in the Civic, windows rolled down, reading through the notes I had made during the past two days.

The memory came unbidden: I raised the board in my hands and hit Lucie's head. The look on her face after. Had she used me? What really happened that day in her barn? My chest felt tight, as though tears welled inside. I loved her and hated her for leaving like she did.

I banged my palm against the steering wheel. "Dumb, dumb, dumb," I said over and over. But I didn't know what was dumb. The day in the barn? My impotent attempts to find Lucie's killer?

Lucie's killer.

I focused on that thought. Lucie's killer. The rest can wait. Find Lucie's killer.

I went back to my notes, looking for the overlooked, trying to make sense of the senseless. Delving into Dale Nowlin's background had been interesting, in the same way that a highway accident is interesting—we all slow and crane our necks to catch a glimpse of mangled bodies and tell ourselves we're lucky it's not us lying beside the road—but if there was a connection between Nowlin's and Lucie's deaths, I was missing it.

"Legends" was one of the cryptic notations. I frowned and then remembered that Lucie had been one of the performers in Legends of the Five Civilized Tribes. It was scheduled to open at the university tomorrow night. Perhaps she had been at rehearsal on Monday; perhaps she had said something that would help me trace her final movements.

I left the Civic parked where it was and walked the two blocks to the Fine Arts Auditorium.

The campus was quiet. Either everyone was studying, or the warm weather had drawn them to the shores of Lake Tenkiller or the Illinois River, favorite drinking hangouts for underage students.

However, inside the brick walls of the Fine Arts Building, the bustle, excitement and uneasiness of final rehearsal pervaded the building. The pale gray walls were covered with posters advertising the performance.

From far down the hall came a cry of anguish, followed by a loud, angry voice. I had been here with Lucie before and knew the way to the backstage area. I took the stairs two at a time. The late afternoon sun filtered through the dusty windows of the stairwell, warming the space and heightening the institutional smell of mineral hot springs and Lysol.

The sound of the ranting voice grew louder and angrier with each step I took.

A tall, thin student, dressed in little more than body paint and a breechcloth, stood at the gray steel backstage door, nervously smoking a cigarette. He jumped when I came up behind him.

"Jesus Christ!" His dark eyes darted from me toward the sound beyond the door.

"Sorry," I said. "Things a little tense here?"

"She's not helping by chewing everybody out." The boy's eyes darted toward the door again. He ground out the cigarette on the tile floor and started biting his ragged nails.

"She?"

"Dierdre Flanagan, the director. She's on a real tear." He shook out a fresh cigarette from his pack of Pall Malls and offered one to me.

"No, thanks."

"I hope you're not one of those crusaders who run to tell mama at the scent of smoke," the kid said while he lit up, "because I'm way beyond that today."

"I'm just looking for some information about a friend. Lucie Dreadfulwater."

"I knew who she was, of course. Everybody knew her. What happened really sucks."

"Did you see her on Monday?"

He shook his head and took a deep drag on his cigarette.

The noise inside had stopped, so I stepped through a gray steel door marked "Authorized Personnel Only," and went backstage. I caught a glimpse of a huddled group in traditional Cherokee clothing before I decided that the proper approach to the director might be through a more conventional door.

Most of the doors around the auditorium were locked, but I found one open and slipped into the back. Two actors were morosely going over their lines on stage, and a woman sat in the center of the auditorium, script in hand, watching them with bright, angry eyes.

I sat in a seat next to her, and she looked at me quickly, ready to add me to her attack list. She was an attractive woman, with upswept dark hair and immaculate grooming, but chronic stress had etched deep lines into her chin and forehead.

"Dierdre Flanagan?" I asked.

"This is a rehearsal," she said. "You're not supposed to be here."

"It's about Lucie Dreadfulwater."

Her eyes softened. "I'm having one of the worst days of my life," she said. "These supposedly serious acting students are behaving as though it's open mike night at the improv, and we're opening tomorrow."

"I know you're busy," I said, "but I need to know if you saw Lucie or heard from her on Monday."

Dierdre dropped her script in her lap and massaged her temples with long fingers. Blue eye shadow was caked in the crevice above her eyes.

"These past few days have all run together. I have no idea who I talked to on Monday or when I last saw Lucie." She paused and straightened the turquoise pin on her paisley silk scarf. "I'm going to miss her. We're dedicating the opening night performance to her. I want everything to be perfect."

"May I ask some of the people backstage if they saw her?"

Dierdre waved her hand in resignation. "Be my guest. Just don't interrupt the flow."

I circled back to the door marked "Authorized Personnel Only." A chubby boy in a brown robe pointed me toward a young woman in a smock, who was using a blow-dryer on a freshly painted cart. She told me she hadn't seen or heard from Lucie on Monday, she was positive, she was so upset over Lucie's suicide, she had never known anyone before who had killed herself. She herself was Osage, not Cherokee, she added as though it were some kind of code I should understand.

I talked to the other people backstage, but apparently Lucie hadn't shown up on Monday.

I was tired of running in circles. I was plain tired. I leaned my forehead against a concrete wall and absorbed the coolness. The voices of the actors on stage droned on like busy bees on a spring day, and I hardly listened until someone said the words I had played over and over to myself the past two days. They weren't exactly the same, but they were close.

"As his body burned up, his spirit began to rise and he was still singing as he ascended. He had created evil and then sacrificed himself to save the people from the evil he had made."

The voices went on, but I didn't hear what they said. I rushed onto the stage and confronted the two actors.

"What did you just say?"

They were shocked into silence.

"About evil."

Dierdre Flanagan marched up to the stage, her mouth set in a grim line.

"You have to leave now." It was an order, but I couldn't obey until I had an answer to my question.

I held out my hands in a conciliatory gesture. "I just need to hear the lines again."

Dierdre gave in grudgingly, perhaps sensing that a lunatic was on her stage and she would get rid of me more quickly by playing along.

The actor repeated his lines. Except for the change in gender, they were Lucie's suicide note, word for word.

"What's that from?"

"It's the legend of Ocasta-Stonecoat," said the actor. "It's part of the performance."

I looked at Dierdre. By this time, the entire cast was alert, wondering what I would do next. "Have you or has anyone here seen Lucie Dreadfulwater's daytimer?" My grand sweeping motion took in the entire room. I was center stage.

The girl in the smock said hesitantly. "You mean like a notebook?"

"Yes! Like a notebook."

"I haven't seen it, like, around here recently, but Ms. Dreadfulwater would write down what she called 'inspiration lines' in a small brown notebook. Then we'd review them when we were constructing the set."

"If anyone finds that brown notebook, hand it over to the Oklahoma Bureau of Investigation. It's very important."

I didn't get an ovation, but I felt the flush of success as I exited the stage.

26

The euphoria didn't last long. I walked back toward the Civic, feeling my energy ebb with each step. The shoulder I had rolled on the day before throbbed. The cut in my foot burned. It had been a long day, and the stakes were high. Whoever had killed Lucie might turn his or her attention toward me next. Utlunta. I looked behind me, with the irrational feeling that something, maybe a black Buick, was creeping up on me. The storefronts on Muskogee Avenue cast long shadows. Tahlequah's 5 p.m. "rush minute" had given way to the sparser evening traffic. No one showed any particular interest in me.

My path led past the open doors of the Creekside Bar and Grill. The sound of "Friend of the Devil" drifted in the air, along with the homey smell of hamburgers. It was an hour before Maggie and I had agreed to meet at the Creekside, but I knew what my body needed. To rejoin the living, to relax in a dark place for awhile, to sort out my thoughts, to take in some carbohydrates.

The door swung open just as I got to it, and Corey sailed out. The odor of beer hung on her like a toxic cloud.

"Hey, Viv!" she said, focusing on me. "Been on any wild plane rides lately?"

"Not today, Corey." I grabbed her elbow to steady her. "Are you all right?"

"I'm A-okay. Just stopped by after work. Now I'm headed home to see my little kiddies." Her voice became a self-pitying whine. "It's always up to me since John lives on the road. Birthdays. Flu. Anniversaries. Emergency room. Just me and the kids. You and Charley are smart not to have any."

Charley didn't feel that way; in fact, more and more frequently these days, he talked about when his stepdaughter Iris was a baby and how she had changed his life and that time was running out for us. Blah, blah, blah. I wasn't about to tell Corey that, though.

"Do you need a ride home, Corey?"

"I got me a ride. One of the girls from the office lives out my way." She swung her head around and almost lost her balance. "She was right behind me. Where did that girl go?"

I had a sudden inspiration. "Do you still have that part-time job at the registrar's office, Corey?"

"Still there. Nothing in my life ever changes."

"Could you do me a big favor?" I took out my card and scribbled Diane Nowlin's name on the back of it. "This woman was a student about twenty years ago. Could you find out who her adviser was?"

"Piece'a cake," Corey said, stuffing the card in her purse.

Just then her friend came out the door. She looked sober, so I told Corey I'd call her tomorrow.

Happy Hour was in full swing in the Creekside, and the after-work, after-school crowd filled most of the tables. I chose a barstool, not even looking around for familiar faces; I wouldn't have been good company.

Betsy and Hank looked as harassed and overworked as I felt. Had Charley been with me, Betsy would have traded jokes with him and comped him a beer; Charley has that effect on people. But she barely managed a smile while taking my order for a chicken sandwich and a Budweiser.

I had finished my sandwich and was into a second beer when

someone jostled my elbow, making me tip over the glass.

"Hutch!"

"That didn't work out like it was supposed to," he said, mopping up the beer with cocktail napkins.

Hutch's dark face had tired creases, and he didn't look like he was in any better mood than I was.

"Lost your rhythm?"

Hutch wedged himself between me and the woman on the next barstool and said in my ear. "We need to talk."

"Yes. We do."

"I have a booth in the back. Two more Buds in the back!" he said to Betsy.

The back room of the Creekside was dark and quiet. We settled into the booth. Hutch's long, slender fingers tumbled a matchbook over and over. The cover was adorned with a bosomy woman wearing a skimpy bikini.

"I thought we had an understanding about amateur investigations," he said.

"I didn't say I wasn't going to ask any questions."

Betsy set the beers down, and we were silent until she left.

"Just about everywhere I've been today, you've been before me," Hutch said in a low, angry voice. He dropped the matchbook and ticked off the list on his fingers: "Truman Gourd, Roy Calico, Johnny Dreadfulwater, the Fine Arts Building, for chrissakes!"

I felt a perverse pleasure that he hadn't mentioned Granny Hillyard or Professor Durant.

"Don't expect me to apologize for my interest in 'your' case," I said. "Did you learn that Lucie's so-called suicide note may be just one of many quotes that she wrote down from a play? Tomorrow or the next day you'll be assigned to some other crime, and eventually you'll forget about Lucie Dreadfulwater, but she was my friend."

"I found out about the note. But it doesn't mean much without the rest of her daytimer." Hutch's hawk eyes pierced me. "I don't suppose you came across that today."

"No." I was suddenly deflated. "Did Johnny Dreadfulwater tell you about the phone call he received today? It could be the same person who called Lucie the night she was murdered."

"He wasn't very happy about his cousin talking to me. Mr. Dreadfulwater seems to think the caller is some kind of sick prankster. That sort of thing happens all too often after someone dies. I offered to set up phone surveillance, but he wasn't interested."

Hutch took my hand and talked to me as though I were a slow but well-meaning child. "What you're doing, Viv, is getting in the way. You could actually be impeding the investigation by confusing the witnesses before we get a chance to talk to them."

I had a sudden thought. "Since when have you been assigned to this case?"

Hutch shook his head and let go of my hand. "You never give up, do you?"

"Well?"

"Since today."

"Here's another piece to puzzle over. Jonathan Marlin was in town last night with his buddy Albert."

"Where?" A sudden, swift dive from the hawk.

"At Menckle's office, after hours. Albert picked the lock and walked in."

"And you didn't find that important enough to mention to anyone?"

It was hard to meet his eyes. "I'm telling you now. Anyway, I don't think they found what they came for."

Hutch tore the matchbook apart, jerking each match savagely and flipping it onto the table. After the matchbook was shredded, he said, "Marlin's bad news. He's the closest thing in Hot Springs to organized crime. Charged but never convicted of racketeering, intimidating witnesses, laundering money, you name it. He has powerful friends. Menckle's gone into partnership with the devil."

We sat in silence and drank our beers. From the jukebox, Don Henley sang about "The End of the Innocence." A very drunk man and woman slow-danced in the corner.

Maybe it was time to grow up and admit I couldn't single-handedly restore the world's moral order. That there was no order to restore. Maybe Hutch was right. Maybe I should leave this to the experts. So far I had been successful in one thing—getting people pissed at me.

"Okay," I said. "I'll back off." I meant it at the time. I just wanted to give in. Maybe the alcohol was going to my head.

Hutch just looked at me.

"You might be a little more grateful," I said.

"I'll be grateful tomorrow when I'm not following you around."

A darker thought sobered me. "What do you make of this Utlunta thing?"

His eyes narrowed. "I thought you were going to back off."

"That doesn't mean I want to read about it in the newspaper."

Hutch sighed and gathered up the pieces of the matchbook and dropped them in the ashtray. "Once Utlunta hits the papers, the crazies will be coming out of the woods. I'd like to put a gag on that Calico character."

Before Hutch left, he scribbled a phone number on the back of his business card. He said he was staying in Tahlequah for awhile; if I thought of anything, I could reach him at that number.

27

I stayed in the booth with my empty glass after Hutch left, too wrung out to move. If I had had the energy and a quarter, I would have plugged the jukebox and played "Friend of the Devil" again.

I was singing to myself, "If I get home before daylight, I just might get some sleep toni-i-ight," when Maggie showed up.

"You didn't give me an easy task," she said, sliding into the booth.

I looked at her. "Jesus Christ! What happened to you?" Her hair was an electric shade of red.

"I was tired of blond." Maggie touched her crimson curls. "A new hair color can change your life."

"You've got to quit reading Cosmo."

"Multiple orgasms: who has 'em and why. This month's cover line. Speaking of which, was that your old buddy Hutch leaving when I came in?"

I felt a flush rise on my neck. "He says I'm impeding the investigation."

Maggie gave me an incredulous look, but before she could say anything, Betsy arrived with her order: a tall, tropical drink. As soon as Betsy left, Maggie picked the maraschino cherry off the end of the swizzle stick and dropped it in the ashtray.

"Three kinds of rum and I forget what else," she said, waving the fruit-laden stick at her glass. "Just what the doctor ordered."

"Rough day, huh?"

Maggie raised her eyebrows at me. "I know that tone. Fine. I don't need your sympathy." She tested her drink and frowned at me. "I've been running all over town, made umpteen-million calls, and now you're going to let Hutch order you around?"

"He's the law."

"He'd better be good," Maggie said. "I came up with nothing, except one interesting little bit. Someone paid cash to have Dale Nowlin cremated. The guy I talked to at the funeral home wouldn't tell me more."

"Surely someone will pick up the ashes."

Maggie had nibbled all the fruit from her swizzle stick, and now she pointed the miniature sword at me. "Furthermore, I called every law office in town with my bogus story about being a relative of poor Dale Nowlin, and I understood they were handling his legal affairs. No one admitted to it. It's enough to drive a person to drink." She put down her glass and lit a cigarette.

"And other disgusting habits," I said.

"Aren't we superior," Maggie said, with an air of superiority. The smoke swirled around her red curls like a malevolent spirit.

Just then, Randy Silvers and Lisabeth Ellis walked past the booth.

Randy did a double take and backed up. "Viv! And little sis. What a treat. We've got a pitcher, and we're headed for the deck. Join us?"

The look on Lisabeth's pale face suggested that Randy was alone in extending the invitation.

Maggie stood. "'Little sis' has gotta go. Coming big sis?"

"Not just now."

She grimaced at me, then shrugged. "Suit yourself."

I couldn't understand the instant dislike that had sprung up between my sister and these two women. Granted, they all had a dysfunctional side. But hold that against people, and you'll lead an isolated life. I followed Lisabeth and Randy out the back door.

"This is obscene," Lisabeth said, turning to go back in the bar. She dropped one of the empty glasses, and it rolled over the edge of the deck. After a second's pause, it shattered on the rocks below.

Randy grabbed Lisabeth's arm, and some of the beer sloshed over the top of the pitcher. "Don't be a baby," she said. Without loosening her grip on Lisabeth's arm, she set the pitcher on a table. "Sit down. I'm going back for more glasses."

Lisabeth sank into a chair and hugged herself as though she were cold.

I sat next to her. "Are you all right, Lisabeth?"

She shivered. "Betsy and Hank should have closed off this deck after Sunday night. What are they thinking?"

"I've been told that was an accident. Besides, Lucie wasn't hurt. Here." The word hung between us.

She gave me a slanted look. "I've heard stories about you. You're always going around digging into people's business. As if you have the right."

"I'm a reporter. I ask questions."

"Yes," she said. "I have a degree in journalism. I know all the usual scripture. But there are lines you shouldn't cross. Some things are private, and they should stay that way."

"It's hard to know where to draw the line."

She brought her knees up to her chest and hugged herself tighter as if she were under attack. "People have a public face and they have a private face. Even celebrities who invite you into their homes and tell you tales of childhood abuse and drug addiction, they still have a private face they hide from you. Maybe it's a fear that they're frauds. Maybe it's a foot fetish. Shouldn't they be allowed their little secrets?"

"No," I said. I didn't really believe what I said, but it had been a long day, and I felt a perverse pleasure in disagreeing with Lisabeth Ellis. I had met her only days before, and I had witnessed an erratic parade of behavior: She had been aloof in

Menckle's office the day we met, nearly hysterical at the Creekside the night Lucie was pushed, and self-important when she broke the news to me that Lucie was dead. I wanted to see her in a new mode: defensive, angry. I didn't care which.

Instead she surprised me again.

"I have secrets, too," she said. She seemed to be shrinking by the minute. Her hands were white with the effort of pulling her body into a ball. "My mother took me away from my father when I was a small child. She saved our lives, she always claimed. If you think out of the frying pan into the fire is an improvement. My father was kind to me, but the men who came later to my mother's house had only one thing on their minds. And it wasn't a home-cooked meal."

"I'm sorry," I said.

She made a little sound that could have been a laugh. But it probably wasn't.

I leaned back in my chair and wondered why I stayed. Lisabeth sank into a stony silence.

The deck held only three tables and no one else was on the deck. The temperature was cool but pleasant, and a slight breeze rustled the bare branches of the trees that topped out at deck level. I could reach out and touch the branches. I broke one off and snapped it into smaller pieces. The sound of water falling over the rocks below played a dark and secret dirge. It reminded me of things I didn't want to think about.

Randy burst back on the deck waving glasses. "Now we're in business," she said, filling each glass until the foam overflowed. If she noticed that her ebullient mood wasn't matched, she gave no sign. She launched into a story about a road trip with the band. I only half-listened. Lisabeth's face was shrouded by her hair, and she looked like she might be crying.

I nursed a beer and watched the sky turn from shell pink to cobalt. I wondered what Charley was doing.

Randy nudged Lisabeth. "See. It's not so bad, is it?"

Lisabeth looked away. "You think you're some kind of therapist? Sometimes you don't have a clue, Randy."

"I'm just trying to help."

"Maybe I don't need your help."

"Babe," Randy said, "you need my help more than you'll ever know."

Lisabeth stood up, bright spots of pink on her cheeks. "I've had enough of this. I'm going home." She turned away and fumbled in her purse for a minute before she turned back to Randy. "I need my car keys." Her voice had grown cold with suppressed anger.

In one fluid movement, Randy tossed the keys to Lisabeth. "Don't worry about me," she said. "I'll just walk home."

Lisabeth snatched up the keys and stalked into the bar, her head high.

"What's eating her?"

Randy looked at me with unreadable eyes. "She's high strung."

Her face gave away nothing.

"What?" she finally said.

"I ran into Neil today."

"Oh?" The breeze ruffled her long hair, and she looked beyond me.

"He said you were back together."

"He's so discreet," Randy said. She stood up. "I gotta pee."

After she left, the deck was quiet again. I looked around, visualizing the scene Sunday night when someone had tried to push Lucie down the stairs.

I stood to look down, and my attention was caught by a rustling in the trees below. At first I thought it was a dog or a deer; the dim light erased detail. Then a man emerged into a clearing beside the creek. The silhouette was unmistakable: Truman Gourd.

Just then, he looked up, and his dark eyes met mine. He

didn't seem surprised; he turned and disappeared around the corner of the building. I climbed over the gate that blocked the fire escape and hurried down the steps. At the front of the Creekside, I looked up and down Muskogee Avenue, but Truman was gone.

I returned to the bar through the front door. Randy sat at the bar, talking to Betsy. She drained her glass when she saw me.

"I thought you had ditched me, babe."

"I'm leaving."

"Give me a ride?"

In the Civic, Randy was keyed up and nervous. She leaned back against the passenger side door and fingered frets and strummed an imaginary bass.

Too much had happened today for me to ease my way into a subject. So the question sounded abrupt. "Did you go to Hot Springs with David Menckle last week?"

She finished a complicated riff on her invisible instrument before she answered. "What if I did?"

"I was wondering if you met a guy named Jonathan Marlin." I turned the Civic onto Basin Street and crossed the low water bridge.

"A little grubworm?"

"That's an apt description."

"We may have stopped by his office on the way to the track," she said. "I didn't actually meet the guy."

"Do you know why Menckle stopped there?"

"Not a clue."

I pulled into Randy's driveway and she turned toward me and put a hand on my shoulder. "Ease up, babe," she said. "You're going around these days with this cloud over your head, treating everyone as though they're guilty of something. 'Where were you when?' 'What do you know about?' 'Do you this?' 'Did you that?' Lighten up."

"I can't lighten up," I said, the words becoming a confession. "I have to know who killed Lucie."

28

It had been a long day. I needed a massage; my injured foot ached. What I should do was run by the grocery store and buy a box of microwave popcorn. Then I would go home, curl up with *Utne Reader*, munch popcorn and let my mind range far from Cherokee County.

The beer had left a dull haze over my mind. Food would help. Instead of the popcorn, I bought a cardboard sandwich at the grocery store and splashed cold water over my face in the bathroom.

I filled the Civic's tank with gas then headed east out of Tahlequah, chewing the sandwich as I drove, going the long way home. I wanted to stop by Neil Hannahan's house and ask him about something that had been nagging me. Surely Hutch couldn't call it butting into police business if I visited an acquaintance and just happened to ask a couple of questions.

"No rest for the righteous, and the wicked don't need it," had been one of my grandmother's favorite sayings. I only knew I was tired as I drove two miles east then turned the Civic north onto Highway 10. The night air was cool, but I drove with the windows down, the wind running like water over my hands and face. The coolness helped sober me.

Highway 10 snaked between the now-sedate Illinois River to the east and rocky bluffs to the west. On summer weekends, the highway was a perpetual traffic jam. On this night it was almost deserted.

The moon was a shadowed face in the sky, and its light glinted off the rippling water and gilded the rows of upside-down metal canoes. The canoes looked like giant white bass beached on the sand bars, silver bellies up.

Lucie's and my wild trip down the river seemed like something that had happened in another lifetime. The flood had receded, leaving behind freshly gouged banks and rotting vegetation as testament to its power.

I almost missed Neil's driveway, although the crooked arrow pointing up the hill and advertising tattoos gave a clear indication of where to turn. The faded sign was a legacy of a former tenant who was now serving time at McAlester for selling drugs. Neil left the sign up, he once told me, because of the interesting visitors it brought him.

I had been here before, with Charley. The driveway cut steeply up a hollow. It led to a clearing with a small geodesic dome in the center, one of the artifacts of a local fascination with Buckminster Fuller. Neil's '60s-era VW bug was parked in front, and light glowed from inside the dome through the triangular windows.

I parked beside the Volkswagen and stood outside for a minute, listening for any sign that Neil was not alone. Warmth still radiated from the engine in the back of the little car.

The night was so quiet that I imagined I could hear the vegetation settling into the autumn-damp earth. A chuck-will's-widow raised its cry in the silence.

I reluctantly knocked on the door. Something about Neil was off-key. He was too eager to please, he tried too hard to be cool, and it was wearing to be around him. But he was weak. If he knew anything, I could tease it out of him.

Neil didn't answer the door, so I knocked again, louder this time. "Neil!" I yelled. "It's Viv Powers. Can I come in?" There was still no answer. He was probably passed-out drunk. Should I just go in?

I solved the dilemma by shouting, "Neil, I'm coming in." I pushed the door open and walked in.

The unfinished house had an open floor plan. Neil decorated in what he called Japanese fashion, with reed mats on the plywood floor and earth-colored cushions piled around. Stacked crates held books, a stereo system and a television. The sheetrock walls were unpainted. A lacquered tea set, with half a cup of tea in one of the small cups, sat on a low black table. I touched the side of the cup; the tea was still warm. Two empty beer cans, crushed Neil-style, lay flat beside the cup. Toward the far side of the room, where the walls curved outward with the shape of the dome, a cluster of clay figures completed the decorating scheme.

The light came from the bedroom, which was closed off by a three-quarters wall from the rest of the house. I yelled Neil's name again. No response. The first prickles of concern started up my back. I remembered every movie that featured a woman in a lonely house. In the movies the dark and menacing music begins, and you think the heroine is an idiot for going through the closed door.

I went through the door.

No body was on the other side, not even a passed-out drunk—just a waterbed and a bedside table that held a ceramic lamp. The lamp cast an indifferent glow on the walls, and it was one of the walls that caught and held my gaze.

It was covered with photos of Randy Silvers. Randy playing her bass with Powers That Be, Randy in a bikini on a sailboat, Randy smiling wickedly and toasting the photographer, Randy, Randy, Randy. I moved closer to examine the collection.

A candle in a sconce hung under a glamour shot of Randy in filmy decolletage. Draped over the picture was a faded white rose. I felt a pang of pity for Neil. It didn't really count that they were back together; from what I knew of Randy, that was temporary.

I moved quickly along the wall, looking at the other photos. One black-and-white photo in the corner caught my attention. There were three people in the picture: Randy and Neil and Lisabeth Ellis, their arms intertwined. They were laughing. I couldn't tell where the picture had been taken. Some room much like this one.

Back in the living area, I looked around at the crates of books and the clay figures. On closer inspection, the three waist-high figures were gargoyle-like. One of the shapes held my eye. It was a male body wearing out-stretched wings and the head of a raven. The name etched into the base was "Raven Mocker." The figure beside it was feminine, slender and wraith-like. At the end of one of the hands was a long fingernail, curved and sharp-edged like a knife. Her face wore a look of unspeakable cruelty. There was no name on the base, but when I saw her, I knew Utlunta.

Neil had told me about the sculptures, but I hadn't imagined that they would hold such malevolent power. I looked around the room quickly, as though an apparition might materialize out of the shadows.

I had a sudden, irrational thought that Neil was outside, perhaps hurt and needing help, or worse, waiting to jump me.

I had to know. I had to know if he was out there. Like a doctor making clinical observations, I noted that my heart was beating faster than usual; my breathing rate was fast and shallow. I felt intensely, gloriously alive.

Darkness and silence are your allies, The Sergeant used to say. I slipped out the back door, crouching low, feeling only slightly silly, not stopping until I was in the black shadows of the forest behind Neil's house. From that vantage point, I could see the moon-washed expanse of Neil's back yard. Broken shards of pottery lay heaped near a kiln. The sky starkly outlined the kiln chimney, making it look like the remains of a burned house. With a gust of deja vu, I remembered the crumbling chimney I had seen earlier in the day on the property next to Lucie's.

A chimney would be a good place to stuff a body. Another obvious place was the outhouse that stood near the line of trees, its weathered, wooden shell leaning precariously off plumb. Other than those two structures and enough crushed beer cans to pave the yard with, the clearing was empty.

I waited in the silent night. The chuck-will's-widow took up its cry again on the slope behind me and after a moment, another answered. Ten minutes passed. I used the cover of the woods to make my way back to the Civic, hoping it was too late in the season for copperheads to be active. I dug my flashlight out of the glove compartment.

A quick look up the kiln chimney and an even quicker look down the hole of the outhouse convinced me that I had overreacted. There was no dead body to be discovered, no bogyman waiting to pounce from the shadows.

All I wanted to do now was go home. I cut across Steely Hollow to connect to the Moodys road, thinking about Neil as I drove. I remembered when Randy had first joined the band and I had gone on a road trip with Powers That Be. Randy and Neil had been living together at the time, and Neil joined us in Eureka Springs, halfway through the tour.

The band had finished its gig, and the band members had loaded their equipment in the back of Charley's Chevy van. The customers were gone; the bar's front door locked. In the hushed silence that was like a vacuum after the earlier din of music and alcohol-enhanced conversation, the employees upended the chairs on the table for the janitor. Outside, Charley tinkered under the hood of the van, adjusting something to his satisfaction.

The night was cold, and I waited inside the bar with Neil. Most of the band had left for the motel. A haze of smoke hung in the air, along with the sharp odor of spilled beer and whiskey.

Randy walked past the table where Neil and I sat drinking beer, the bar manager trailing her. He had been watching her all evening. Randy wore a mocking smile.

Neil said, "Randy."

She looked over her shoulder past the manager and said, "Later, babe."

Randy and the manager disappeared behind a thin wall. Neil looked at me then looked away. A few minutes later came the unmistakable thumping, moaning sounds of sex.

I had been trying to carry on a conversation with Neil, but we both fell silent. The misery on his face aged him. I felt anger and sorrow for him at the same time.

"Let's see how Charley's coming along," I said as I would to a child.

"Go ahead."

I shrugged and left. After awhile Randy and Neil came out of the bar, and we rode in silence to the motel. It was as though nothing had happened.

29

Half an hour later, when I pulled into my own driveway, I was yawning and fighting to keep my eyes open. I stopped to check the mail through force of habit. As though a check might be in the box. As if that ever happened.

The dim light from the interior of the Civic cast a pale glow inside the mailbox. There were envelopes inside, and toward the back of the box, something round-shaped lay on top of them, something like a furry ball.

I was suddenly wide awake. A feeling of dread swept over me. I reached under the seat of the Civic and pulled out the ice scraper. I poked at the ball. No movement. I used an old newspaper for a dustpan while I drew the ball out with the scraper.

I let out a cry of disgust. It was a rabbit head, still dripping red blood, smelling of iron and warm animal. I almost flung the whole mess into the woods before I realized I should give it to Hutch. It was evidence. Whoever did this might be the same person who left a rabbit head in Lucie's mailbox. Whoever did this might be the same person who killed Lucie.

My maneuvers around the perimeter of Neil's house had been a game; I was playing for keeps now.

I peered through the dark woods as I slowly drove up to the house. My headlights caught the twisted shapes and sinister shadows of black jack oaks. I was on guard now. Spooked. What I remembered most vividly was that I had left the house unlocked.

Only a few days earlier I had told Charley, "We don't own

anything valuable, and if someone wants our junk enough to steal it, they must be in pretty bad shape." He had raised one thin eyebrow. "And furthermore," I added, "way out here in the woods, there's nothing to prevent someone from breaking a window or kicking the door in, so in addition to whatever was stolen, we would have to repair the damage." I now regretted my carelessness.

The house looked quiet from the safety of the Civic. The engine was running, and my foot was on the clutch, ready to roll if I saw any movement. The moonlight reflected off the stark planes and angles of the house, giving it a ghostly fluorescence like the negative of a black-and-white photo. The sharp black shadows of the leafless branches framed it.

The rational part of my mind told me that whoever had placed the rabbit head in the mailbox was probably long gone. The head was either a warning or a prank. The animal part of me, though, the part that put survival first, was pumping epinephrine through my body, making my palms sweat, my heart beat faster, putting every sense on alert.

A cloud swept across the moon, casting running shadows on the ground. I couldn't enter the dark house. I had already turned the Civic around to leave when my pride took over. How would it look to let someone run me off from my own home? What if I called the Sheriff's Department to search the house and no one was there? Sheriff Wes Turner would never let me forget that.

I switched off the Civic, dug around in the junk piled in the back and pulled out a tire iron.

I stood on the porch for a minute in the darkness, straining to hear any sound inside. There was nothing: no movement, no sound. Images of Marlin and Albert, Menckle, Truman, and Neil and his sculptures ran through my mind.

I held the tire iron up like a club, gripping it so tightly that my hand ached. I took a deep breath, turned the door handle and pushed the door open so hard it crashed against the doorstop on the wall. I flipped on the light switch to the right of the door and quickly surveyed the house.

I was grateful for the openness of the design; the only part of the house I couldn't see from where I stood was the bathroom and the back half of the sleeping loft.

The familiar surroundings relaxed my guard. I could almost laugh at myself. As soon as I checked the bathroom and loft, that's what I would do, have a good laugh. I walked around the house, turning on lights as I went, opening cupboard doors, looking behind the sofa. The bathroom was deserted; the silence broken only by the steady drip from the tub faucet, waiting for repair.

The loft had me worried. If anyone waited at the top, I would be at a disadvantage while I climbed the steep stairs. What I needed, I thought, was a stun grenade: throw it over the rail and then check out the loft. Desperation breeds macho fantasies.

I grabbed the tire iron again and started up the steps. Take a step. Stop. Listen. Take a step. The silence was deafening. If anyone popped up, I planned to bail off the steps and hit the floor running.

At first glance, the loft was deserted. I turned on the two lamps and threw the closet doors open. Then I checked under the bed. Yellow animal eyes glowed in the dark corner. My heart raced. Then Mack hissed at me.

I pulled him out from under the bed, enduring his scratches and stroking his rigid, trembling body before I thought to wonder how he got in the house. He had been outside when I left in the morning. And why was he so freaked out? Mack was generally as mellow as melted butter; the only other time I had seen him behave this way was the night he narrowly escaped the talons of an ambitious owl.

Someone had been in the house. Someone had frightened Mack half to death. I looked around to see if anything had been disturbed or stolen. The only things I valued—my Macintosh computer and my hidden stash of grandmother's gold jewelry—were still in their places. Charley's guitars and other musical instruments still stood in their corner cases and hung from the walls.

One thing was different from the way I had left it that morning. And in its own way, it was as disturbing as the rabbit head. I moved closer to the bed. The sheets and blankets were still wrinkled and thrown back like I had left them, but something was sprinkled across the crease my head had left in the pillow. It looked like dry, crumbled leaves. I pinched some of the leaves between my fingers and sniffed. The scent was similar to tobacco, but harsher. Traditional Cherokees use a ceremonial herb, "grandfather tobacco," for several purposes: to work spells, to ward off evil spirits. Was someone working witchcraft on me? I scooped some of the leaves onto a paper, folded it up and stuck it in my pocket.

The windows were in a transitional period between their summer screens and winter coverings of 10 mil plastic. I opened one and shook the rest of the leaves into the night air. The realization that someone had invaded my house was more than frightening: it was a form of psychological rape. My anger drove some of the fear away.

Mack followed me as I went downstairs to lock the doors, meowing loudly. I reached down and picked him up.

"You big baby," I said.

Maybe Mack wasn't a wimp; maybe he was smarter than I was about some things. It wouldn't be much of a retreat, would it, to spend the night at Maggie's house? If I closed my eyes, I could still see the rabbit head dripping blood as I pulled it from the mailbox. I didn't want to stay here alone, reliving that image all night.

I was headed for the phone to call Maggie when it rang. I jumped. I had the uncanny feeling that someone was watching me, anticipating my moves. I stood over the phone, looking at the blank windows as though someone might be peering through them. On the sixth ring, I picked up the phone.

"What?" My voice was rough.

From the other end of the line came a faint rattling sound, a threatening buzz, like the time I had almost stepped on a timber rattler in front of the garden shed. Mack yowled and clawed out of my arms and streaked up the stairs.

"Go to the garden," said a harsh voice. It was soft and as abrasive as sandpaper on stone. I remembered Rachel's description of the phone call Lucie had received the night before she went to meet her killer. "Such a strange, whispery voice," she had said.

It was impossible to tell whether the caller was male or female. I wanted to hear it again.

"What did you say?"

"Go to the garden." The rough voice was more emphatic.

"Why?"

The line went dead.

"Fuck you," I said.

My mind sped up. The garden could wait. I was after one thing right now. The Sergeant had been thorough in his training. He had always seemed more like my commanding officer than my father. And in true military form, he had given me a college graduation gift that he thought would serve me well through life. I had been hoping for a trip to Europe. But The Sergeant gave me a .38 Special and trained me to use it. It was in a metal case under a pile of sweaters at the back of my closet shelf.

I hadn't touched it in years, but there was nothing I wanted more at this moment than to feel its hard, cold steel. I planned my next movements as though every second counted. There was no time to be afraid, no time to dwell on the voice on the phone, no time to wonder why I should "go to the garden." At that moment, all my thoughts focused on the gun.

I scrambled up the stairs as fast I could, feeling like my back was exposed with each leap. I threw the sweaters aside and grabbed for the metal box.

For a minute, I couldn't find it, and I had the sinking feeling that whoever was in the house earlier had taken it, but my searching fingers finally reached deep enough, and I pulled it down to the floor with a cry of triumph.

I fumbled at the clasp and opened the box. The gun was still there, wrapped in white muslin, with a box of ammo beside it. In my panic, I forgot for a minute how to release the cylinder so I could load it, but then my thumb found the catch and it fell open.

I shook the cartridges from their styrofoam container onto the floor, sliding six into the chambers. I heard myself saying, "Okay, okay, okay." Once the .38 was loaded, I ran my fingertips over the sides, feeling for the safety. Then I remembered there was none. It was a double-action; all I had to do was pull the trigger.

It was reassuring to have the gun. I felt calmer, but it was the false calm at the center of the storm. I sat on the floor of the loft with the gun in my hand, trying to think what to do next, when I heard the sound of metal striking stone. The sound was rhythmic, constant, and it came from the garden.

Three windows overlooked the garden: two upstairs and the bathroom window downstairs. If someone were stalking me, I didn't want to be an easy target. Once again, I raced around the house, gun in hand, this time switching the lights off. The bathroom light was the last to go off; therefore, I reasoned, I should look out one of the other windows. Besides, the view would be better from the loft.

I knelt below the east loft window and looked out. In the bright moonlight, a dark shape hacked at the garden beds with a hoe, slashing my strawberry plants, sending clumps of earth flying, striking rocks so hard that sparks exploded.

He worked his way down a raised bed, chopping at the apple trees I had planted just days before. I was certain it was a man; I could see only his bare back, but the shoulders were too broad and the body too tall for any ordinary woman.

I watched the destruction of my garden as though I were in a trance. Once, after Charley and I made love, he had said: "In the moment of transcendence, time stands still." I had said, "Hmmm?" And Charley said, "On the other hand, if time is linear, we can always seek to improve on ecstasy." The inane memory ran through my mind until the man turned toward the house, his chest heaving. It wasn't until then that I realized he was wearing a mask.

The mask wasn't your usual thug-with-pantyhose-over-the-head mask; from a distance, it looked like a wooden ceremonial mask with lighter-colored slashes down the cheeks.

I was suddenly outraged at the wanton slaughter of my garden. I hefted the gun; I heard again in my mind the whispery voice on the phone.

The window I had opened to shake the tobacco off my pillow was still open. I scooted along the floor until I was underneath it. With one smooth motion, I rolled onto my knees, pointed the gun at the ground below me, and fired. I wanted to scare the hell out of the guy.

The explosion split the night and echoed through the room. The man in the garden dropped the hoe and stumbled backward, and for one moment, I thought my bullet had struck him. But he recovered his footing and took off in a lurching run.

I watched him until he disappeared into the forest, and then I watched awhile longer, staring into the dark shadows of the oaks. He might come back. And whoever had phoned might be with him. My decision to spend the night at Maggie's seemed better than ever.

After I was safely at Maggie's house, I would call Hutch and tell him about the man in the garden.

I stuffed a few necessities into a canvas bag, including the gun, and called Maggie to let her know I was coming. I told her the details would have to wait. Then I dragged the reluctant Mack out from under the bed again and put him in his carrying cage. I reconsidered the gun and pulled it out of the bag. I would feel safer leaving the house with the gun in my hand.

The bag, the caged cat and the gun made an awkward load, and I cursed when, in my haste, I banged my head against the steel frame of the Civic. Mack wasn't happy when I started the engine, and he meowed loudly and constantly to tell me so.

I backed up the Civic to the garden and surveyed the broken plants. I had always thought of the darkness as friendly, but it didn't seem that way now. Somewhere in the darkness was a man in a mask. There was a white-hot core of anger inside me. The garden was my route to peace with the world, and for some-one to violate it was about as personal as anyone could get.

30

I often dwell on the pain-in-the-ass side of my sister, but when Maggie saw me at her door carrying Mack in his case as though I were a war refugee, she took over.

"What the hell's been going on?" she said. She was dressed in a long filmy robe, with silky pink slippers. Her hair was wrapped in a towel and something slimy was smeared across her face. She saw me looking at it.

"Mashed avocado," she said. "Moisturizes the skin. Hand me your bag. Put the cat down."

Jake wagged his tail and sniffed at Mack while Mack arched his back and hissed through the spaces of the carrier.

"Jake, no!" Maggie said.

Mack swiped at Jake's nose, and Jake jumped back, knocking over a delicate side table and upsetting an African violet. Potting soil spilled across the floor.

"Shit!" Maggie threw my bag at Jake, who high-tailed it to the kitchen.

While Maggie jailed Jake on the screened-in back porch, I swept up the soil and repotted the plant. Some of the leaves were broken, but it should survive. Salvaging the violet reminded me of my own broken plants, and outrage rose in me again. Tomorrow I would return to the garden and see what damage had been done, but more important, I would see if the man in the mask had left any sign behind that would help me identify him.

I dug Hutch's number out of my pocket. Everything else in the pocket came out with his card: the packet of grandfather tobacco, the torn picture of Nowlin's wife and daughter, the Pearl Beer bottle cap. I placed my hard-won trophies beside the telephone while I dialed. I could hear Maggie running water in the kitchen and the clink of ice against glass.

Someone picked up on the other end. "Candace Fl-rez," said a voice as silky as molasses.

The surge of disappointment caught me off guard. "I'm calling for Mr. Hutcheson."

"I'm sorry, he's left for the night. Could someone else help you?"

I realized now that the number Hutch had given me hadn't been for a motel room but was a business number.

"It's important that I talk to him. Can you reach him and give him my number?"

"I can try," she said noncommittally.

I left my name and number and hung up. Maggie stood at my elbow with a Scotch and soda. "You need something to pick you up," she said. "Now. What's this all about?"

She beckoned me to follow her, and I trailed after her to the bathroom where she scrubbed off the avocado. I sat on the closed toilet lid and sipped my drink.

"It's a long story," I said.

Maggie straightened up over the sink and gave me one of her looks.

"How long could it be? It's been two, three hours since I saw you at the Creekside. Why don't you run a bath and tell me about it?"

While the tub filled with steamy water, I stripped, feeling the tension of the day ease with each piece of clothing removed. Maggie shook some bubbles into the water and took her turn on the toilet lid seat while I settled into the bath.

"Now, tell all." She lit a cigarette and leaned toward me.

While I sponged suds over my body and luxuriated in the healing warmth of the water, I told Maggie about the sculptures at Neil's house and about the man in my garden. Maggie's eyes grew big, and she forgot a cigarette was dangling from her manicured fingers. The ash dropped to the floor.

"Jesus, Viv," she said. "Do you have any idea who the guy was?"

I resurrected the image of the man: the bare back, broad shoulders, the mask. I blew some bubbles off my chin. "No."

"Have you called Charley?"

"I can't run to a man every time I have a problem." Conveniently forgetting I had just tried to call Hutch.

"Works for me."

"I find inspiration in the question asked by Germaine Greer: 'If a woman never lets herself go, how will she ever know how far she might have gone?'"

"I think we're getting closer to the truth." Maggie regarded me through half-closed eyes. "But there's more."

Taking a last drag off the cigarette, she stubbed it out and watched me.

I squirmed under her scrutiny. "What?"

"Why are you doing the Lone Ranger thing?"

I took a deep breath. "At some point, I have to take responsibility for my stinking life. I'm attracted to men who can't make commitments. I have a cat for a pet because cats don't give a damn if you're there or not. My only real friend was Lucie. I can't let her down."

"You're too hard on yourself," Maggie said. "Nothing short of perfection suits you."

I slid down in the tub until only my face was above the bubbles.

"Remember the last trip we took together as a family? We went to Colorado for Thanksgiving. Must have been ten years ago."

"Of course I remember. I was a junior in high school, and I lost my virginity on that trip."

"Yes. That's the one. Anyway. On Thanksgiving Day we were headed up Thompson Canyon out of Loveland—mother and The Sergeant in the front seat of that old Pontiac station wagon and you and me in the back. Just before the road narrows and there's nothing but river and rock on either side, we saw a log cabin sitting on a clearing next to the river. It had a stone chimney with smoke threading out of it, and there were bare cottonwood trees in the yard. The road curved there, and we had plenty of time to observe the house. As we watched, flames shot out of the roof around the chimney, and a man ran out of the house. He looked like a cartoon figure waving his arms and jumping up and down. None of us said anything. It was like we were watching TV, and the car never even slowed down.

"It wasn't until later that I thought to ask The Sergeant why we didn't stop to help. He looked at me as if it were the most obvious thing in the world, and said, 'There wasn't anything we could do.'"

Maggie was watching me as though I were an alien who had just materialized in her bathtub. "I don't remember that," she said.

I sat up straight, soap bubbles sliding down my breasts, and looked at her in disbelief. "You must remember! It struck me later that what we had done wasn't even human. You must remember."

"Maybe you dreamed it."

"Maybe you blocked it out."

"Now wait a minute." Maggie lit another cigarette. "You can be so self-righteous. How did we get off on this?"

I sighed and gave up. "The bottom line is that I won't—I can't—let anyone scare me off. I have to finish this."

"I think you need a good night's sleep," Maggie said. "We'll talk about it in the morning."

Maggie found me a robe, a substantial, comforting terry cloth, probably one she kept on hand for male guests, and I settled in among the ruffles of the Laura Ashley sheets in her guest room. Mack stretched out on the bed, his earlier terror forgotten. The .38 lay on the bedside table on top of one of Maggie's Danielle Steel novels.

It was a long time before I could sleep. I thought about Lucie and the time we had spent together. I knew I would never find another friend like her. We're lucky, someone once told me, to have five good friends in our lives. I was an Army brat, and The Sergeant moved us every year or two. You don't make friends that way, not real friends. I was nowhere close to five. And my best friend was dead.

Of course on an intellectual level, I knew we all die at some point, but I had felt Lucie and I had some kind of special protection. There is no such thing as special protection. If there was none for Lucie, there was none for me. Life is goddamned unpredictable.

That didn't make me any less determined. If anything, it made me less afraid of what might happen. A kind of fatalism set in. What happened wasn't so important as how I reacted to what happened.

31

During the night, the wind picked up. I awakened to the mo notonous tap-tap of a branch against the bedroom window. The fluorescent tips of the clock hands pointed to 4:30 a.m. From far in the distance came a low roll of thunder. The air was warm and heavy, and I threw back the covers.

I closed my eyes and willed sleep to return, but instead, the conversations of the past few days replayed through my head. Something was just at the edge of my memory, some connection I was missing but couldn't capture.

At some point I fell asleep again, and when I woke, the bedroom was lit with the diffuse light of morning. I drew aside the ruffled curtains and looked at an overcast and angry sky.

Mack was pacing back and forth by the door, crying to go out. I slipped on the terry cloth robe and dug in my bag for his leash. He didn't like it, but I couldn't take the chance of him dashing off in a strange place. The town cats would eat a little country cat like him for breakfast. I half-dragged him outside and fastened the leash to Maggie's fence, leaving Mack to sulk.

From his prison on the back porch, Jake began to bark, an anguished yelp of false imprisonment. All I needed to complete my morning, I thought, was an argument with Maggie. It wasn't until then that I noticed Maggie's car was gone.

The phone was ringing when I entered the house. Before I had a chance to say more than hello, Maggie was bubbling on the other end: "Viv. You're finally up. I didn't have the heart to wake you. Help yourself to breakfast. There's bagels in the cup-board and fruit in the fridge. Hutch called, but I told him you were sleeping."

I tried to insert a question, but she rattled on.

"I had an appointment with my acupuncturist, or I would have stayed. Wait for me. I know you, Viv, and the first place you're going to want to go is to your house. I also know that patience is not one of your virtues. If you'll wait until I get home, I'll go with you. You shouldn't go out there alone; it's not safe. Promise me?"

"When will that be?"

"Elevenish."

I considered. "I'll wait until eleven," I said. "But punctuality is not one of your virtues. So be on time."

When I hung up, I saw the collection I had emptied from my pocket the night before still lying beside the phone. With a gri-mace, I remembered my other piece of evidence, the rabbit head in the Civic. The packet of tobacco and the torn picture went in my bag. The Pearl Beer cap went in my pocket. As for the rabbit head.... I dialed Hutch's number.

This time a man's voice answered, but it wasn't Hutch. I left my phone number and cursed Hutch.

Then I brought Mack inside, threw a load of clothes in the washer, brewed some coffee, ate a bagel, showered and impa-tiently waited for the clothes to dry. By the time I pulled on the freshly laundered sweatshirt and jeans I had worn the day be-fore, it was after ten. I sipped a third cup of coffee and remem-bered the thoughts I had had while lying awake and listening to the branch tapping the window. Something about the timing of events didn't add up.

On the trip to Hot Springs, Probst had told me Marlin called him Monday to say the trip was on. By Monday evening, Lucie had a letter from Jonathan Marlin, along with a plane ticket to Hot Springs. Even with the modern miracles of Federal Express and fax machines, the events were compressed.

I called Truman. His voice on the phone was reluctant. I asked what time the mail was delivered. "Usually by noon," he said. "Why?"

"I'm still trying to figure out where Lucie went on Monday," I said.

"I still can't help you on that one," Truman said, as though he had given up wondering.

"Here's one you can help me on. What were you doing behind the Creekside last night?"

A small pause. "Passing by."

"Someone came by my house last night. Was it you?" It's useless to ask questions like that over the phone. Judging the truth of something requires a host of signs: eye movement, body language, facial expression. The voice is the slightest of indicators.

"I was here the rest of the evening," Truman said. "Not that it's any of your business, but I was drinking and cursing and kicking the dog." He hung up on me.

I stood by the phone. The day before, when I was talking to Neil at the crafts co-op, I had looked across the town square to the offices of the *Green Country Journal*. Jonathan Marlin's partner, David Menckle, could have made the arrangements and hand-delivered the packet to Lucie. Marlin's signature could be reproduced easily with a scanner and a laser printer, and Menckle had both. I decided to pay him a visit.

I dashed off a be-right-back note to Maggie and headed for the Civic. Before I could get to it, Hutch's pickup pulled into the driveway to block me. He climbed out of the truck, looking more than ever like a junkyard dog. His clothes were wrinkled as though he had slept in them, and there were dark circles under his eyes.

"Rough night?" I asked.

We stood beside the Civic.

"What was it you wanted?"

I opened the door and gingerly pulled out the rabbit head wrapped in newspaper. In the daylight, it looked pathetic rather than frightening, like a worn and ragged remnant of a child's stuffed toy.

Hutch took it from me. "Where'd it come from?"

I told him about going by Neil's house, the rabbit head in my mailbox and the man in the garden.

Hutch listened carefully, interjecting a question now and then. I dashed in the house and brought out the packet of tobacco, feeling as though I were giving him a gift he didn't really deserve.

"You didn't recognize the guy?" Hutch asked one more time.

"He was too tall to be Jonathan Marlin or Albert."

"It couldn't have been them."

I grabbed his arm. "How do you know that?"

Hutch looked at my hand on his arm and I dropped it. "The city police had them in custody by 10 p.m."

"Why?"

"They were at your buddy David Menckle's office, roughing him up. He didn't want to press charges, but we trumped up something to keep them locked up for twenty-four hours. Maybe they'll be eager to leave town when they get out this evening."

"I have to leave, Hutch."

"Wait. Just wait a minute." Hutch's long fingers closed around my wrist. He looked at me. "You understand what's happening? Whoever killed Lucie Dreadfulwater is after you."

He said it so calmly that I shivered.

"I kind of figured that out."

"You're staying with your sister?"

I nodded.

"Don't go anywhere alone. Don't do anything stupid. Get it?"

"Yes, Hutch. I get it." I pulled away from him. "I'm just going downtown."

His eyes narrowed. "You see what you're doing, don't you?"

"What am I doing?"

"You're playing detective to keep from thinking about your friend. As long as you keep the excitement going, you don't have to mourn her."

"That's amateur psychology bullshit."

"Whatever you want to call it. I'm going to check back with you this afternoon, and we're going to go over this whole thing again, line by line. You probably know more than you realize."

"Fine," I said. "If I'm not here, I'll be at my house."

I saw the look in his eyes.

"With my sister," I said.

The thunder that had growled in the night rumbled again, closer this time.

After Hutch left, I walked to Menckle's office. It was only a couple of blocks away, and I needed the exercise.

In the gray sky, the stacked domes of cumulus toppled and rebuilt; on the ground, the humid wind pushed discarded fast-food wrappers down the street and tore gold leaves from the weeping willows hanging over Town Branch. I hadn't heard any forecasts, but every indication pointed toward tornado weather. In eastern Oklahoma, the heart of Tornado Alley, tornado watches and warnings are a fact of life; nothing to be too concerned about.

I pushed open the glass door of the *Green Country Journal*. The thought I had had the night before was still with me, giving me the courage to face Menckle: What happens isn't so important as how I react to what happens.

Unfortunately, Menckle wasn't in.

Tanya Webster's head jerked around when I came through the door, and the secretary dropped the stack of mail she had been sorting and burst into tears.

"Thank God, it's you," she said, mascara streaking her face.

"When I got this job as secretary at an honest-to-god, four-color, regional magazine, I was so proud. Now I just want out of here."

I took her arm, her bracelets jangling with false cheerfulness, and guided her to her desk. "Where is everyone?"

"That's just it!" she said, dropping into her chair. "Lisabeth didn't show up for work this morning, didn't even call in. Then I sent a call to Mr. Menckle's office, and he was furious. He yelled at me." She dabbed at the tears with a wadded pink tissue while she talked.

"Where is he now?"

"He left. Just left without saying where he was going or when he was coming back. You could hear his tires leave a trail of rubber." Tanya's plump hands fluttered. "What am I going to do about his appointments? And what about his lunch date?"

"Let him deal with the fall-out," I said. "You're his secretary, not his mother." I patted her shoulder. "Don't let it get to you, Tanya. You're a talented lady. Look for another job."

"It's not like there are other jobs in this town," she said.

"Don't remind me. I'm in the market, too, remember?"

I changed the subject. "I dropped by to ask Menckle about Monday afternoon."

She started sorting the mail. "What about it?"

"Were you here on that day?"

Her brow furrowed. "Yes," she said, tossing the last envelope in the trash. "I'm here every day."

"Did Lucie Dreadfulwater come by?"

"Lucie Dreadfulwater? The storyteller?" Her eyes widened. "I hadn't even put that together. Yes! She was here in the afternoon. It must have been nearly three because I was going on break, and Lisabeth said she was buying if I would pick them up. You know, Redmen Shoppe limeades.

"When I came back, Ms. Dreadfulwater was in Mr. Menckle's office with the door closed. I remember because she left her handbag on that table over there." She gestured to the light table across from Lisabeth's desk. "She forgot it when she left. No one even noticed it was there until she came back for it."

"Did she have papers in her hand when she left Menckle's office?"

"I don't know."

"Where was Lisabeth?"

"She was at her computer."

"Did she talk to Lucie?"

"I don't know. I don't think so. But like I said, I was gone part of the time."

I told Tanya I would be back later to see if Menckle had returned and was halfway out the door when I realized this was the perfect opportunity to pick up my personal files. I didn't know if Menckle would let me have them, but he wasn't here to stop me. I told Tanya what I was after and went to the bank of file cabinets. I pulled out the drawer and let out a cry of surprise.

"What?" Tanya said.

"Where are my files?"

Tanya rushed to see. "Oh! Those files." Her hands flew to her cheeks. "Lisabeth told Jim Ray to get rid of everything in this drawer."

"But they're mine."

"I'm sorry, Viv. I didn't realize." Tanya's eyes welled again with tears.

"Don't worry about it," I said, gritting my teeth. "I'll talk to Lisabeth. When did Jim Ray empty these drawers?"

"Yesterday."

"You know Jim Ray. They're probably in a box in back waiting for him to sort them for recycling."

Jim Ray Wheeler was the thirty-three-year-old custodian. He was a hulking man with a haircut that looked like someone had put a bowl over his head and whacked off whatever stuck out. Everything about him was slow: his walk, his thoughts, the way he pushed a broom.

He also was the ultimate recycler. Barrels in the back room held aluminum, paper and glass. I found him sorting through the office trash one day, looking for things that had been thrown out before their usefulness was done. He begged me not to tell Menckle because he was sure he would be fired for stealing.

Tanya and I went to the loading dock in the back of the office, looking for the files. I even went to the alley and looked in the dumpster. No luck. Trash day was Monday, so the files were probably around somewhere. I wasn't too worried about them, but I was angry at Lisabeth. What gave her the right to throw out my papers?

32

I was trudging up Maggie's driveway when she pulled in be hind me. "You're still here!"

"I can follow directions."

Maggie jumped out of her car. "When you choose to."

She started pulling grocery bags out of the back, moving like she was charged with energy and goodwill. "I thought I should pick up some food if I'm going to have a house guest."

"I'm not sure you have a house guest," I said. "I'm not going to let that jerk in the garden scare me off."

"You don't have an ounce of sense."

"I beg your pardon, oh mistress of rectitude."

She ignored me and pushed the porch door open with her back. Jake saw the opening and dashed through it to freedom. Maggie ignored him, too. I followed her into the kitchen and helped put things away while she kept up a running monologue of reasons why I should stay at least another day. The common theme was safety.

I finally held my hands up and said, "Enough! I'm staying. But I need to go out to the house and pick up a few things, take a look around."

"I'm going with you."

"Haven't we already had this conversation?"

We decided to drive the Civic and take Jake along for protection. As Maggie pointed out, "He's so big that most people don't stop to realize he wouldn't even bite his own fleas." Mack stayed at Maggie's—even though he complained loudly when we wouldn't let him go outside.

I didn't say anything to Maggie, but I slipped the .38 into the glove compartment.

Maggie changed into a flowered short set that showed off her tanned legs. She donned a straw hat and tied the broad ribbon under her chin. Harlequin sunglasses completed her costume. With her newly red hair, she looked like Lucille Ball setting off on some screwball adventure. Jake and I were her straight men.

I headed up Highway 10, the same route I had used the night before.

"This isn't the way to your house," Maggie said. The wind from the open window flapped the ribbons around her face.

"I want to stop by Neil's."

"Haven't you seen enough of that creep?"

"Yes, but after what I saw last night, I have a couple of questions."

Maggie lit a cigarette and subsided into silence until the Civic was climbing Neil's driveway.

"Tattoos," she said, when we passed the sign. "I've been thinking about getting a tattoo."

Neil's VW was in the same place it had been the night before. Maggie and Jake waited in the Civic while I knocked on his door. No one answered, so I gave the door a push, and it swung open. I stood in the doorway and looked around. The first thing I noticed was that the clay statues were gone.

"Neil?" I ran into the bedroom. The room was empty.

The fate of Utlunta and Raven Mocker and the third statue was immediately obvious when I walked out Neil's back door. Shards of smashed statuary lay everywhere, as though someone had dropped the figures from a height or taken a sledgehammer to them, leaving no pieces large enough to identify.

Maggie was waiting impatiently when I returned to the Civic.

"Well?"

"Neil's not home, and the statues are destroyed."

"Wow," Maggie said. "Do you think Neil did that?"

"I don't know." I started the engine. "But now I want to talk to him more than ever. When we get to the house, I'll make some phone calls."

I was tired of abandoned houses, but that's just what mine looked like when we parked in front of it. The wind had scattered leaves across the front porch and flapped the screendoor open.

Maggie let Jake out, and he disappeared into the woods, barking at squirrels and birds, reminding me why I didn't have a dog.

We walked around back to the garden to assess the damage. I left the gate open and swiftly walked up and down the rows of raised beds. The apple trees were shredded. I'd have to replant.

The hoe—my Smith & Hawken hoe—that the man in the mask had used the night before was lying on the ground. I bent to pick it up, but Maggie's voice stopped me.

"Don't touch it! It probably has fingerprints on it. Don't you know anything about evidence?"

"Fine. I'll leave it right here for the Sheriff's Department, whom I didn't call."

"What if your friend Hutch wants to examine it? And you shouldn't be tramping around in the garden," Maggie said. "There may be footprints or something."

I didn't want to admit my sister was right, but I joined her at the gate and closed it. "Let me guess. Having sex with a cop has made you an expert at evidence."

"Among other things," she said with false modesty.

The wind kicked up again, and the sky darkened. Raindrops spattered my face.

"Jake is deathly afraid of storms," Maggie said. "Jake! Jake! Come here!" Her voice was drowned by a heavy roll of thunder.

A curtain of rain advanced toward us from the west like a charging army, pushing the smell of wet earth ahead of it. We ran for the house. Jake did not appear.

While the rain pounded the roof and the thunder rumbled, I made lunch—a pot of coffee and microwave popcorn.

Maggie made a face. "Is this what you live on? How do you stay in shape?"

"It's all a front. When no one's looking, I eat only organic fruits and vegetables and whole grains."

"In that case, I won't worry about you," she said, stuffing a handful of popcorn in her mouth. "I am worried about Jake, though. It's not like him to stay out during a storm. Usually he hides under my bed."

I roamed the large room, coffee cup in hand, propping a window open on the leeward side of the house and peering out for a wet black lab. I was eager for action. I had been spinning my wheels since I got out of bed, and the day was half gone. I wanted to talk to Neil. His disappearance and the destruction of his statues made me wonder what role he played.

I've heard that you shouldn't make phone calls during a thunderstorm—something I probably read in an Ann Landers column—but I tried Neil's number. There was no answer at his house. Then I dialed Randy. Again no answer. Lisabeth might know where she was, and there was also a matter of missing files I wanted to talk to her about.

I had never called her home before. No Lisabeth Ellis was listed in the book, and when I called information, a mechanical voice told me the number was unlisted.

The rain was short-lived, leaving behind the monotonous sound of runoff dripping from the eaves. I was poised to call the magazine office to get Lisabeth's number when I heard Jake.

He howled, a note of panic in his voice. I had never heard him make a noise like that. It was an insistent cry charged with meaning, sounding more like coyote than dog.

"Maggie! Go check on your dog."

Her voice was muffled. "I'm in the can."

"Something's wrong. I'm going out."

My running shoes slid on the wet grass. I followed the sound of Jake's cries through the dense second-growth forest behind the garden.

Wet branches slapped my face and tore at my clothes, and I stumbled over a deadfall. I hurried, certain Jake was either hurt or had treed some helpless animal. The ground sloped upward, and the wet leaves and rocks were slippery. And all the time, Jake howled.

I was yelling his name and scrambling through the brush when I came out on the abandoned logging road near the top of the hill. The track contoured around the hill, and I followed it. Jake's cries sounded closer, more desperate, as though the sound of my voice renewed his energy.

The road curved around an enormous oak that had somehow been spared by the loggers. On the other side of it, Jake sat on his haunches, muzzle lifted to the sky, lips pulled back over his sharp teeth, crying for help.

He was guarding a still form.

Jake stopped barking when he saw me, but the hairs on the back of his neck bristled.

"Hey, Jake, it's okay now." My voice sounded like it was coming from somewhere else. It was anything but okay.

The still form was a man, and even from a distance he looked dead. He lay on his side with his arm thrown over his head, shirtless, a beer belly bulging over the top of his jeans. His chest was almost hairless. Jake had blocked my view of the man's head, but now Jake whined and moved back from the body.

It was Neil Hannahan.

The skin of his face was mottled and bluish, and the rain had plastered his blond hair against his forehead.

I tried to be analytical, pushing the fear into a corner of my mind. I walked around his body from a distance, noting the worn white tennis shoes, green stains on the rubber soles. I sucked in my breath with the realization that Neil must have been the masked man who had torn up my garden the night before.

It wasn't until I saw his back that I lost my composure. He was ripped open as though a wild animal had torn at him, like a rabbit gutted by a hawk. Utlunta. I turned away and stumbled back in the direction of the house, calling Jake after me in a voice that was as soft and porous as a wet sponge.

Maggie burst out of the forest onto the road only a few feet away. "Jake!" she scolded. "What have you been up to?" She knelt, and he licked her face and whined like a repentant child.

She lifted her face to look at mine and stood abruptly. "What?"

I gestured with my head, and she looked beyond me to Neil's body.

"Christ! We've got to help him." Maggie started toward him, but I grabbed her.

"Don't go any closer."

She was confused. "What happened?"

"He's dead."

"Do you know him?"

"It's Neil Hannahan. Now let's go." This time I pulled her roughly, and she followed me through the dripping, gloomy forest.

33

It seemed like a long time before Sheriff Wes Turner arrived with one of his deputies. The Chevy Caprice tore up the driveway with sirens screaming and lights flashing, as though their urgency would make any difference to Neil. In the meantime, I had changed into dry clothes.

It was another three hours before the medical examiner was finished, evidence gathered, photos taken and the body removed. A very unpleasant three hours.

I told Turner everything I knew about Neil. After all, my fingerprints were probably all over Neil's house. Turner only grunted when I told him about the statues.

"Let's go over this one more time, Powers," Turner said, the match stick in his mouth pointing at me. He leaned back in a kitchen chair, his hands folded across his belly, legs outstretched and his muddy cowboy-booted feet crossed. Maggie sat on the front porch petting Jake and chatting up Turner's deputy, a pimple-faced, skinny kid I didn't know.

"What was your relationship with the deceased?"

"I knew him. He was an acquaintance."

"He wasn't really a friend, but last night you visit his house and waltz right in, and you claim he tore up your garden later. Now he's dead on your property."

I didn't say anything.

Turner's glasses made his eyes look soft and unfocused, but there was no warmth in his voice. "There's been three murders in Cherokee County in the past week. Now maybe I ain't no genius, but my instincts tell me there's more to be known than you're telling." He worked the match in his mouth for awhile, and I sat at the kitchen table, looking at a cobweb hanging from a corner of the room.

"How about I do this," he said finally. "I get some deputies out here to walk every one of your acres. You and that hippie boyfriend of yours might have a little marijuana-growing operation going on here."

"You wouldn't find anything unless you planted it yourself, and you know it."

He grunted and sat up straighter. "You're not telling me shit, and it's pissing me off, Powers. You can tell me now, or I can take you down to the county jail and let you think about it. You decide, and decide damn quick. I've got work to do."

There's no telling how it would have ended, but Hutch showed up then, careening up the driveway in his white Chevy pickup. Turner cursed and walked out to meet him, and I joined Maggie on the porch while they conferred.

A fresh line of thunderheads advanced from the southwest. The sky was midnight blue over Spring Creek.

"How's it going?" she asked me in a low voice.

"He's threatening to take me in."

"That's ridiculous. On what grounds?" She appealed to the deputy who stood at the bottom of the steps. "He can't do that, Curtis."

Curtis looked hungrily at her tanned legs and at the low-cut line of her flowered blouse. "He's a good guy, really," he said.

"He's trying to intimidate me," I said.

"So you live around here?" Curtis said to Maggie.

I went inside. It didn't seem like my house at the moment; I wondered if it would again. I found a quart bottle of Mountain Valley Spring Water in the refrigerator and lay on the couch, occasionally pulling from the bottle as though it were something stronger. I tried not to think about how Neil's body had looked.

It seemed like a long time later when Hutch came in and sat in the rocking chair opposite me. Outside, an engine roared to life and tires crunched on the gravel as a vehicle left.

"So now do you believe me?" he asked. There was an undercurrent in Hutch's voice, anger perhaps.

"I always believed you, Hutch. Am I free to go?"

"Tell me what you know."

I told him everything from where I lay on the sofa. He rocked while he listened. He was like a psychologist making a house call. He frowned when he heard about Dale Nowlin's daughter and ex-wife, and about the back-and-forth transfer of property between Nowlin's and Lucie's families.

"I'll follow up on that," he said. "What else?"

"That's it," I said, watching his face. "You've wrung me dry. So what's my status? Are you going to turn me over to Turner?"

His smile was sardonic. "Turner's going to leave you alone for now—under two conditions. One, you stay in the county. Two, you keep me informed of your whereabouts."

I sat up and swung my feet to the floor. "I can live with that for now."

"This was a careless murder, and it's only a matter of time before we nail the asshole. In the meantime, play it safe, stick with your sister."

"Like a Band-Aid, like super glue, like a shadow."

"Why do you have to be so sarcastic?"

"There's a certain safety in sarcasm."

"And in loneliness, too."

I studied the wall. I didn't want to see Hutch's face. I liked feeling indifferent about him.

34

I dropped Maggie and Jake off at her house over Maggie's protests. I told her the same thing I had told Hutch: I was going by the offices of the *Green Country Journal* to pick up some files, and then I would return to her house.

I parked in front of the office building and watched lightning split the sky to the west. It was late afternoon, and the only way to forget the way Neil's body had looked was to stay busy. Very busy. So I was following my original plan to find Jim Ray Wheeler and retrieve my files. I was leaving the search for Lucie's and Neil's murderer to the OSBI.

The swinging glass door closed behind me, for the last time, I hoped. A man in a suit sat stiffly in one of the outer office chairs, with a briefcase balanced on his knees.

"Mr. Menckle specifically asked that I deliver these bids in person," he was saying to Tanya.

Tanya twisted her bracelets. "I so terribly sorry," she said, looking toward me for help, "but Mr. Menckle was unexpectedly called away. Perhaps I could reschedule your appointment?"

Not my problem. I edged past her to the loading dock in search of Jim Ray. It was dark in the cavernous room; the dock door was pulled down and the lights were off. A single shaft of light glowed from the open door of the janitor's closet in the corner. I headed toward it, calling Jim Ray's name.

He stuck his bowl-shaped head out of the closet and peered into the dark room.

"It's Viv, Jim Ray," I said. "Who turned off the lights?"

"Oh. Viv," he said, focusing on me. "I don't want to waste no electricity. There's a hole in the ozone, you know." He set a broken stapler on his workbench.

"I know, Jim Ray." I moved forward into the pool of light. "I'm looking for something I lost, and I think you might be able to help me."

"People are losing things all the time, aren't they?" Jim Ray had the wide, innocent eyes of a child, but his hands were as large and powerful as a boxer's.

"This was more like a misunderstanding," I said. "Lisabeth told you to throw out some of my files, and I was hoping you still had them around here somewhere."

"I just do what they tell me," Jim Ray said, worry in his voice. He popped his knuckles, working one hand and then the other.

I tried to reassure him with a smile, but he was staring at the floor. "It's no big deal, Jim Ray, but if you still have those files, I'd like them back."

"I just do what they tell me."

"I know, Jim Ray. You do a good job."

Jim Ray flipped on the lights and led me to a stack of boxes in the corner. "These them?"

I cracked a box open and peeked inside. "These are the ones. How about if I pull around back, and you help me load them?"

"Okay." But he stood still, staring at the floor and popping his knuckles until I asked him what was wrong.

"Uh… did you maybe lose something else the other day?"

"I don't think so. What kind of something?"

He headed back to his closet, and I followed. He lifted a stack of newspapers from the corner. Underneath was a manila envelope.

"It's a good envelope," Jim Ray said. "It's still good enough to mail somethin' in. Folks just throw things away."

"I don't think that envelope's mine, Jim Ray."

"No. Inside." He reached in and drew out a small leather-bound book. "I found a calendar book. Maybe someone lost it." He looked at me with wide eyes. "Mr. Menckle don't like me to go through the trash, you know. He might fire me."

"No one's going to fire you, Jim Ray." My heart beat faster as I reached for the book.

It was a daytimer. The front panel had been torn out, but I recognized Lucie's handwriting. I wanted to flip through it, but I realized I might be destroying valuable forensic evidence. I slipped the daytimer back into the envelope.

"Where did you find this?" My voice sounded strained.

Jim Ray looked helpless. "I don't know. It was in the trash this week."

"Think, Jim Ray! It's important."

That was the wrong thing to say to Jim Ray. He began stuttering, "I j-j-just emptied the trash like I always do, all the small cans into the big one, and when I got it back here I looked to see if there was anything important. I don't know where it came from."

I squeezed his shoulder. "Don't worry, okay? I'll make sure this gets to the right person, and I promise, Jim Ray, you did the right thing. Forget about those files for now, and just hang onto them for me."

I rushed back out to the front office. The man with the brief-case was gone, and Tanya sat staring into space.

I had no patience for preliminaries.

"Tanya, I need Lisabeth's phone number."

"I'm not supposed to give that out."

"Then I need her address."

"She told me not to give it to anyone."

I lost my temper. "Would I be asking you if it weren't impor-tant? Dammit, Tanya, just give it to me."

Tanya set her lips in a stubborn line. "You're putting me in an impossible situation, Viv. If you want her address, I'll have to get

Mr. Menckle's permission." She looked toward his office.

"Menckle's here? You just told that man he wasn't in." I realized how naive that sounded even as I said it.

"He said he didn't want to be disturbed."

"Well, I'm going to disturb him."

"Remember," she called after me, "I told you."

Menckle crouched in front of an open file cabinet, stuffing papers into a box. The shelves and walls were stripped, and the desk was bare except for a phone and an oversized calendar pad. Cardboard cartons were stacked beside the desk.

He looked up when the door opened, but he didn't say anything. He didn't seem surprised to see me. His face was grim and pale, and an angry bruise stained his cheek. One arm was wrapped in a bandage.

"You're leaving," I said.

"Who the hell invited you in?"

I stood over him. "In just a minute, I'm going to call the OSBI."

He stood to face me. "They've already been here. Now get the hell out."

"There's a thing or two they don't know yet. Murder has been committed because of Lucie's land, and whatever unethical dealings M&M Investments was into, I don't think you stooped to murder." I was talking off the top of my head, but it sounded right.

"In Hot Springs, I was nearly run down by your partner. If I get some straight answers from you, I may be able to leave a few things out when I talk to the OSBI."

His shoulders slumped. "I've done nothing wrong. Marlin was upset when you showed up in Hot Springs; anyone would be. You were stupid to pull that shit."

"Is that why he was working you over last night?"

Menckle sank into the chair behind his desk and buried his face in his hands. "That was just a little disagreement."

"Why did you buy Dale Nowlin's land in the first place?"

"The location was perfect. The price was right. The old man convinced me the eighty acres next to it would be available. What a laugh."

"Tell me about the meeting you had with Lucie on Monday," I said softly. I sat in one of the chairs in front of Menckle's desk.

Menckle made a dismissive motion. "I told her to go to Hot Springs, look around, no strings attached."

"Why didn't you sell the land next to Lucie's and find another piece?"

He looked at me with contempt. "You people here dream so small. You've forgotten what prosperity looks like. Go to Tulsa. Drive down the freeways. Look at the new glass and steel office buildings. Smell the money in the air. That's what Lucie Dreadfulwater's land would have done for me."

Thunder rattled the windows and a handful of fat raindrops spattered against the panes.

There was hate in Menckle's voice. "I'm sick of you women pushing me around. First Lisabeth, now you. Just go to hell."

My voice matched his. "There are two people dead now, Menckle, and leaving you alone is not an option."

His eyes flickered. "Two?"

"Neil Hannahan, Randy Silver's boyfriend."

"She doesn't..." he began. And then he stopped.

"She doesn't what?"

He shook himself as though he was recovering from a blow. "What?"

He was silent.

"The night I came to your office, Wednesday night, Randy Silvers was here."

"That's none of your damn business."

"Let's pretend it is for a minute. Have you heard of a Cherokee witch named Utlunta?"

"Lisabeth's working on that," he said impatiently. "Didn't she tell you we're doing a special issue on Cherokee tales?"

"And one of those stories is about Utlunta?"

"Yes, dammit!"

"Have you seen this before?" I showed him the envelope that held the daytimer.

Menckle reached for it, but I pulled it back.

"It's Lucie's daytimer," I said. "It was in the office trash."

"I don't get it."

"What if I told you someone in this office tore out a page and tried to make it look like a suicide note?"

"Shit." Menckle sounded boxed in and hopeless. Against my will, I believed he was leveling with me.

"I need to talk to Lisabeth. Where does she live?"

"You should talk to Randy."

"What does that mean?"

"Randy talked me into hiring that slut in the first place. Let her give you the address."

I took the envelope with the daytimer and headed for the Civic. It was not quite 5 p.m., but the sky was dark. The rain had stopped for the moment.

35

Randy Silvers' house sat on the Town Branch flood plain, at the end of Basin Street. Its in-town location and Randy's fondness for entertaining had made it a popular party spot. After the bars closed, the Powers That Be sometimes brought their instruments to Randy's house and made music and drank until dawn, with other local musicians sitting in and hangers-on spilling into the street.

I joined the after-work traffic toward the south side of town and parked on the street behind Randy's car. Two dark-haired girls in the yard next door stopped jumping rope and stared at me.

The small house Randy rented was constructed of fieldstone. The mortar was crumbling and the wood trim needed paint. There was no doorbell. I stood on the steps and knocked on the wooden door.

I was becoming superstitious; I rubbed the Pearl beer bottle cap in my pocket. "F-wren-Ds 4+ever."

No one answered the door, but I could hear the low thumping beat of a bass guitar. I knocked again, louder.

I followed the sound around to the side of the house where it drifted out an open window. I cupped my hands against the screen and peered in. Randy sat on the floor against the wall, wrapped in a quilt, while beside her a reel-to-reel played what sounded like Randy thrumming her bass. It was a mournful, tuneless sound.

I rapped on the wooden screen frame, and Randy slowly looked up. Her eyes didn't seem focused, and she rose and glided toward the window, the quilt falling behind her, as though she were sleepwalking.

Her hair hung lank on her shoulders, dirty and uncombed. She was dressed in black. Black tank top. Black leggings. Bare feet. When she reached the window, she pressed her fingers against the screen and leaned down until her hands framed her pale, oval face.

"Randy," I said. "I need to talk to you. Let me in."

It wasn't until then that her eyes registered recognition. I wondered what she was on. She nodded slightly and turned away.

When the front door swung open, Randy had pulled the quilt around her head again, and she clutched it under her chin. She looked sick and frightened, like she had just been pulled out of the river and resurrected.

"You look like hell warmed over."

"It's been too much," Randy said. "So many things have happened."

"What has happened?"

We sat on her sofa. A baby grand piano took up most of the room. Her bass guitar case leaned against it. Framed sheet music hung on the wall. A cool wind fluttered the white curtains and blew the smell of rain-damp earth through an open window. A pale sun came out for a moment, casting the image of windblown trees on the curtains like flickering monochrome flames. Just as quickly, the day was gray again.

I waited for Randy to talk, but she sat huddled in her quilt. She reached for a bottle of rum on the low table in front of us, and poured a shot into a cup of tea.

"Join me?" she asked, after she took a sip.

"Not right now, Randy. I'm here to talk about Lisabeth."

"I don't think you can blame her." Randy's husky voice was lifeless.

"Blame her for what?"

"For what she did," Randy said, as though she were talking to a child. "Last night after we left the Creekside, I went by her house, but she wasn't there. It was after midnight when she finally came in. I've never seen her so upset. I said, 'What is it?' and she said not to worry. She said if anyone asked, I was to say she had been home all evening. She begged me to say that, and I told her I would. What else could I say?"

Randy studied her hands. "I'm worried about her, babe. She hasn't been herself. Ever since she started working on that story about Utlunta. She would come by after work and talk about Utlunta. She wanted to buy Neil's sculpture for the magazine. It was like she was obsessed."

"Where was she last night?"

"I told her I wouldn't say."

"She went to my house, didn't she?"

Randy nodded. "I think so."

"Did she kill Neil?"

"He's an idiot," Randy said. "Lisabeth said he was drunk, and she told him it was a joke to rip up your garden, that she would win a big bet, that she would make it up to you. Now he's dead."

"Neil was one of the people you've been sleeping with. Aren't you upset?"

"It appears I'm losing all my lovers. Of course I'm upset." She pulled the quilt more tightly around her.

"Menckle told me he gave Lisabeth a job because you asked him to."

"She was new in town, and she needed a job. She was like a lost puppy. I just wanted to help."

"Did Lisabeth ever talk about Lucie Dreadfulwater?"

"She hated her."

"Why?"

"She wouldn't tell me."

"Did she kill her?"

"She scares me. I thought if I told anyone about last night she would kill me." Randy shivered under her quilt.

"Where's Lisabeth now?"

"She's gone, babe."

"Gone?"

"She came by this morning. She was crying. She told me she was leaving, that she knew a place where no one could find her."

"Why didn't you tell me earlier?" Lucie's murderer was slipping through my hands. I felt a moment of panic.

Randy pulled the quilt over her head and lay down on the sofa.

I shot across the room and grabbed the phone, digging in my pocket for Hutch's phone number.

He answered on the first ring.

"Lisabeth did it," I said without preliminaries.

"Lisabeth?"

"Lisabeth Ellis! She killed Lucie, and now she's leaving town. It may be too late, but we've got to find her." I turned to Randy. "Lisabeth's address. What is it?"

She listlessly gave me a number on West Delaware.

Hutch wasn't as rushed as I was feeling. "How do you know?" I filled him in on my conversations with Menckle and Randy.

"I'll get a team together, and we'll find her," Hutch said.

"I'll meet you at her house."

"That's not wise."

"Don't deny me now."

"Have it your way. You usually do," he said. "But come here. It's going to take some time to prepare, and in the meantime, I won't have you scaring her away."

36

It was one of those hurry-up-and-wait situations. By the time I made it to Hutch's temporary headquarters, which turned out to be a motel room on Downing Street, he had dispatched a team of three agents to West Delaware to stake out Lisabeth's house and to follow her if she left.

A fourth agent sat at a desk, listening intently on the phone.

Hutch looked at me. He sat on the motel bed, pulling on a shoulder holster. His unruly hair was damp, as though he had just showered. There was a crooked smile on his thin lips.

"You're coming with me," he said. "You're going to tell the judge what you told me, and he's going to give us a search warrant."

"All I have is what Menckle and Randy told me. And this." I handed him the manila envelope with the daytimer.

"Where did it come from?"

"The offices of the *Green Country Journal*."

Hutch's face fell. "That's it? By the time a defense lawyer's finished with that, it could have been left there by almost anyone. Unless there are fingerprints, it's worthless as evidence. And you've probably screwed up any prints that may have been there.

"Furthermore, the information from David Menckle and Randy Silvers will have to be checked out. Just because they say it, doesn't make it so. I've already checked with Judge Clark. No matter how eager he is to have an arrest, hearsay alone won't be enough to obtain a warrant."

He sat in thought for a minute, drumming his fingers on his thigh. "If Menckle's as cooperative as he claims to be, he'll let us search his offices. We'll just have to see where things lead from there."

He turned to the man at the phone. "Ron, run a background check on Lisabeth Ellis. Radio me as soon as you find out anything."

Hutch headed out the door at a trot, and I followed.

Hutch radioed the sheriff while we were en route to Menckle's office and asked him to send two deputies to help with the search. Menckle reluctantly allowed them in. At Hutch's insistence, I stayed in his pickup while the officers searched. Menckle looked out at me once through the office window. It was a look filled with venom.

I tried to be patient. Lucie's killer would soon be arrested, I told myself. All I could do now was stay out of the way and let the professionals handle it. But my nerves were on edge. Every time a voice squawked on the shortwave radio, I jumped.

Not long after Hutch went inside, the radio crackled a long set of numbers. All I understood was the last, impatient plea: "Hutch, do you copy?" I looked at the array of dials, buttons and wires running out of the radio. The only identifiable object was a microphone. I picked it up, held down the button on its side and said, "Yes?"

"Miss Powers?"

"Yes?"

The man talked to me as though I were a three-year-old. "Miss Powers, do you know where Hutch is?"

"Yes."

"Tell him to call Ron Eubanks. It's important."

I opened the door of the *Green Country Journal,* grateful for an excuse to see what was going on. Hutch and the two deputies from the Sheriff's Department looked up when I came in.

Menckle was apparently in his office with the door closed, and Tanya and Jim Ray were nowhere in sight. Hutch frowned when I gave him the message. He picked up the phone on Lisabeth's desk, and I sidled up beside him, eager to know what Ron Eubanks had discovered.

"That's it. That's the connection," Hutch said, hanging up the phone. He looked at me. "Lisabeth Ellis is Dale Nowlin's daughter."

So many things fell into place in that moment. "Lucie killed her father. No wonder she hated her."

I followed Hutch out the door and into his truck. I waited until the engine was running before I asked what else he had learned on the phone.

Hutch guided the truck smoothly into traffic. "Information is sketchy at this point. We do know that she lived with her mother, Diane Ellis Nowlin, in Kansas City for several years and graduated from high school there. College was the University of Missouri. She dropped out of sight for a few years before she turned up here. We'll fill in the holes; it just might take awhile."

"You guys work fast when you're on the right track."

Hutch shot me a dry look. "Marvels of technology."

"So is she also Alexandra Nowlin?"

"We'll ask her."

With the new information, Hutch had no trouble getting a search warrant signed. He lay it on the seat between us, and when I picked it up, he didn't stop me.

I read the document. "You're searching for the missing bottle of Rompun and syringes."

"The smaller the item," Hutch said, "the more thorough the search you're allowed to make."

In the courthouse parking lot, I looked at the sky. A storm still threatened; a billowing bank of dark clouds hung over the west side of town, the side of town where Lisabeth Ellis lived.

Hutch radioed ahead to the three agents who were watching Lisabeth's house, and then he retreated into silence. He had hardly seemed aware of my presence since I had walked into Menckle's office.

We parked on West Delaware in front of a small white frame, two-story house. From the outside, Lisabeth's house looked sterile and unlived in—there were no flowers on the small front porch, nothing in the windows but pulled-down shades. Her car was parked in the driveway.

"Stay here," Hutch said. He glared at me with his hawk-like eyes. "I mean it. Don't get out of the pickup."

"I know I'm a pain in the ass," I said. "I'll stay."

From the rolled-down windows of Hutch's pickup, I watched two of Hutch's men walk toward the back of the house while Hutch and another man knocked on the door. After waiting on the stoop a few minutes, Hutch returned to the truck and pulled a small black bag from under the seat.

He looked at me and started to say something, but the moment passed. I didn't help him out.

He used the tools from the black bag on Lisabeth's door. A moment later he and the other man disappeared inside.

Darkness came early, a long-lasting, eerie twilight, punctuated by threatening growls of thunder from the west. A gust of wind ripped a dead branch off the elm tree the truck was parked under and threw it into the bed. I wondered if I should move the truck then realized I had no keys. I had promised to stay in the truck, but I didn't plan to wait until the tree toppled.

Until now, I hadn't had time to think about Lisabeth murdering Lucie. Lisabeth, the emotional train wreck. I couldn't imagine how I would act if someone murdered my father. Would I want to exact revenge on behalf of The Sergeant? On one level, it seemed incredible that Lisabeth could do such a thing, on another level, I was just relieved to see it coming to an end.

Lights came on upstairs in Lisabeth's house, and shadowy figures moved behind the window shades. What was taking so long?

After what seemed like forever, a black Chevy pulled up alongside Hutch's pickup. Behind the wheel was the tired face of the medical examiner who had earlier in the day investigated Neil Hannahan's death. I knew what that meant, but I wanted to be wrong. Across the street, a white-haired couple sat in metal chairs on their porch and watched as though it were a reality-based TV show that was taking place in the white frame house.

There was another wait while the sky deepened into a purple stew and the minutes slowed to a crawl. I remembered that when I left Maggie's house, I had told her I was going to Menckle's office. Period. I hoped she wasn't too worried. The street lights flickered on and a steady rain began. Hutch walked tiredly to the pickup, ignoring the rain, and looked in at me.

"I need you to identify a body."

"Is it Lisabeth?"

"Follow me, please."

The look in Hutch's dark eyes allowed no options. I had already seen enough death for one day, but I climbed out of the pickup and followed him inside.

37

The entry hall allowed a glimpse into the two front rooms. The light fixtures were bare bulbs hanging from the ceiling. In the harsh light, the rooms looked spartan, as though Lisabeth had been camping in the house. There were no rugs on the hardwood floors, no pictures on the walls, no furniture. Instead, unopened cardboard boxes were piled haphazardly in the rooms. I ran my finger along a box in the hall and left a snaky trail in the dust.

Hutch led the way up the narrow staircase. The stairs opened into a large room. The furnishings were spare and uncluttered: a plain white desk with chair, white dresser and mirror, a full-size bed. The bed was neatly made up with a white coverlet. Stretched out on the bed, as though she had lain down for a nap, was Lisabeth.

She was wearing a pastel-flowered robe that gaped open to reveal her underwear. Black lace. It looked new. Black heels were paired beside the bed.

"Don't touch anything," Hutch said.

I stood near the bed for a minute looking at Lisabeth's pale face, at her long slender fingers resting on the white cover, the left thumbnail chewed and ragged. She looked plastic, like a mannequin version of Lisabeth Ellis. I thought I should feel something, but I was empty inside.

In the background I was dimly aware that men were working, picking items up in sterile, gloved hands, placing them in bags. A flashbulb went off beside me, and I jumped.

Hutch's hand grabbed my elbow and steadied me.

"I.D.," he said.

"It's Lisabeth Ellis," I said in a voice that was not mine. "How did she die?"

Hutch snorted. "Have you thought of going into police work, Viv? I could use someone like you."

"Yeah. I'm all machine. How did she die?"

The medical examiner nudged me aside, none too gently, and Hutch led me to a window at the back of the room.

"We won't know for sure until after the autopsy. But Thomas," he nodded toward the M.E., "is fairly certain it was Rompun. We found a bottle that may be the one missing from the Dreadfulwater place. It was lying beside her body, empty, and there was a needle in her arm."

"Are you saying it was suicide?"

"That's likely."

"Did you find a note?"

"There was something."

"May I look?"

He shot me a look. "Not a chance."

"Give me a hint."

Hutch paused and glanced toward the other men. "This is between you and me. Understood?" His voice was just above a whisper.

I nodded.

He indicated a bracket on the windowsill beside us.

"See that? A telescope was mounted here. What you can't see right now because it's dark is Dale Nowlin's backyard." Hutch pointed to the southwest. "It's just over there. I looked through the telescope before dark. There's a great view of his back rooms."

I struggled to grasp the meaning. "Lisabeth was spying on her father?"

"Apparently."

"Why?"

"All we know is what her letter to him said. Lisabeth Ellis had been watching her father since she moved here about four months ago, apparently fantasizing about a reunion with him when the time was right. Just what she was waiting for, we'll never know. The letter was never sent.

"Before the reunion could occur, Lucie Dreadfulwater killed him. That explains Lisabeth's motive for killing Lucie. Now all we have to do is match the evidence."

"She had opportunity," I said. "While Lucie was in David Menckle's office, Lisabeth could have gone through her purse and found the daytimer. The quote she found must have seemed perfect. It was ambiguous enough to sound like the sort of thing an artistic person like Lucie might use for a suicide note."

Hutch looked at me. "Somehow she lured Lucie Dreadfulwater to the eighty acres. She may have hit Lucie on the head with a rock, then injected the Rompun. She shoved her over the cliff to cover up the injury caused by the rock."

Hutch's description was too graphic, the details too painful. I didn't want to think about Lucie's last moments. I must have been holding my breath because I suddenly felt lightheaded.

"I need to use the bathroom," I said.

"Jeez, Powers, I thought you thrived on this kind of stuff."

"Go to hell," I said, heading toward the bathroom.

"You can't go in there!" Hutch grabbed my arm and said more gently. "They're not through in there, you'll have to go downstairs."

I stumbled down the stairs and found a small bathroom off the kitchen. I sat on the stool and dropped my head between my legs. After awhile my breathing steadied and I could sit upright. I leaned back and closed my eyes, taking slow, deep breaths. I knew the details would come back later, but for now, I tried to shut Lucie's death out of my mind.

I wondered when Lisabeth had died. When she went by Randy's house this morning, had she already decided to kill herself? Is that what she had meant by a place where no one could find her?

I ran some cold water in the sink and lifted a double handful to my face. It felt good so I did it again.

Hutch's voice came through the closed door. "Are you all right?"

I dried my hands and pushed my hair back. The person in the mirror didn't look like me. Her eyes were dark-ringed, and there were new lines across her forehead.

Hutch's fingers were performing an impatient tap dance on the kitchen counter when I came out of the bathroom.

He walked toward the door, motioning me to follow. "I've done all I can do here," he said over his shoulder. "The guys can wrap things up; I need to talk to some people."

"Randy?"

"She may have been the last person to talk to Lisabeth."

"When did Lisabeth die?"

"That will take time to determine. All the medical examiner would say is sometime this morning." He paused and turned toward me. "I'll drop you off at the motel to pick up your vehicle. You look like you could use some sleep."

"Yeah, well, you look like crap, too."

Outside the rain fell like tears. Hutch switched on his headlights and wipers and pulled out into the street just as a car stopped in front of Lisabeth's house.

"Randy Silvers."

"That saves me a trip," Hutch said.

He backed up and parked again.

I jumped out of the pickup and headed toward Randy. Even if we weren't close friends, she might need someone familiar nearby when she heard the news about Lisabeth.

Randy stood beside her car with the door open and looked

at the house. She was still wearing black, but she had left the quilt behind.

"What is it, Viv? What's wrong? Why are all these people here?" Her voice was strained and urgent.

I took her hand. I hadn't realized it would fall to me to break the news.

The dome light from her car cast dim shadows on her face. She looked ghostly. "Lisabeth is dead, isn't she?"

"I'm sorry, Randy."

Randy's slender body slumped, and she stumbled against her car. I caught her with my free arm and hugged her. Hutch watched us while Randy made inarticulate, choking sounds into my shoulder. After awhile, the sobs slowed and stopped, and she pushed away from me.

"Poor little waif," she said. It was not clear whether she was referring to Lisabeth or herself.

Hutch stepped forward and identified himself. "Let's get out of the rain," he said, taking her elbow and steering her toward the porch.

The elderly couple across the street still watched from their metal chairs. I wanted to tell them the show was over. The bad guys won.

I followed Hutch and Randy, not expecting to hear anything new. Hutch noticed me and remembered that he had promised to give me a ride.

"I'll only be a few minutes if you want to wait in my truck."

"I'll walk to Maggie's."

"I can have someone drop you off."

"I want to walk."

"It's raining."

"I know!" I said it forcefully enough that he shrugged.

"Make yourself available tomorrow," he said. "We need to talk."

I gave a half-hearted wave to indicate that I had heard, and then I headed down the hill in the rain.

I thought I would feel triumphant when Lucie's killer was found. But instead an uneasy feeling was fighting its way up through the sludge in my mind. The question of Alexandra Nowlin still was unanswered. If Lisabeth's mother had been named Diane, and Dale's mother was Alma, how did Alexandra fit in? Perhaps it was Lisabeth's middle name. Or even her first.

I felt tired and empty and used. By the time I reached Maggie's house, a half mile away, I was also cold and wet. I came in through the back door, startling Jake, who barked at me. When he saw who it was, he wagged his tail.

Maggie, however, was not so welcoming. She stood at the stove, wearing skimpy shorts, a halter top and high heels, stirring something in a pot with one hand and clutching her phone with the other.

She paused when she saw me and said to someone on the other end, "Hold on. She's here." She laid the phone down and looked me over with the same expression our mother had used years earlier when we had violated her sacred trust.

"So. You're alive." Her lips were pursed. "I was worried sick, although I don't know why."

"We found Lisabeth Ellis. She killed Lucie, and now she's killed herself."

Maggie sucked her breath in. "What happened?"

My wet clothes dripped on the floor. "It's a long story, so you might want to wrap up your phone conversation."

She gave me a strange look. "It's Charley. He's been trying to reach you."

I frowned. "And you told him I was playing Nancy Drew."

Her eyebrows raised. "I didn't lie, did I?"

I took the phone as though it might be rigged with explosives. Charley. Even the name sounded foreign. I tried it out loud.

"Charley?"

"God, it's good to hear your voice."

It felt unexpectedly good to hear his, too. "What's going on?"

"That's the question I should be asking you."

I said enough about Lucie and Lisabeth to satisfy him. Maggie listened in, her eyes wide as she stirred the pot. I stood up and wandered over to the stove while I talked. Maggie handed me a spoon. Chicken gumbo. My mouth watered for more.

"I'll fill in the details when you come home. Sunday night, right?"

Charley hesitated. "That's what I was calling about, Viv. We're staying another week. They've been really good to us down here. We've been invited to sit in on a recording session with Asleep at the Wheel. It's too good to pass up. Come down and join me. Bring Randy along. You both need to get away from Tahlequah."

"Lucie's funeral is tomorrow."

"Come after."

"Maybe."

Charley launched into a description of the Austin music scene, and I sat down and closed my eyes and let his voice flow over me, as warm as shower water, as refreshing as ripe strawberries. After a few minutes, he abruptly stopped. "I'm boring you."

I felt a rush of tenderness. "What I would like to do right now," I said, "is lie under a tree with my head in your lap. And I would listen to your voice until I fell asleep. That would be good."

There was a short silence. "Come down to Austin."

"I'll call you tomorrow."

"Viv, be careful."

"It's over now, Charley."

"I dreamed about you last night. I can't shake it."

Maggie fed me, begged for more details, and then argued when I asked her to give me a lift to the Civic so I could go home. I told her I wanted nothing more than to sleep in my own bed, and she finally gave in, grumbling under her breath. I gathered my things, retrieved Mack from the bedroom, and headed out the door.

A piece of paper fluttered from the phone desk when I walked by. Maggie, directly behind me, bent to retrieve it.

"Shit!" she said.

"What?"

"I forgot to give you this message from Corey. It's beside the point now, but the name of Diane Nowlin's adviser was Dr. J.P. Durant."

38

Perhaps two bodies in one day had unhinged me. I only know that anger swept over me with the force of a tornado tearing through a town.

Maggie dropped me off at the motel so I could pick up the Civic. She watched me as I threw my bag in the back.

"Viv, you've done nothing but curse since I gave you Corey's message. What the hell is going on?"

I set Mack's cage down hard. He hissed.

"I asked Professor Durant yesterday if he knew Diane Nowlin. He lied to me."

Her eyes widened in recognition. "He's that nice little man you visit."

"That nice little man." My voice was a bitter echo.

Maggie looked at me. "Come back home with me."

I combed my hair back with my fingers. "Not now."

Maggie jumped out of her car and grabbed my arm. "You're not going to harass that old man, are you?"

I shook her off. "Maybe Lisabeth wouldn't be dead now if we had known earlier that she was Nowlin's daughter."

"So the state's been spared the expense of a trial." Maggie shook out a cigarette and lit it.

"Jesus Christ. You just don't get it."

By the time I turned onto Normal Street and pulled into J.P. Durant's driveway, the rain had stopped, and the rays from the streetlights reflected in the puddles like artificial moons.

The professor's house was dark, but I pounded on the door until I heard his footsteps.

"Who is it?" His fretful voice was muffled by the door.

"Viv Powers." I didn't trust myself to say more.

He fumbled with the locks on the door and finally swung it open.

The small patches of hair on his head stood up, and he was wearing a robe. While I watched, he fitted his glasses over his ears.

"My dear, what brings you here at this hour?" His voice was slurred with the remnants of sleep.

I pushed past him into the house and slammed the door. "You lied to me."

The light from the hallway illuminated the fear on his face. "Lied?"

"Diane Nowlin," I said. "You were her adviser."

He slumped into a chair and gripped its arms with shaking hands. His eyes looked past me. "That was a long time ago."

A wave of anguish swept me. "Why did you lie?"

His voice was almost inaudible. "My past is none of your business."

"Another person is dead. Diane and Dale Nowlin's daughter. She didn't have to die."

He sucked in his breath as though someone had punched him. "Lisabeth. Little Lizzy is dead?"

"She killed Lucie Dreadfulwater and Neil Hannahan. Then she killed herself."

Professor Durant didn't seem to take it in. It was as though he were talking to himself. "She was a quiet little thing. She used to visit me at the office with her mother. Her mother suffered a lot before she left that terrible man. But it wasn't true what they said about Diane and me. It was a lie."

"Why did Diane leave him?"

"He drank. He beat her." The professor looked up at me. "He

chased off his first wife, and then he continually compared Diane and Lizzy to his first wife and child. As though his new daughter had to make up for the loss of his other."

"He had another daughter? What was her name?"

"I never met her. There was no reason for our paths to cross."

Professor Durant continued on his own path of memories. "She told me that whenever he drank too much, he would tell them that someday he would come into a great deal of money. That he was the son of a rich man and other such ravings. Well, his father was dead, of course, and Diane had to beg and borrow just to get the money to go to the university."

"Did you know that Lisabeth had moved back to Tahlequah?" My voice was quieter now, and I felt the first twinge of guilt for my roughness.

He wrung his hands. "No. When I last talked to her mother, Lisabeth was living at home."

"When was that?"

"Dale Nowlin's mother died about a year ago. I knew Diane would want to know."

"So you called her?"

"I did. There may have been some small inheritance, even though Diane didn't get along with her mother-in-law. They were entitled to their share."

"There was a will," I said. "It left everything to Dale and Alexandra Nowlin."

"Alexandra Nowlin?"

"Have you ever heard the name?"

He looked at me. "No, I have not."

We studied each other for a moment.

"I found Neil Hannahan's body this morning," I said. "And identified Lisabeth's this evening. I'm not myself." It was as close to an apology as I could come.

I let myself out the door.

39

A mile north of Moodys, an owl flew from a fencepost beside the road, almost sweeping the windshield with its outstretched wings. I wrenched the steering wheel to the right and nearly lost control of the Civic. It yawed sickeningly before I fought it back on the road.

I pulled off to the side until my hands stopped shaking.

The night was calm now, but clouds obscured the stars, and a heaviness lay in the air. Another storm brewed; long tongues of lightning slashed the hills to the southwest.

I rolled down the window and breathed in the electric air. It smelled of damp rot and death.

As soon as I got home, I let Mack out of his cage. He darted around the end of the house as though I might change my mind.

I slipped out of my clothes and into the shower. The hot water sluiced over my hair and shoulders and down my back. I stood under its pressure until the hot water was gone. It should have been relaxing, but when I stepped out of the steaming stall, I still felt tense and uneasy.

Justice had been served. Lucie's killer was dead. Yet so many questions were not answered. What had Lucie and Dale Nowlin been fighting about? Why had Johnny Dreadfulwater kicked me out of his house just for bringing up Nowlin's name? Who was Alexandra Nowlin? Alma Nowlin had left her thirty acres to

Dale and Alexandra, and both had signed the papers when the land was sold to Menckle's investment company.

The weather was as unsettled as I was. Outside a lightning bolt struck nearby with a sickening crash, thunder rattled the windowpanes and the electricity went out. Coming home hadn't been such a good idea after all.

I peered through a window into the dark yard, just as the rain started pounding the roof, and another bolt of lightning lit the sky. I saw in the flickering light that the earlier strike had splintered one of the oaks on the west side of the house, a white scar streaking the trunk.

I groped my way across the dark room to check the phone. The line was as dead as the silence in a lovers' quarrel. Not an unusual occurrence during a storm. Lightning-struck trees and phone outages were minor annoyances after the past few days. I felt my way up the stairs. I needed sleep.

As bone-tired as I was, sleep didn't come. Its edge held dead bodies and a witch with a long, sharp nail who kept changing form. It held the moment I'd struck Lucie Dreadfulwater with the board she had handed me. It held the look on her face after.

I tossed and turned and finally gave up. I dragged a pillow and blanket downstairs and lay on the sofa. Still I couldn't sleep.

Eventually I lit the Aladdin lamp—a glass heirloom handed down through my grandmother Powers—and set it on the edge of the cherry side table by the sofa. The table's broken leg wobbled. The lamp tipped and the light flared. Wide awake now, I set the lamp on the cold, solid top of the wood stove and adjusted the flame until it put out a steady glow.

I sat at my desk and nursed a glass of Johnny Walker. One of the early warning signs of alcoholism, I reminded myself, is using it as a sleeping pill. I sipped the Scotch anyway and doodled on a sheet of paper. Lisabeth, I wrote, and scrawled a huge black question mark after her name. The pencil lead snapped.

How much hate does it take to murder another person? How

much cunning and planning? How much left to chance?

I knocked back the rest of the Scotch, blew out the lamp and lay on the sofa. Mack curled on my belly and purred.

At some point, the storm subsided to a steady rain, and I drifted off to sleep.

Maybe I was dreaming. A woman walked on the logging road above the house. It was dark, and I couldn't see clearly.

She stood in the moonlit clearing. Her face and hair were hidden behind a mask with horns sprouting on top, and a tangled mass of dried rushes served for hair. Her nose was long and hooked. Folded clothing lay in a plastic bag at her feet; the pale light caressed the highlights and contours of her naked body.

She laughed to herself, a low, throaty sound. She wanted to dance in the moonlight to celebrate her success, but the rocks hurt her feet. She slipped her shoes back on and gyrated toward the moon.

Utlunta was pleased. She had changed shape, carelessly discarding the friend-form. "Witch. Goddess. Bitch," she sang.

The silence of the woods was broken by the sound of a large animal crashing through the underbrush. A man staggered into the clearing. His features also were hidden by a mask, with jagged scars on the cheeks. He tore off the mask and flung it on the ground.

"She tried to kill me!" He gasped for breath, and his white belly, hanging over his belt, blew in and out.

"You did well." Utlunta's voice was enervating, like a third glass of wine. "You were perfect."

"She fucking shot at me! You didn't tell me she had a gun." He looked at her for the first time. "God, you're beautiful. Take off that stupid mask. Let me look at you."

He moved closer and reached for the mask.

Utlunta kicked aside the bag of clothing and grabbed something. Swooped upward. Slashed again and again.

The man screamed in surprise and pain. He fell to the ground, and soon the forest returned to its sepulchral silence.

Utlunta gathered her plastic bag and the man's mask and made her way downhill through the darkness to a creek. She splashed water on her body, shivering in the cool air. The creek turned red with blood.

I woke from the nightmare drenched in sweat, as though I had witnessed Neil Hannahan's murder. I pushed aside the covers and looked outside. The wind pushed the treetops back and forth, slapped by a giant's hand. Far below, Spring Creek was rising. I couldn't see it in the darkness, but I could hear its growing power as it ground the rocks and carved the banks.

I read somewhere that the earth's magnetic poles sometimes reverse themselves. That over the past 9 million years the earth's magnetic fields have flipped at least nine times. The North Pole becomes the South Pole and south becomes north. The evidence is recorded in ancient volcanic rock formations, which align with magnetic fields as the molten rock is cooling.

I felt a sudden reversal taking place deep inside. I rubbed my hands together to see if the sensations were still the same. And then I did what I could to prepare for Utlunta.

She came in the hour before dawn.

She cut through the dark forest like a phantom, a shadow among the black tree trunks, and had I not been watching so closely, I would have missed her.

I gripped the .38 Special, The Sergeant's gift that I had never wanted. It was now my only friend. The nightmare was still with me, as real as if I had been there, and I felt shaken and weak as though it had been me whom Utlunta had slashed with her sharp and bony finger.

I sat on the sofa. The door was open, and she walked in as though she knew she was expected.

"Hey, babe," she said.

"Randy."

I had been sitting in the darkness; she had been out in it. Her eyes didn't need the light to see that I carried a gun.

Nevertheless, I felt along the wall with one hand until I found the Aladdin lamp and the box of wooden matches. I struck a match against the box and held it up. The dim light cast dark pools around Randy's eyes.

"We don't need the light, babe," she said.

The fire burned down to the end, singeing my fingers, and I dropped the match.

I deliberately turned my back to her, struck another match and lit the lamp. "What are you doing here, Randy?" My voice was as calm as the eye of a hurricane.

"It's not over." She sat down against the wall, her legs splayed. She looked helpless, but her presence subtly threatened. Anger crept into her husky voice. "I have to tell you a story."

"Fine. Tell me a story." I went to the window by the door and peered out. Trees screened the driveway. I couldn't see whether her car blocked mine.

"Sit down, babe." She gestured toward the sofa. The mantle on the lamp was flaring, burning a smoky hole in the fine net. I adjusted the flame and picked up the lamp and placed it on the edge of the cherry table between Randy and me. I set it down carefully so the leg wouldn't wobble.

"I had a lonely childhood," she said. "My mother sang with the Lenny Schuster Orchestra. Perhaps you've heard of it."

I shook my head. No.

The steady light from the Aladdin shone on her eyes, the highlights of her face. "We traveled all over the country with the band, living in hotels, eating in restaurants, seldom staying long in one place.

"I was left on my own much of the time. I learned how to order room service, how much to tip and how to live out of a suitcase. By the time I was fourteen, I learned that sex makes a suitable, though unpredictable, substitute for money.

"I have my mothers' genes." She held out her long, slender fingers. "I was playing with a band in Dallas when I met Neil. But I didn't follow him up here; I came for my own reasons."

She shifted her position so she was kneeling. My muscles stiffened, ready for fight or flight.

"Now, it's time to move on, babe," Randy said. "I know how to disappear." Her voice was cold and matter-of-fact.

"Was that the story? It's a bit incomplete. Kind of like a ballad without a last verse." My voice sounded conversational but inside the adrenaline was racing through my body like water through a broken levy on a flooded river.

She was quiet for a minute, and in the silence I could hear the rain resume, a gentle pattering on the roof.

"You want to know about Lisabeth. When she came to Tahlequah, she started hanging out wherever the band played, and she followed me home one night. She told me how her mother had taken her from her father. That she hadn't known where to find him until a man called to say her grandmother was dead.

"Lisabeth moved to Tahlequah thinking that she could claim her legacy. But the legacy was mine. And then last week…" Randy's voice trailed off, and she shifted positions, as though she was in pain. "She knew the courts in this county wouldn't serve up justice to the mighty Dreadfulwater family. It was up to us."

I watched the kerosene lamp cast shadows on Randy's face. "Us?"

She laughed. It was like flat stones falling on concrete. "Perfect plan, no guts. I had to do it all."

At that moment, I figured it out—a few hours late. "She's

your sister."

She smiled. "Half-sister. I came here after grandmother died, and Lisabeth saw me visiting Dale. That's why she started following me."

"Randy's a nickname for Alexandra."

She looked at me. "And Silvers came from my first husband. Makes a nice stage name."

"Charley's going to miss you," I said.

"And he's going to miss you."

We sat in silence for awhile, the lamplight shining on our faces, the sound of rainwater dripping from the eaves.

Finally she stirred. "You're ruining everything, Viv. I heard you and Lisabeth talking that day on the deck. 'You're always going around digging into people's business,' she said. 'As if you have the right.' There is no right! You've been digging through the trash, and you haven't even come close!"

"If something happens to me now, the OSBI will figure out the truth." I thought of Hutch and of how angry he would be.

"They'll never figure it all out," she said, "and this cannot go unpunished."

She flicked something toward me then, something that moved faster than a snake's tongue and burned like fire when it hit my wrist. My gun clattered to the floor. We both dived for it, and Randy was the winner.

Her triumph was short-lived.

I breathed an apology to my grandmother and made my move. I kicked the leg out from under the table, and the Aladdin lamp crashed to the floor. I dived to the side of the sofa. The kerosene from the broken base splattered on Randy, and the fire ran up her bare legs like she was a wick. She screamed and dropped the gun, slapping at the fire.

I kicked the gun and it disappeared under my desk; then I threw the blanket from the sofa over Randy to smother the flames. She was still, and I checked to see if she was conscious.

The acrid smell of singed hair hovered over her like a shroud.

"Randy," I said.

Her hands came up like a striking snake, grabbing my hair and pulling me down. She smashed my head against the floor, and I yelped in pain and surprise before I was able to tear myself from her grasp.

I like to think that we were evenly matched: two desperate women fighting for our lives. She lunged after me, catching hold of my shirt, and we rolled across the floor in the darkness, clawing and tearing at each other. I was dimly aware of the sound of breaking glass around us.

Randy fought with a ferocious strength that didn't match her slender build. She aimed a punch at my face; I twisted to the side and the blow glanced off my shoulder. I broke free, scrambled to my feet and ran to the kitchen. In the darkness, I groped above the sink and wrapped my hand around the handle of the butcher knife.

I had expected Randy to attack me from behind, but the only noise in the thick night was a raspy, gasping sound that was my breathing.

A shadow moved across the living room window, and Randy came into view. She held something long and slender over her head. It was the iron poker from beside the woodstove.

We faced off in the dark with the kitchen table between us. She had the advantage of reach. Randy's teeth gleamed briefly, and she stalked me around the table, poker held high.

I ran for the stairs and took them two at a time, thinking of nothing except escape. At the top, I paused and looked down.

Randy walked confidently toward the stairs, poker in hand. She had me cornered, and she knew it.

Behind her, the front door swung open and a dark shape filled it.

"Utlunta," said a man's voice.

Randy whipped around. The quick lethal explosion of a gunshot filled the air. She fell to the floor and didn't move.

I was shocked into immobility, and my ears rang from the after-effects of the gunshot. The man still stood in the doorway, his ponytail askew.

"Truman," I said, "put down the gun." Inside I was churning; my heart pounded against my rib cage.

He took two steps inside the room, the gun pointed at Randy. "Not until I know the witch is dead."

The electricity flickered, then came back on, and the sudden light left us blinking like miners emerging from the ground into the sun. I slowly descended the stairs, holding the butcher knife at my side. A red blossom spread across the front of Randy's shirt. I checked her throat for a pulse.

"You didn't have to kill her."

"It is better that I did." Truman's voice was flat.

One leg was twisted under Randy, bowing her back. I started to straighten it out, then decided not to and pulled a blanket over her head. I turned my back on the pathetic heap.

"Tell me that's not my gun," I said to Truman.

He looked at the gun he still held in his hand, as though he were surprised to find it there.

"It's a Smith & Wesson .357 Magnum," he said.

"You could have just as easily killed me in the dark." I was trembling.

"You were lucky."

"Put the damn thing on the table; you're making me nervous." My voice had a tremor in it, and I took several deep slow breaths while Truman followed my orders then went to the front door and looked out as though he were expecting someone.

I stood beside him. "You realize I'm going to have to call the cops?"

He looked at me mildly. "Of course."

"The phone's out."

"Use mine."

I must have looked dense.

"My cell phone."

Hutch's voice, thick with sleep, quickened when I told him what had happened. He ordered me not to touch anything and to keep Truman at the scene, if possible. "But no heroics," he said before he hung up.

I slumped on the sofa and Truman sat stiffly in the rocking chair while we waited for Hutch. The rocker creaked, and Truman put both feet on the floor to stop its movement.

After a long silence, Truman lifted his head and looked at me. The acne scars pitted his cheeks like gravel thrown into still water; his black eyes were unreadable. "I saw a woman push Lucie that night at the Creekside, and I saw her again last night when you were on the deck. So I followed her. She went home and stayed there. It was Lisabeth Ellis. After a long time, Randy Silvers let herself in the door.

"I have a friend on the police force. He called me tonight and told me about the Ellis woman's death. This time I did the right thing; I went to Randy Silvers' house. When she left with a suitcase and a guitar, I followed her." He grunted. "Good thing for you I did."

"I was handling it." I sounded surly.

"She was Utlunta. She would have killed you." His voice was flat with assurance.

"Thank you." If he wanted to pass it off as self-defense, I wouldn't stand in his way.

"She and Lisabeth were sisters," I said. "The daughters of Dale Nowlin."

Truman thought for awhile. "That makes sense then."

At one point it had seemed to make sense to me, too. Now it no longer did. I looked at Truman's scarred face. "What hold did Dale Nowlin have over Lucie?"

"Over Lucie?" Truman considered my question. "Ask what

hold he had over Johnny Dreadfulwater. My wife got caught in the middle."

I felt like we were slowly moving toward the truth. That Truman wanted to tell me. "What hold did he have over Lucie's father?" I asked.

Truman smiled slightly. "All Johnny ever cared about was his family's good name. He always hated his father for what he did."

"His disappearance?"

"No. Before that. The bastard he fathered with Alma Nowlin."

"Dale was Johnny's half brother?" Finally it began to make sense.

Truman nodded. "Johnny would have gone to any length to keep that from becoming public. I wonder what price he paid all these years for Dale Nowlin's silence."

The body of Dale Nowlin's daughter lay under a blanket in the middle of the floor, a testament to the price of silence.

The first flush of dawn bled across the sky by the time the OSBI left with Randy's body. Truman followed them. Hutch lingered behind.

"I never should have let her leave." He pushed back his uncombed hair, and a frown creased his forehead like a fan.

"It's not your fault, Hutch."

He looked for the truth in my face. I raised his hand to my lips and kissed it. He looked at his hand then looked away.

"I had someone look into David Menckle's affairs," he said. "He's in major financial trouble. He used his partner's money at the track, trying to raise capital. He lost it all. From what I hear about Jonathan Marlin, Menckle better find a deep hole to hide in."

"What will happen to Truman?"

"It sounds like a case of self defense to me, but it's out of my hands."

I didn't tell Hutch that Dale Nowlin and Johnny Dreadfulwater were half-brothers. If Truman wanted the news broadcast, he would have to find another route.

40

Lucie Dreadfulwater's memorial service was held at Oaks at the Spring Creek Baptist Church. The small white frame church couldn't accommodate the crowd, and it overflowed into the churchyard. Rumors flew among the mourners, rumors about Lucie's death, rumors about a rift between Truman Gourd and his father-in-law Johnny Dreadfulwater over where Lucie was to be buried. The old man had won out in his insistence that Lucie be buried in the family plot at Ross Cemetery. The historic cemetery was near the Dreadfulwater home, and it held the bones of many of Tahlequah's early prominent citizens.

Maggie and I stood behind Truman and his daughters at the cemetery. An old man and woman, Truman's parents, stood beside Truman. Off to the side, Johnny Dreadfulwater slumped in his wheelchair and Faith stood over him like a guard.

I listened to the minister's droning voice and silently said whatever prayer there was to say. We are born and we die, and in between is the ambiguous kaleidoscope through which we play out our lives. Already Lucie was rushing from me; she was a warm spot in my memory to be visited from time to time whenever some moment in time or place or object resurrected her.

The compulsion that had kept me moving in the past week was also fading. I was left with a nagging feeling that I was owed something.

I took Maggie home, and then I returned to the cemetery to the mound of floral arrangements and pushed the Pearl bottle cap into the damp earth. "F-wren-Ds 4+ever." It was the only way I knew to say goodbye. I listened to the crows in the nearby trees, and the shadows lengthened in the graveyard.

There have been a handful of people in my life I could truly call friend. Where do they come from these people whose way of thinking fits ours like a glove? Who, when we find them, feel like coming home to a well-loved place. Why are they so rare and precious? Despite her faults, Lucie had been my friend. My rare and precious friend.

Lucie Dreadfulwater was now in the company of her ancestors. I stood up and read the headstones in the family plot: Lucie lay next to her mother, and the earlier generation formed a neat line behind them. Lillian Ross Dreadfulwater, beloved wife of John Dreadfulwater, born April 17, 1901, died July 1, 1969. John Watie Dreadfulwater, born Jan. 23, 1894, disappeared July 4, 1945. It seemed odd to have a headstone and no body. The family had found its own way to commemorate their patriarch.

Nineteen forty-five. Randy Silver's words came back to me like a distant echo. "The legacy was mine." I suddenly realized it wasn't finished.

The windows were closed at Johnny Dreadfulwater's house, despite the warmth of the day. Silence covered the sprawling house like a cloak. But I felt certain he was home. His van hadn't been parked in front of the Southern Gothic Mausoleum. He had nowhere else to go.

No one answered when I knocked above the carvings on the wooden door, but when I tried it, the door swung open. I walked down the dimly lit hallway to his office.

Johnny Dreadfulwater bent over the chess board, rolling a fallen bishop under his fingers, and he didn't even turn around. "I told you to get out of here, Faith," he said.

"Faith isn't here."

He started and wheeled his chair around to face me. "Miss

Powers," he said. "Who let you in?" I saw the beginnings of alarm deep in his eyes.

"You didn't hear my knock, so I let myself in."

"I'm busy." He gestured at his desk.

"This won't take long." I remained in the doorway. "I just came by to tell you that when I grab hold of something, I don't let go until it's finished."

He looked at me defiantly, his eyes a brilliant black under the aged folds of his lids. The effort seemed too much for him, and his face creased in pain. "The price will never be paid for my father's weakness," he said.

"It cost your father 110 acres in return for Alma Nowlin's silence."

"She was just as weak as he was. She couldn't keep her mouth shut when her bastard asked who his father was."

"And then your father disappeared."

He looked at me.

"On the land where Alma Nowlin lived," I said, "all that remains of her house is a chimney that sits on a block of concrete. A date is engraved in the concrete. July 4, 1945. I think if someone chipped away the block, they would find a skeleton with shrapnel in the skull."

The proud set of Johnny's shoulders gave way, and he slumped in his wheelchair. "My mother was a good woman," he said. "How he could prefer that whore over her…"

"Alma left a legacy to her granddaughter," I said. "That was Randy's word: 'legacy.' Alma knew where the body was buried, and she knew who killed John Dreadfulwater. Were they blackmailing you? How much did Lucie know?"

"You should leave now." Johnny's palsied hand reached toward the telephone and then fell to his lap.

"What will you do?"

He made a strangled, laughing sound. "Do? There's nothing to do but wait here until I die." He raised one gnarled hand and slowly swept the chess pieces from the board. They hit the floor like hail.

When I got home, I changed into shorts and a T-shirt and walked to the garden. I had two new apple trees, and I replanted the bed Neil Hannahan had destroyed. I worked until the oaks etched black scars against the dusty light.

A part of me felt sorry for Johnny Dreadfulwater. His daughter was dead, and his pride was a thin gruel that could not sustain him.

Lucie had been my friend, and because of whatever debt I owed to friendship, the body of her grandfather would remain encased in its concrete tomb. I knew the truth, and for me that was enough.

I was suddenly eager to get out of Tahlequah. I would leave Mack with Maggie and head to Austin for a few days. There, I would become a connoisseur of sensuality: sleep late, bathe long, max out the charge card, drink until the bars closed and make slow, sweet love to Charley until dawn.

At least I had a plan.

Letha Albright has worked at newspapers, in a sawmill and as a wilderness guide. Since 1989, she has been the editor of *School & Community*, a magazine for Missouri teachers. She earned an undergraduate degree in psychology in Oklahoma and a master's degree in journalism from the University of Missouri. Albright lives in Columbia, Missouri, with her husband, two children and a cat. In her free time, she climbs rocks and hikes. Albright lived in Cherokee County, Oklahoma, the setting of her books, for eight years. The first Viv Powers mystery, *Tulsa Time*, was highly praised.

Recommended Memento Mori Mysteries

Luanne Fogarty mysteries by Glynn Marsh Alam
DIVE DEEP and DEADLY
DEEP WATER DEATH

A Katlin LaMar Mystery by Sherri L. Board
BLIND BELIEF

Matty Madrid mysteries by P.J. Grady
MAXIMUM   INSECURITY
DEADLY SIN

A Dr. Rebecca Temple mystery
by Sylvia Maultash Warsh
TO DIE IN SPRING

INCIDENTAL   DARKNESS
Cynthia Webb

AN UNCERTAIN CURRENCY
Clyde Lynwood Sawyer, Jr.
Frances Witlin